SCENTS AND SENSIBILITY

SCENTS AND SENSIBILITY

A CHET AND BERNIE MYSTERY

SPENCER QUINN

ATRIA BOOKS

New York   London   Toronto   Sydney   New Delhi

ATRIA BOOKS
An Imprint of Simon & Schuster, Inc.
1230 Avenue of the Americas
New York, NY 10020

First Atria Books hardcover edition July 2015

ATRIA BOOKS and colophon are trademarks of Simon & Schuster, Inc.

For information about special discounts for bulk purchases, please contact Simon & Schuster Special Sales at 1-866-506-1949 or business@simonandschuster.com.

The Simon & Schuster Speakers Bureau can bring authors to your live event. For more information or to book an event contact the Simon & Schuster Speakers Bureau at 1-866-248-3049 or visit our website at www.simonspeakers.com.

Manufactured in the United States of America

10 9 8 7 6 5 4 3 2 1

Library of Congress Cataloging-in-Publication Data

Quinn, Spencer.
  Scents and sensibility : a Chet and Bernie mystery / Spencer Quinn.
    pages ; cm
  1. Dogs—Fiction. 2. Private investigators—Fiction. I. Title.
  PS3617.U584S29 2015
  813'.6—dc23
                          2015010341

ISBN 978-1-4767-0342-8
ISBN 978-1-4767-0344-2 (ebook)

To Lily, with many thanks for all the help.

SCENTS AND SENSIBILITY

ONE

Home at last! We'd been away so long, first in swampy country, then in a big city—maybe called Foggy Bottom—that
confused me from the get-go. Is there time to mention the air in
both those places before we really get started? Soggy and heavy:
that sums it up.

Where were we? Was it possibly . . . home? Yes! Home! Home
at last! Our home—mine and Bernie's—is on Mesquite Road.
Mesquite Road's in the Valley. Quite recently I might have heard
that the Valley's in Arizona, but don't count on that. What matters is that right now I was inhaling a nice big noseful of Valley
air. Light and dry, with a hint of greasewood and just plain grease:
perfect. I felt tip-top. Bernie opened our door, kicked aside a huge
pile of mail, and we went in.

"Ah," said Bernie, dropping our duffel bag on the floor.
I did the first thing that came to mind—just about always my
MO—which in this case meant sniffing my way from room to
room, zigzagging back and forth, nose to the floor. Front hall,
our bedroom, Charlie's bedroom—mattress bare on account of
Charlie not being around much since the divorce—office, with

the circus-elephant-pattern rug, where I actually picked up a faint whiff of elephant, even though no elephant had ever been in the office. I'd had some experience with elephants, specifically an elephant name of Peanut, no time to go into that now. The point was: somehow I was smelling elephants in the office. Had to mean I was on a roll. Chet the Jet!

Sniff sniff sniffing gets your nostrils quivering real fast, a nice feeling, as you might not know, the human sense of smell—even in huge-nosed dudes and gals—always turning out to be shockingly weak, in my experience. Take Bernie, for example, and his lovely big nose, somewhat crooked, although he plans to get it fixed when he's sure no more dustups are in his future, which I hope is never, on account of how satisfying it is to see that sweet uppercut of his, followed by some perp toppling limp to the floor, all set for me to grab him by the pant leg, meaning case closed, closing cases being what we do at the Little Detective Agency. Little on account of Bernie's last name being Little. I'm Chet, pure and simple. As for Bernie's big crooked nose: What's it for? Just beauty? Is that enough? I tried to think about that, got as far as: Why not? Hey! Beauty was enough! And of course Bernie's the most beautiful human I've ever seen. Hold on to that fact, if nothing else.

I sniffed my way over toward the wall where we've got our safe, hidden behind a framed picture of a waterfall. We've got lots of waterfall pictures, water being one of Bernie's biggest worries. Why worry, you might think, when we had bright green golf courses out the yingyang here in the Valley, sprinklers on full blast morning and night, making beautiful rainbows? A lovely sight, but not to Bernie. What was the aquifer, again? Maybe Bernie and I should go find it, put things right. Wow! One of my best ideas ever! The next thing I knew I was flat on my back, wriggling around on the elephant-patterned rug to my heart's content. After a while I thought: Why? Why am I doing this? I tried to remember, came up blank, stopped wriggling, and in that blank and motionless pause, I caught another unexpected smell, this time not of elephants but of Iggy.

Iggy? Iggy's my best pal, lives next door with the Parsons. The fun we used to have! But that was before the Parsons—a real old couple—bought an electric fence that they never managed to work right, so now Iggy didn't get out much. And even in the old days, had he ever been in our house? Not that I remembered. So what was his smell doing here, not a faint, long-ago kind of smell by the way, but strong and recent?

I rolled over, popped up on my feet, barked one of my barks, of which I've got many, one or two that can tear the roof off, as Bernie says. The truth is he only said it once, but it led to a whole night of me trying to bark the roof off where we were, which happened to be a hotel—possibly the Ritz—where we'd gone for a special weekend with Suzie, Suzie being Bernie's girlfriend, a crack reporter now working for the *Washington Post* . . . which . . . which might be in Foggy Bottom! I came real close to figuring out something about the past. But no cigar, which didn't bother me at all. Once I chewed on a cigar butt, and believe me it's not something you'd want to repeat. Although I did. And then again.

Back to this particular bark. Not close to my loudest, but sharp and quickly cut off, sending a message. I was about to try it again, even sharper, when Bernie stuck his head in the room.

"You okay, big guy?"

There he was! My Bernie. Hadn't seen him in way too long. My tail started wagging, closed in on blur speed. The room got breezy, not sure why, but that breeze carried Iggy's scent. My tail hit the brakes in mid-wag, stood tall and stiff, and I was back to barking that sharp bark, eyes on Bernie.

"Going through some mood changes, huh?" he said.

Which I didn't get at all. I was about to bark one more time—Bernie! We've got a problem!—when he took a gun from his pocket and moved toward the waterfall picture. We'd had several guns in our career—including the .38 Special, now at the bottom of the sea for reasons I couldn't remember even if I tried, which I did not—and for a while quite recently we'd been completely gunless, not good in our line of work, but that .45—a big stopper—in Bernie's hand meant we were good to go again. A big stopper, by the way, that I'd taken off a perp or . . . or possibly a cop of some sort? I was wondering about wondering about that, as Bernie reached for the waterfall painting. A gun not in use belonged in the safe, where we also kept some papers, plus our most valuable possession, Bernie's grandfather's watch.

Bernie removed the painting, spun the dial on the safe, put the gun—but no. What was this? No safe? No safe behind the waterfall painting, but instead just a hole in the wall? Bernie went still. So did I. We're a lot alike in some ways, although the only one actually panting was me.

Bernie lowered the painting, leaned it against the wall. He put the gun back in his pocket, all his movements real slow now, his gaze on the hole in our office wall. I could feel his thoughts. He was thinking his hardest. When Bernie thinks his hardest, the air feels like a storm's coming on. Then he gets an idea and you feel light as a balloon when someone lets go of the string. Feeling light as a balloon when someone lets go of the string—Charlie, for example—is the best. I waited as patiently as I could for Bernie to get an idea. All I knew was that Iggy couldn't be the perp. He's way too small, for one thing, and not much of a leaper. Leaping is my best thing, although I'd somehow flunked the leaping test at K-9 School on my very last day. Was a cat involved? And maybe some blood? It didn't matter. That was how I'd met Bernie, meaning it was the best day of my life, except for all those that followed. But I still wouldn't mind a do-over on the leaping test.

Bernie went to the desk, checked all the drawers. Then he walked slowly around the room, eyeing everything real careful, the way he does when we're on a case. Was this a case? If so, who was paying? The Little Detective Agency is the best in town, not counting the finances part. We'd had some bumps in the road when it comes to finances. Don't get me started on Hawaiian pants or tin futures in Bolivia. In fact, I'm never mentioning them again.

We left the office and went through the whole house, starting with the front door—not a mark on it—and going all the way to the back door, off the kitchen. No marks on the back door, either. Bernie opened it, worked the lock a few times.

"Are we dealing with a pro?" he said.

I had no idea, wasn't sure I understood the question. We walked out onto the back patio. The swan fountain—pretty much all Leda had left behind after the divorce—wasn't running. Bernie reached for the faucet on the side wall and was just about to start the water flowing out of the swan's stone mouth, when he noticed something shiny on the tiles of the empty pool bottom. He picked it up, and held it so we could both have a good look. A small but thick silver snakehead on a broken chain?

"Pendant," Bernie said. He took a closer look at the edge of the pool, bent over, and pointed to a reddish patch on a blue tile, although I can't be trusted when it comes to red, according to Bernie, so skip this part. "See what happened here? Dude doesn't see the fountain—meaning nighttime and maybe not a pro after all—falls in, scrapes off some skin, loses the pendant. On the way out or the way in? I'm thinking the way in. On the way out he'd have the safe, and a dropped safe leaves marks. So, not a pro, plus no sign of forced entry." Bernie rose. "Meaning he had a key." He gazed at the silver snakehead—who would want that around his neck?—and the heavy broken chain lying on his palm. "Yeah. He for sure."

"Leda?" Bernie said. "It's me."

We were back in the kitchen. Leda came over the speaker. "I recognize the voice," she said.

"Uh, right. It hasn't changed."

"What does?"

"Sorry? Not quite following you."

"My point exactly."

Bernie laughed. "You're in a good mood."

Silence.

"The thing is, we're back," Bernie said.

"I know that. You texted me an hour ago. I'll bring Charlie over Saturday morning, as agreed."

"Right. Good. Thanks. But that's not why I called."

"No?"

"I was wondering if you still had a key to the place."

"Your place?"

"Um, yeah."

"Another one, you mean?"

"Huh?"

"You sound a little slow today, Bernie."

Bernie's voice got a bit edgy. "I'm just trying to find out about the key."

Leda's voice got even edgier. "And I'm not in the mood for one of your blamefests. I humbly apologize for my indiscretion, but I had no idea I even still had a key until last week. I was sending some things over for the homeless, and the stupid thing fell out of an old Gucci bag. I drove by to drop it off with Mr. Parsons. That's the only key I had. Unknowingly, as I'm trying to make clear."

"Why him?"

"Mr. Parsons? One—he was outside. Two—I'd tried your slot, but it was blocked by the mountain of mail in the hall. Three—if you don't trust Mr. Parsons, you've got paranoia issues."

"Okay, okay, I was just—"

Click.

Bernie looked at me. I looked at him. "Started well but cratered fast," he said. "Where do I go wrong?"

Bernie going wrong? That made no sense to me. I pressed my head against his leg, pressed my very hardest. It was all I could think of to do. Bernie recovered his balance in a flash. He's quick on his feet, just another wonderful thing about him.

We went over to the Parsonses' house. "Wow!" Bernie said. "This is new." A big saguaro stood in the Parsonses' front yard, freshly dug earth piled around the base. I'm not a fan of saguaros, especially the kind that look like giant green men, such as this one. I laid my mark on it in my quickest and most efficient manner, and we walked to the front door.

Bernie knocked. Right away I heard Iggy start up on the other side. How I'd missed that amazingly high-pitched *yip-yip-yip yip-yip-yip*, a *yip-yip-yipping* Iggy could sustain all night if he wanted, and he often did! But now it was saying *Welcome home, buddy! Let's do something fun!* Like dig up old man Heydrich's lawn, old man Heydrich being our neighbor on the other side. Dig it up so it stayed that way! What a brilliant idea, especially coming from Iggy.

"Chet! What do you think you're doing?"

Uh-oh. Possibly standing on my back legs, pawing at the door?

Maybe more like clawing into it, somewhat deeply? If that was really happening, I got it under control and pronto. If you'd looked, you'd have seen me standing silent and still beside Bernie, like a good citizen, whatever that happened to be. You'd have thought I'd been like that the whole time. And . . . and hadn't I? Hey! You'd have been right! And me, too! Which made me like you! What a day I was having, and it had hardly begun! It was great to be home.

Stump stump stump. That was the sound of Mr. Parsons on his walker, stumping toward the door. Stumping mixed with yipping in a way I found quite pleasant. Then came some grunting, the grunting of an old dude bending down to do something, and after that the door opened. Not much, but enough for Iggy to shoot through. Iggy! My best pal. We bounced off each other, Iggy spinning high in the air, and took off for parts unknown—my favorite kind of parts!—ears flat back from the wind we were making with our own speed, knocking over this and that, chasing every living—But no. None of that happened, except Iggy shooting through and bouncing off me. Why? Because Iggy was on a leash. A leash in the house? I'd never heard of such a thing. And even so, it almost didn't matter because the leash slipped from old Mr. Parsons's hand. But Bernie grabbed it, and Iggy came to a sudden halt, hanging in midair for what seemed like the longest time, before thumping back down.

"Uh, sorry to bother you, Daniel," Bernie said.

"No bother," said Mr. Parsons. "Nice to see you back. Read a rather hair-raising account of your recent adventures in the Sunday paper."

"You know how they exaggerate," Bernie said. "Didn't amount to much."

"Nice to see you anyhow."

And it was nice to see old Mr. Parsons. Was he getting skinnier? His shirt, buttoned to the neck, hung kind of loose on him. So did his long pants. His feet were bare, nice broad feet I'd always liked. I was considering giving them a quick lick when he said, "Anything I can do for you?"

"Actually," Bernie said, getting a tighter grip on the leash, Iggy's stubby legs now churning at top speed, although he was going nowhere, "I was hoping to pick up the key Leda left with you."

"Sure thing," Mr. Parsons said. "Come on in."

We entered the Parsonses' front hall, me first, after a little confusion in the doorway. Bernie tugged Iggy in after him and closed the door. Meanwhile, Mr. Parsons went to a small corner desk and opened the front drawer.

"That's funny," he said. "I know I put it here."

TWO

M r. Parsons straightened, scratched his head. That's a human thing for when they're confused. In the nation within—which is what Bernie calls me and my kind—we scratch our heads, too, but only if they're itchy. And wouldn't you know? Seeing Mr. Parsons scratching his head made my own head itchy! So for moment or two we were both scratching away, me and old man Parsons. What a life!

Mr. Parsons—a wisp of his thin white hair now standing up—went through the drawer again. This time he took all the stuff inside and laid it on top of the desk, stuff like papers and pens and a flashlight and—and a tennis ball? I eased my way over there, eased a little quicker when I noticed Iggy easing in the same direction.

"That's funny," he said again.

"One of the other drawers?" Bernie said.

Mr. Parsons shook his head. "They're for Mrs. Parsons's knitting supplies. Verboten territory."

"Maybe she's seen it," Bernie said.

Mr. Parsons picked up a scrap of paper and gazed at it. "Seen what?" he said.

"The key," said Bernie. "That Leda left with you."

"Afraid not," Mr. Parsons said, putting everything back in the drawer.

At the last moment, Iggy made a play for the tennis ball, leaping the highest I'd ever seen him leap. But he just didn't have it in him, poor little guy. As for me, I'd already noticed that the knob on the drawer was kind of big, like a mushroom—don't get me started on mushrooms—with a narrow stem. We'd done lots of work on knobs like that, me and Bernie, work meaning a Slim Jim every time I opened a drawer. In short, I could have that tennis ball anytime I wanted. I'm a good worker.

". . . back in the hospital before Leda dropped by," Mr. Parsons was saying. "The docs have got some new procedure they want to try, but she has to get stronger first." He turned to Bernie, his eyes a bit watery. "How's she going to get stronger in the hospital? Answer me that."

"I don't know," Bernie said.

"She hates the hospital," said Mr. Parsons. "Edna's a free spirit, maybe something hard to spot in an old woman. But she was a cowgirl when I met her—folks had a ranch outside Sierra Vista. Could rope and ride good as any man or better." Mr. Parsons paused, took a deep breath. On the way out, it turned all wheezy. He put a hand to his chest.

"How about a glass of water?" Bernie said.

"I'm all right," said Mr. Parsons. "Sorry if I got a bit exercised there. It's just that we . . . we . . ."

"Nothing to be sorry about," Bernie said.

Iggy sat down beside Mr. Parsons's feet, leaned sideways, gave the nearest one a quick lick. What a tongue Iggy had! Enormous, especially considering how runty the rest of him was. Hard to imagine having a better pal than Iggy.

"Nice of you to say so," said Mr. Parsons. "Couldn't ask for more in a neighbor than you, Bernie." He glanced down at the desk. "Where the hell is that damn key?"

"Maybe you put it somewhere else."

"Nope. I remember distinctly. There was a whole thought process. Directly in the top drawer, Danny boy—that's what I said to myself."

"Could someone else have moved it? A cleaning lady, for example?"

"Flora's having some health issues herself—hasn't come in three weeks now."

"Has anyone else been in the house?"

"No," said Mr. Parsons. "Other than . . ." He paused, licked his lips.

"Other than?" said Bernie.

Mr. Parsons spread his hands, then brought them together, fingertips up. "Had Billy here for a few days."

"Who's Billy?"

Mr. Parsons met Bernie's gaze for a moment, then looked down. "Our son."

"You've never mentioned a son."

"No," said Mr. Parsons. "He's been . . . living far away. And we haven't been . . . how would you put it?"

"In communication?"

"I was going to say 'close.' But 'in communication' is better. We haven't been in communication for a long time."

"None of my business, but has something changed?"

Mr. Parsons thought about that. "I've been asking myself the question—what's changed? Aside from the obvious, of course."

"The obvious?"

Mr. Parsons opened his mouth to reply, but before he could,

someone knocked on the door. A real quiet someone—how could they get so close without me knowing? I went right to the door but didn't bark. Bernie wouldn't want me to—I just knew that. And don't forget it wasn't my job here at the Parsonses' house. It was Iggy's. So why was he trotting down the hall toward the back of the house? That was Iggy: full of surprises.

Knock knock.

"Want me to get that?" Bernie said.

"I'll handle it," said Mr. Parsons, maybe a little annoyed, for reasons I didn't know. He reached for his walker, stumped over to the door, and opened it. On the other side stood a woman in a khaki uniform. She had light hair, blue eyes, white teeth, and other things, too, all adding up to the kind of woman Bernie tended to have trouble with.

"You the property owner?" she said to Mr. Parsons.

"That's right," he said.

"What's your name?"

"Daniel L. Parsons."

She took out a notebook and wrote something down. "I'm Special Investigator Newburg, Department of Agriculture," she said, flashing a badge. "What can you tell me about the cactus on your front lawn?"

"It's a saguaro," Mr. Parsons said.

Which I knew to be true, but the answer didn't seem to please Special Investigator Newburg. "I'm aware of that," she said. "I'm asking about its provenance, meaning where did you—"

"I know the meaning of 'provenance,'" Mr. Parsons said, his back straightening and his voice losing some of its wispiness.

"Then answer the question," said Special Investigator Newburg.

"Can we ramp down the attitude?" Bernie said. "Mr. Parsons here is not a criminal."

Special Investigator Newburg turned slowly to Bernie. "Who are you?"

"A friend."

Another answer I could see she didn't like. Her eyebrows kind of went together in the middle, and her mouth opened in that lippy way humans have when something sharp is coming, but then she noticed me and seemed to change. She blinked a couple of times, gave her head a quick shake—the only good thing I'd seen from her so far—then turned back to her notebook.

"It's a simple question," she said. "Where did you get the cactus?"

"It . . ."

Mr. Parsons's hands tightened on the walker, like things had gone wobbly. He licked his lips again, maybe on account of how dry and cracked they were. I licked my own lips. They felt just fine.

"It just arrived," Mr. Parsons said.

"Just arrived?" said Special Investigator Newburg. I wasn't liking Ms. Newburg as much as I liked most humans, but then I picked up a faint scent coming off her, the scent of a member of the nation within, a member of the nation within who smelled a lot like . . . me. Have I described my scent yet? Hate to slow things down when by now we've definitely gotten started, but my scent is pretty important. Scents are not so easy to describe, but this will give you some idea about mine: a mix of old leather, salt and pepper, mink coats—I knew about mink coats on account of Bernie had one, his grandma's, that he gave to Leda—and a soupçon—a favorite word of Bernie's, meaning, I think, a tiny drop of soup: in my case, cream of tomato. Plus there's the faint scent of gator, coming off my collar, but no time to get into that now. The point is I was smelling a member of the nation within who smelled a lot like me, minus the gator part.

". . . more or less a gift," Mr. Parsons was saying.

"More?" said Newburg. "Less?"

Mr. Parsons began to tremble a little. He bent over the walker, hanging on harder.

"A gift," he said.

"From who?" said the special investigator.

There was a long pause. Mr. Parsons glanced at Bernie—who was watching with one of those complicated expressions you sometimes see on his face, complicated expressions that I never understand and wish would go away fast—then gazed down at his feet.

"Anonymous," he said.

"Speak up, please," said Newburg. "I didn't catch that."

Bernie spoke up, spoke up plenty. "Then there's something wrong with your hearing. He said 'anonymous.'"

Wow! Bernie had better hearing than Special Investigator Newburg? Made sense since his ears were bigger than hers—by a lot, actually—but Bernie's hearing had never been one of our strengths. I got the feeling that the Little Detective Agency was just getting started.

Special Investigator Newburg gave Bernie a hard look. "If you're really a friend, you'll stay out of this."

"And what is 'this,' exactly?" Bernie said.

That hard look stayed on Bernie. "How about I show you?" she said. "Then, if you're a true friend, you'll persuade Mr.—" She checked her notebook. "—Parsons here to cooperate."

After a brief moment of confusion in the doorway, we went outside, first me, then Newburg, Mr. Parsons, and Bernie. Just as Bernie closed the door, Iggy, somewhere back in the house, must have figured out, too late, what was going on. I knew that from the heavy thump against the door, followed by yip-yip-yipping.

We stood by the saguaro. Special Investigator Newburg took

out her phone, held it so Mr. Parsons could see. "Check this out," she said.

"I'm not certain what I'm looking at," said Mr. Parsons.

"An app we created at the department," said Newburg.

"I've heard of apps," said Mr. Parsons, "but can't say as I truly—"

"Never mind all that," Newburg said. "Were you aware that it's illegal in this state to move or transport a saguaro cactus from public or private land without a permit?"

"No," said Mr. Parsons.

"Ignorance of the law is no excuse."

"I know," said Mr. Parsons. "And that law sounds right to me, now that I think of it."

"You don't have a permit for this one, do you, Mr. Parsons?"

"No ma'am."

"Right answer," said Newburg. "One hundred percent verifiable—there's a chip planted in this cactus, and when I open the app and point the phone like this, it fires right up. Like that. See?"

"I see some numbers," Mr. Parsons said.

"Those numbers are GPS coordinates. This particular cactus was dug up out of the desert at 32 degrees 13 minutes 12 seconds north and 110 degrees 32 minutes 28 seconds west, give or take, meaning just east of Rincon City." Special Investigator Newburg tucked the phone away. "That's what I've got, Mr. Parsons. What have you got?"

Mr. Parsons licked his cracked lips again. "I don't know what to say." He turned to Bernie.

"Is there any chance," Bernie said, "the person who gave you the cactus had a permit?"

"I . . . I don't know."

"How about making a call or two?" Bernie said.

"Is there a listing for 'anonymous'?" said Newburg.

Which didn't sound at all friendly to me, but then came a surprise, namely Bernie laughing a quick little laugh. Newburg's eyebrows rose in surprise and, at least for a moment or two, she didn't seem so annoyed. Hey! Her eyebrows were kind of like Bernie's, speaking a language of their own, even though she had way less going on when it came to eyebrow size.

Meanwhile, Mr. Parsons just stood leaning on his walker, still trembling a bit.

"Go," said Newburg, but for the first time a little gently. "Make a call or two."

Mr. Parsons made his way back into the house. That left me, Bernie, and Newburg standing by the cactus, meaning there were more than two of us. Two was best, in my opinion, and also as far as I go when it comes to numbers.

Bernie and Newburg exchanged a glance. I thought of Silent Sammy Cipher, a perp of our acquaintance who spoke to us once and once only. "Whoever talks first is a loser, pal." You can find Sammy over at Central State Correctional, breaking rocks in the hot sun, and if you can't get there soon, no problem.

Bernie, the farthest from a loser you'll ever see, spoke first. For a moment, I had this picture in my head of Special Investigator Newburg in an orange jumpsuit, no telling why.

"I know you're just doing your job," Bernie said.

"Spare me," said Newburg.

One of Bernie's techniques—mine, too! No wonder the Little Detective Agency is so successful, other than the finances part, in case I haven't mentioned the financial part already!—is plowing right along. That's what he did now, continuing as though Newburg hadn't said a word. "And it's an important job. I respect it. I admire it."

"Stop already."

"But he's an old man in poor health and his wife's dying in the hospital."

"Everybody has a story."

"That's no reason to tune out."

Newburg's eyes shifted slightly, like she was paying attention to something inside.

"How about going easy on him?" Bernie went on. "We'll do whatever we can to help you."

"Is that the royal we?"

"It's me and Chet here, commoners both."

We were commoners? I was just finding that out now? But whatever commoners happened to be, for sure it was something good, if the group included Bernie. So: just one more reason to be in a fine mood, which I was already.

"Chet's your dog?" Newburg was saying.

Bernie nodded. Newburg turned my way. Her head tilted to one side, a sign she was trying to get a different angle on things; we do that, too, where I come from. She seemed about to say something, but at that moment, someone popped up into view in the shotgun seat window of her truck, parked by the side of the road. Did I mention her pickup truck already, all dusty, painted the color of her uniform except for a green and gold shield in on the side? If not, I should have. Don't be mad. The whole truck thing isn't really important anyway. The important part was this someone who'd popped up into view. First, he was a member of the nation within. Second, he was just a puppy. After second came a lot more, including the fact that his ears didn't match, one being white and the other black. Also I'd come upon this little dude before, out in the canyon behind Mesquite Road. We'd even had a playful dustup, if memory serves, which it hardly ever does in my experience.

He saw me and barked. I should have liked the sound of that bark, on account of how similar to mine it sounded—nowhere near as powerful, of course, hardly seems necessary to throw that in—but for some reason it annoyed me. I barked back at him, sending a clear message. Meanwhile, both Bernie and Newburg were looking from me to the puppy and back again.

"I'd heard something about a puppy matching that description being loose in the neighborhood," Bernie said.

"Shooter is never 'loose,'" said Newburg. "But that shoe most certainly fits someone else in our happy little scene."

Shoes were the subject? Bernie wore flip-flops, Special Investigator Newburg boots, and Shooter—if I'd caught the little dude's name—and I had no need for shoes of any kind. That was as far as I could take it. Meanwhile, all eyes were on me, for some reason. I thought of rolling over and playing dead, a trick I hadn't performed since my own puppy days.

THREE

"My neighbor," Special Investigator Newburg said, "had a bitch—since deceased—"

"Sorry to hear that."

"—who got knocked up a while back by a perpetrator unknown."

All eyes still on me? That made no sense. Wasn't a perpetrator something like a perp? That ruled me out—I was the number one enemy of perps here in the Valley, had grabbed so many by the pant leg that I'd lost count! Actually losing count after two, but that wasn't the point. The point was: Why me? In moments of uncertainty like this, a go-to move that usually works—as you may or may not know—is marking something. The only good marking post around was the big saguaro, which I'd already marked, but now I marked it again. Humans often say you can't have too much of a good thing—and I'm sure they're right—but from the looks on their faces as they watched me with one back leg raised, I got the feeling that Bernie and Special Investigator Newburg had forgotten all about that saying, at least temporarily.

"Shooter being the result?" Bernie said.

"Correct."

"How big was the litter?"

"Just Shooter. My neighbor was having problems at the time. I took him."

Bernie glanced my way. "Any point in a DNA test?"

"To confirm the obvious?" said Newburg. "I'm not paying."

Bernie nodded like that made sense, whatever it was. I finished what I was doing and sat by myself in the Parsonses' front yard. I would have preferred sitting by Bernie, but . . . but sort of wanted him to call me over. Which he did not. I sat up tall and alert, a total pro. It was all I could think of to do.

"I didn't think this could happen," Bernie said.

"That's what they all say," said Newburg. "You owe me child support."

"You're joking, right?" Bernie said. Newburg didn't reply, and her face showed nothing, at least to me. "Where do you live?" Bernie said.

"On Wildheart Way," said Newburg.

"That's the other side of the canyon?"

"Correct."

"And your neighbor?"

"Down the block from me."

Bernie nodded again. "Got a moment?" he said. "I want to show you something."

Special Investigator Newburg checked the Parsonses' door, still closed, then turned toward Shooter. The passenger-side window was cracked open enough for him to stick his muzzle way out, which he was doing. It was the right move, and I'd have done the same. "Okay," Newburg said.

We walked over to our place and around to the back gate. Bernie unlocked it and we went inside. "Welcome," he said. "I'm Bernie Little, by the way."

"Ellie," said Special Investigator Newburg. "I like your foun-tain," she added as they shook hands.

"It's a swan."

Ellie Newburg quickly let go of Bernie's hand. "I can see that."

"A bit abstract," Bernie said. "This particular rendering, which was why I mentioned it."

"It's not abstract to me," said Ellie. "And it captures the es-sence of swans very well, in my opinion."

"The essence being?"

"That beauty can be nasty inside."

Then came a silence in which they both quickly looked at each other and quickly looked away. No idea what that was all about. What were we even doing? I had no idea. But it was always nice to be on the patio. No complaints, amigo.

"I grew up on a lake near Pinetop," Ellie said. "We had swans out front all the time, so I got to know them." She pointed her chin at the fountain. "This is what you wanted me to see?"

Bernie shook his head. "Check out the gate."

"What about it?"

"The height."

He hurried into the house. I stayed where I was. A no-brainer. We had a stranger on the property and security's my job; also, no-brainers are my favorite kind of brainer. I kept my eye on Ellie. She took a look at the gate, then turned to me.

"An interesting guy," she said. "The most interesting guy I've come across in some time, matter of fact, but is he nuts?"

I had no idea who she was talking about, was unable to help.

She took out her phone. "How about a quick search?" She tapped at the screen, then gazed at it for a few moments. "Well, well," she said, which was around the time Bernie came back out, and she put the phone away. Or maybe not. All my attention was on Bernie, on account of what he had in his hand, namely a Slim Jim. The day, already off to a rockin' start, was about to get even better! I couldn't believe my luck, except that I could. I've had a very lucky life, especially after joining up with my partner Bernie.

"What's going on?" said Ellie.

"Just trying to explain what happened here," Bernie said. "Sit tight, Chet. Ms. Newburg and I are going out for a bit."

"Huh?" said Ellie.

Bernie led her through the gate and then closed it. I sat tight, which I took to mean was all about trotting right over to the gate and pawing at the wood.

"Chet—cool it."

I paused, one paw in the air. They started talking, talking with me not there. That was bothersome.

"Did you check out the gate?" Bernie said.

"What about it?"

"No way under, right?"

"Not that I can see," said Ellie.

"And would you call it high?"

"Gotta be six and half feet."

"Seven," said Bernie. "I used to let Chet sleep out by himself on nice evenings. Hard to imagine that gate being leapable."

"No way."

"Exactly my point—a . . . a black swan event, if you see what I mean"

"I do not," said Ellie.

"You will," Bernie said. Then he called to me: "Hey, Chet. Got a Slim Jim here, big guy. Come and get it."

Well, of course I knew he had a Slim Jim: I'd seen it and I could smell it. Normally Slim Jims can't be resisted. But right now resisting seemed the way to go, although I had no idea why.

"Come on, Chet—jump!"

The Slim Jim smell grew stronger, as though Bernie was waving it in the air. My mouth started getting wet. Did I even drool a bit? I'm not denying it. But I stayed where I was, actually sat down in this special way I have of making myself very hard to move. And I would have stayed like that as long as it took, but a commotion started up on the other side of the gate.

First came the sound of running, not human running but real running, no offense.

"Oh my God," said Ellie. "Shooter! How did you get out?"

Bernie laughed. "Two peas in a—"

"Shooter!" said Ellie. "Sit! Sit down this minute. Do you hear me? I said sit." And a lot more like that, accompanied by the sounds of a chase, specifically the special kind of chase where a human tries to corral a member of the nation within, one of the very best games going.

"Sweet moves for a little guy," Bernie said. "A budding Crazy Legs Hirsch. But not very obed—"

"Are you going to commentate or are you going to help?"

Or something less than friendly like that. I might have missed it on account of Crazy Legs Hirsch. First I'd heard of him, but clearly a perp. News flash for Crazy Legs: get measured for an orange jumpsuit. But not right now. Right now I was caught up in more fun sounds—they'd reached the wild scrambling stage—and the next thing I heard was Bernie saying, "Hey, Shooter—how about a Slim Jim?"

"He's not allowed any damned—"

All it once it got very quiet and still outside the gate, like the chase was over. How could it have been over so fast? I knew chases: this one was just getting started. Something was very wrong.

"Good boy, Shooter," Bernie said. "Come on over and get

your Slim Jim. Attaboy. Now sit. Excellent. Funny little guy. Here you—"

Some things in life can't be tolerated. At the top of the list would be an upstart puppy getting hold of a Slim Jim meant for me. I'm sure you'd feel the same way, feel it so strongly that there'd be no holding you back from jumping that gate. Which you couldn't do. Sorry for pointing that out. But there happened to be a gate-jumping dude extraordinaire on the premises: namely Chet the Jet!

Bird's-eye view: The next moment I finally got to understand what it meant, on account of that's what I now enjoyed! What a life birds had! So why were their eyes mean and angry? No time to puzzle over that. Instead I just delighted in my view from above, a view of Bernie, Special Investigator Newburg, and Shooter, all standing in a sort of circle, completely unaware of me way above them. One correction: Shooter was sitting, not standing, in fact sitting just as Bernie had suggested, sitting up nice and proper in anticipation of the Slim Jim which Bernie was about to hand over right that instant. What's an instant? Something pretty quick is all I know, meaning less than an instant had to be even quicker! Wow! Was I on fire or what? All this going on in my mind and at the same time I was dive bombing down like . . . like a dive bomber, whatever that might be. I snatched that Slim Jim out of Bernie's hand just as Shooter's cute little jaws were closing on it, one of the very best things I'd ever done! This Slim Jim was mine!

I cut one way, then the other, raising a dust cloud, the Slim Jim hanging out one side of my mouth but completely secure, baby, better believe it. Did Ellie throw up her hands in fear and scream, "Oh! Oh!"? Did Bernie yell, "Chet! Stop! For God's sake!"? Did Shooter come zooming after me, zigging and zagging with every one of my zigs and zags, plucky little dude, actually jumping up to make a play for that Slim Jim, and . . . and whoa! Snatching it right out of my mouth. None of that, amigo! I snatched it back, bowling him over in the process, and then without another thought, always a sign I'm at my best, I took off into the canyon at top speed, or even faster. And what do you know? The little fella took off right after me! We charged up a long rise, scrambled, and rolled down the far side, flew over a dry wash, and headed for points far distant, leaving the whole world in our dust.

"CHET!"

"SHOOTER!"

"CHET!"

We came back much more slowly, Shooter and I side by side, our tongues possibly hanging out the slightest bit. It's also possible we had thorns of some sort in our coats—I was pretty sure I did—and Shooter had learned a hard lesson or two involving javelinas and those pesky tusks of theirs. But most of all we were filled with the feeling you get from a job well done, although what the actual job had been wasn't superclear to me. Something about a Slim Jim? That seemed right. As we climbed over the crest of the last rise and came to our back gate—mine and Bernie's—I wondered about the chances of another Slim Jim real soon. Pretty good, right? I could think of no reason why not.

The gate was closed and no sounds came from behind it. We walked alongside the house—Shooter giving me a little bump for no reason and me bumping him back for the reason that . . . that he'd bumped me! Phew! Almost forgot!—and found lots happening in the Parsonses' front yard.

For starters, we had some workers digging up the saguaro cactus, watched real closely by Special Investigator Newburg who was telling them to be careful and watch what they were doing and take it easy for chrissake. Then we had Bernie standing by the front door, watching her. And old Mr. Parsons in the open doorway, hunched over his walker. He didn't appear to be watching anything, but he was the first one to see us.

"The happy wanderers return," he said.

Hey! Mr. Parsons nailed it. He turned out to be one smart old customer. Shooter went trotting over to Ellie, and I trotted over to Bernie. But what was this? She took a quick glance at Shooter, then looked away? And Bernie did the same thing to . . . to me? I did the first thing that came to mind, which was to grab him by the pant leg. Gently, of course. Bernie was no perp, although wasn't there something a bit perpish about not making a fuss over the return of a happy wanderer? I tugged at his pant leg a bit, still gently, and he steadied himself easily by getting a quick grip on the front step. Then I felt his other hand giving me a quick scratch between the ears, as only Bernie can do.

"You're incorrigible," he said.

Which had to be something good. I lay down at his feet.

"And it's going to take hours to get all those thorns out of you."

Life was perfect, or even better. As for Shooter, he was sitting over by Ellie and kind of whimpering. She wasn't giving him the time of day—it was maybe afternoon, in my estimation, but no guarantees—and was in fact looking at Bernie. "See that look, Chet?" he said in a low voice. "It means I caved."

What was this? Caves were in the picture? We hadn't done any cave exploration in some time and now didn't seem right, but here's something about me: I can make just about any time seem right!

"Easy, Chet. What's with you today?"

Nothing. Nothing at all. I sat, calm, silent, but at the same time totally in charge of everything that was happening on the Parsonses' front lawn. It's always fun to watch humans at work. They tend to snap at each other at times, and flash dirty looks. Dirty looks: a fascinating subject, but not now. In short, after some snapping—mostly from Ellie at the workers—and some dirty looks—mostly from them back to her when she wasn't watching—the saguaro got moved to a flatbed truck and driven away. After that, Ellie scooped up Shooter and carried him to the pickup. He gave her face a lick on the way over—almost always the right approach in this sort of situation, but she said, "That crap won't work on me." Then she plopped him down on the shotgun seat—leaving the window cracked open, but not as much as before—and came over to us.

"Any word on your 'anonymous' benefactor having a permit?" she said to Mr. Parsons.

"No ma'am."

"We have other ways of IDing the thief," Ellie said, "but if you gave up the name, it would make all the difference in your personal case. Think about your answer."

Mr. Parsons stood straighter and for a moment let go of the walker. "I have nothing more to say."

"Then get ready to be cited for receiving stolen property." Ellie headed for the pickup. "Among other charges," she called over her shoulder.

Bernie walked after her. I went with him, of course, hardly seems necessary to mention. We caught up to her by the pickup. Bernie lowered his voice.

"I hope that was an idle threat on your part."

Ellie's eyes, blue, as I hope I've already pointed out, now

seemed more like the color of ice cubes. "Hope away," she said, not lowering her voice at all. Was that why Bernie lowered his even more?

"I'm asking you to give him a break. I told you I'd help."

"Uh-huh. I looked you up. You're a private detective of mixed repute, although you seem to get results. But it's all moot, because there's no line item in the budget for private detectives."

"We'll work for nothing," Bernie said.

Ellie shook her head. "No, thanks. I'll handle this myself. But—" She glanced over at Mr. Parsons. "But if you can get me the name within twenty-four hours, I'll cut him a break." She got in the pickup and drove off. Shooter looked my way as they turned the corner at the end of the block and let out a series of barks I didn't appreciate. How come he got to ride in the shotgun seat? Which maybe didn't make a lot of sense since I had no desire to be in that pickup at all. But what can you do?

Bernie turned to Mr. Parsons. "Don't know if you caught any of—"

"I'm not saying anything and that's that," said Mr. Parsons.

"Understood," said Bernie. He gazed down at the hole in the ground where the saguaro had stood.

"Suppose it's too much to expect them to fill it in themselves," Bernie said.

"Government," said Mr. Parsons.

"Got a shovel?"

"That's not necessary."

"Be my pleasure."

Bernie ended up filling in the hole. I did what I could to help, but undigging turns out to be different from digging in ways I have yet to master. When we were done, Bernie said to Mr. Parsons, "When was the last time you had a nice home-cooked meal?"

Mr. Parsons shrugged.

"Steak and eggs at our place," Bernie said. "Fifteen minutes."

Fifteen minutes? Was that like now? I was already at our front door.

FOUR

"You're quite the chef, Bernie," said Mr. Parsons, wiping his mouth on a napkin. "I didn't realize I was so hungry."

We sat at our kitchen table, me actually under the table and closer to Mr. Parsons's end, in case he turned out to be a messy eater. Which he did not. But you have to learn to deal with disappointment in this life, and I was just starting to wonder how that might be done, exactly, when all of a sudden, in a sneaky, quiet way, there was Mr. Parsons's hand down under the table, holding a nice fatty glob of steak practically right in front of my mouth. I snatched it up, and pronto. So that was how you dealt with disappointment? I'd learned a valuable lesson.

"Maybe you haven't been eating enough, Daniel," Bernie was saying.

"The thing is I enjoy sitting down to a meal with Edna. It's not the same by yourself."

"There's Iggy."

"And I love him. But . . ."

But? What was that but? I loved Iggy, too, but with no buts

about it. I wriggled myself out from under the table, kind of wanting company.

"How about a beer?" Bernie said.

Mr. Parsons checked his watch. "Isn't it a little early?"

"Planning on operating heavy machinery this afternoon?"

Missed that one, myself, but it made Mr. Parsons laugh. Bernie got two bottles from the fridge, snapped off the caps with the opener—loved that sound! Snap off more caps, Bernie, more, more, more—and gave one to Mr. Parsons.

"Cheers," said Mr. Parsons.

"Cheers."

Mr. Parsons took a little sip. "Do you think she's serious?" he said. "Special Investigator whatever her name was?"

"Newburg, Ellie Newburg," Bernie said. "And yes is the answer."

"Not that I blame her—can't have people digging up saguaros out of the desert, willy-nilly."

"True," Bernie said. "But you had nothing to do with it."

Mr. Parsons gazed at the beer in his hand, then drank again— this time not a sip, more like the rest of the bottle, tipping it up, his throat exposed. I'm always interested in exposed throats, not sure why, which is how come I noticed that Mr. Parsons was one of those unlucky humans who—if I'd heard right—had some sort of an apple caught in there. Poor guy. Just watching it bob around made my own throat uncomfortable.

"What's that squeaky sound Chet's making?" said Mr. Parsons. "Think he's all right?"

"Chet—cool it."

Squeaky sound? Me? I cooled it, so fast no one could have noticed anything.

Mr. Parsons put down the empty beer bottle. "As for my involvement . . . " he said in a very low voice, almost like he was talking to himself, which humans often do, especially with just me around. Like I'm not there! Hello? Mr. Parsons shot a quick glance at Bernie, maybe to see if he was watching; which of course he was, being Bernie.

"What about it?" he said.

Mr. Parsons sighed. "Depends how broad the definition is."

"I'm all ears," Bernie said.

What was that? I studied his ears, not small in human terms, but nowhere close to being all of him. And of course what they were actually for was a puzzler. I was a bit lost.

"You're a good neighbor, Bernie."

"You said that already."

"And that's all I've got to say. Last thing I'd want to do—and Edna would never forgive me—would be to drag you into . . . anything."

"My money's on Edna forgiving you pretty quick," Bernie said.

Mr. Parsons laughed. Human laughter is one of the best things they've got going for them, and I always enjoy the sound and the looks on their faces, usually kind of wacky— the insides of their mouths, packed with tiny teeth! And those feeble little tongues!—but in this case Mr. Parsons's laughter turned with no warning into tears. Mr. Parsons put his head in his hands, went silent, a bit of moisture leaking through the spaces between his fingers.

"Tell me about Billy," Bernie said.

Mr. Parsons went still. Then he slowly spread his fingers and looked at Bernie, his eyes drying fast. "He fell in with bad people."

"When was this?" Bernie said.

Mr. Parsons lowered his hands and sat up straight. "You're

relentless, Bernie, in the nicest way. Edna pointed that out to me."

Bernie nodded. He's the best nodder I've ever seen, has many different nods signaling this or that. There's one for yes that actually means no! As for this particular nod, I had no clue.

"In answer to your question," Mr. Parsons went on, "Billy fell in with bad people more than once."

"You mentioned that he's been living far away. Was he in prison?"

"Northern State Correctional."

"You're from up that way originally, as I recall?"

"Yes."

"How long was the sentence?"

"Fifteen years."

"So it began around the time you moved here?"

"Six months earlier. We . . . we needed a change, Edna and I."

"What was the crime?"

"Kidnapping. Billy drove the getaway car—he was always a very good driver." Mr. Parsons got an inward look in his eyes. "I taught him how to parallel park. He got it on the very first try." He gave his head a little shake. "That was years before, of course. At the time of the . . . the event, Billy was on his own, living down here in the Valley. He admitted to driving the car but claimed ignorance of any kidnapping. The jury didn't believe him."

"Did you?"

"I . . . I've never been sure. Edna believed him one hundred percent. We hired the best lawyer money could buy. Not a hardship—I was still working at the time. Shouldn't even have mentioned it. She—the lawyer—wanted Billy to take a plea deal the DA offered, but Edna . . . but we, Edna and I, argued against that.

Falling in with bad people can't be the same as being a bad person yourself, can it?"

"Depends on whether you judge by results," Bernie said.

Mr. Parsons's voice sharpened. He didn't even sound like himself. "Easy to say when it's not your flesh and blood. Just imagine if it was Charlie instead of—" Mr. Parsons covered his mouth with his hand. "I'm so sorry, Bernie. Way out of line. Please forgive me. No excuse for . . ."

"Nothing to forgive," Bernie said. "Bottom line, I'd like to help you."

"I'm very grateful, but there's nothing I need help with."

"Understood. But maybe at least I could get Ellie Newburg to back off."

"How?"

"Leave that to me."

Mr. Parsons shook his head. "I can't have Billy implicated in any way. He's on parole."

"I've had some success in preventing people from getting implicated," Bernie said. "But only when I knew the whole story."

Mr. Parsons just sat there. Silence went on and on. I heard a squirrel run across the roof. How I hated when that happened! Like they owned the place. They did not own the place. We owned the place, me and Bernie. I lost myself in thoughts of how to keep squirrels from running across the roof and was getting nowhere when Mr. Parsons finally spoke.

"Iggy loves him, followed him around constantly the whole time he was here," Mr. Parsons said. "If that makes any difference."

"It does," Bernie said.

"You have to promise me, Bernie."

Bernie said nothing.

"Not a small request, I'm aware of that," Mr. Parsons said. "But when you've only got a few moves left in life, you want them to be right."

"How do you know that's where you are?"

Mr. Parsons smiled. His teeth were very yellow, but his smile was nice. "It's good to be optimistic. Gives you some lift over the years. But it's no help in the end to be a Pollyanna."

Pollyanna? A new one on me. A perp? Sounded that way, if I was following things right. In which case: heads up, Pollyanna. Hope you look good in orange.

Meanwhile, Bernie was still saying nada.

"It's not just about the legal consequences," Mr. Parsons went on. "A child is your investment in the future. We have just the one. No one wants their investment wiped out."

Bernie nodded, a short nod that means he's come to a decision. "I promise," he said.

Mr. Parsons nodded the same sort of nod. "It was a gift," he said.

"The saguaro?" said Bernie.

"A thank-you gift."

"From Billy?"

"A landscaper just drove up. No warning. All paid for, including the planting."

"What was Billy thanking you for?" Bernie said.

"You may think we're very foolish," said Mr. Parsons. "A foolish old couple, long past it."

"How much did you give him?"

Mr. Parsons stared at Bernie for a moment. Then he started laughing. What was funny? I didn't get it. Maybe nothing was funny and tears were on the way again. But that didn't happen this time. Mr. Parsons's laughter wheezed to a stop. "We had to open a home equity line of credit," he said. "We gave Billy twenty grand. But it's in the form of a loan."

"Written form?" said Bernie.

"More like a handshake. And a kiss for his mom—he came to the hospital, sat with her for practically the whole afternoon, just holding her hand and talking about long-ago times. Billy remembers polka-dot socks she knit him in kindergarten. Can you imagine?"

Bernie was silent.

"It meant the world to her," Mr. Parsons said. "I took a picture of the two of them." He held up his phone so Bernie could see. I saw, too: Mrs. Parsons sitting up in bed, dark patches under her eyes and a big smile on her old face, plus a man leaning in, one arm around her shoulder, and an even bigger smile on his face. He had long fair hair down to his shoulders, and . . . and a small tattoo on one cheek, small but strange, perhaps a snakehead. I could feel how hard Bernie was looking at the picture.

"Did Billy say what the money's for?" he said.

"Why, to get him back on his feet, of course," said Mr. Parsons.

"Why that specific amount?"

"Accreditation, a cheap car, living expenses—it all added up."

"What sort of accreditation?"

"Forestry management," said Mr. Parsons. "Billy's always loved the outdoors. They've got a program down at Rincon City College. Classes start next week."

"Sounds promising," Bernie said. "Except for the saguaro. I take it you called him when you went in the house?"

"No answer. I left a message. But shouldn't we be keeping an open mind? What if he bought the thing legitimately from a garden shop? He'd have had no way of knowing it was stolen."

"We need to hear his side, no question," Bernie said. "Any idea where he's living?"

"Nowhere permanent at the moment. He's looking for a place in Rincon City. Are . . . are you thinking of going down there, Bernie?"

"If we can't reach him by phone. How about trying again?"

Mr. Parsons took out his phone, tapped at the screen. "Hello, Billy? It's me, your fa—your dad. I'd like to talk to you, son, if you've got a minute or two. Nothing too . . . urgent, but, uh, at your earliest convenience." He clicked off.

"Can I get that number?" Bernie said. Mr. Parsons read out the number and Bernie wrote it on a scrap of paper. "Does Billy know about me?" he said.

"Know about you? Just that you're a wonderful neighbor—and that includes Chet, too."

Another no-brainer? And the day was still young: had to be a good sign.

"Does he know what we do for a living?" Bernie said.

"I don't think that ever came—wait a minute. Maybe it did. Was he in the house when Leda dropped off the key? I was outside when she drove up. We talked, I took the key in, and . . ." Mr. Parsons closed his eyes tight, a human thing meaning they're trying hard to remember something. Humans try so hard at all sorts of things! You really have to feel sorry for them sometimes. "And . . . yes, Billy came out of the kitchen." Mr. Parsons's eyes opened. "He saw Leda's car driving off, made some remark about how fancy it was, and that's when I think I mentioned you were a detective."

"In the context of Leda's fancy car coming with her second marriage."

Mr. Parsons smiled. "You're amazing, Bernie. Figuring how things were from just a few random pieces."

Message to Mr. Parsons: Tell me something I don't know!

"Makes me certain I'm doing the right thing," Mr. Parsons went on, "although I may not tell Edna on my visit today."

"The right thing being?" Bernie said.

"Hiring you, of course," Mr. Parsons said. "To sort out this whole saguaro matter in a way that . . . in the right way."

"I'd like to do that, Daniel. But money won't be changing hands."

Whoa! What was that?

"I insist," Mr. Parsons said.

Bernie? Hello? He's insisting. Wouldn't it actually be rude to—

"No way," said Bernie. "We won't hear of it and that's that."

We being? They both turned to me. "What's he barking about?" Mr. Parsons said.

"Probably wants you to slip him another piece of steak," Bernie said.

No, no, it wasn't that at all. But, funny thing: then it was! What a life!

"Bernie and Chet!" said Mr. Singh, clapping his hands as we entered his shop, pawn brokerage at the front, tiny kitchen hidden by bright-colored hanging cloths at the back. "It's been entirely too long since I've laid eyes on that beautiful timepiece."

The beautiful timepiece being Bernie's grandfather's watch, our most valuable possession. It lived in two places, either at Mr. Singh's or in the safe at—Whoa! I'd forgotten all about the safe! Eye on the ball, big guy, as Bernie always says, although nose on the ball works better for me. Maybe not for you. But forget all that, because at that very moment Mr. Singh was calling to his wife behind the brightly colored cloths.

"Dhara, would we have any curried goat at hand? Chet is here. And Bernie, of course."

"Only by reheating," Mrs. Singh called back. "Which is never as good, no matter what you say."

"It's really not necessary," Bernie said.

What did he mean? Reheating wasn't necessary? I was with him on that. Really, who cares? But if he meant—

"Just be patient," said Mrs. Singh. "I am doctoring up as we speak."

Now doctors were in the picture? In a cooking situation? I was not in the picture myself. I went closer to the brightly colored cloths and took a sniff or two. Mrs. Singh was the only human on the other side, as I'd thought. So therefore? Oh, no, not a so therefore! So therefores were Bernie's department, me bringing other things to the table. But wouldn't you know? Just when I was at a total loss, the cloths suddenly parted and there was Mrs. Singh—one of my very favorite people in the whole Valley!—laying a plate of curried goat at my feet.

My memories of goings-on at Mr. Singh's pawn brokerage were a bit hazy after that. Did Mr. Singh say something about seeing a watch similar to ours but not as nice going through the roof on *Antiques Roadshow*, and because of that he was now prepared to come across with way more green? Did Bernie tell him that we actually no longer had the watch? Was that followed by a less than happy discussion of our current insurance policy? Maybe, maybe not. All I'm sure of is that after I'd finished licking the plate clean, Bernie said, "If you're in touch with any of your competitors, I'd appreciate an alert."

"Colleagues, Bernie, not competitors. We are a band of brothers in our little world, and—"

Is there a kind of laugh called a snicker? If so, that was what I heard coming from behind the brightly colored cloths.

"—and I will inform each and every one to be on the lookout."

They shook hands. I took a last lick of the plate, a long, careful lick, and maybe a few more after that. Do things right: that's one of my core beliefs.

FIVE

We hopped in the Porsche, me in the shotgun seat, Bernie behind the wheel, always our arrangement, with the exception of one time I'd rather forget when we got it reversed. Usually I'm brilliant at forgetting, so why couldn't I forget that particular episode? Don't ask me. Let's drop the whole subject. What to remember is that riding shotgun in the Porsche just happens to be my favorite thing in the whole world. Our ride's been a Porsche ever since the start of the Little Detective Agency, which had to be when I joined up, unless I was missing something. We've had three so far, each one older and more dinged up and nicer than the one before. The first went off a cliff—with Bernie in it!—and the second got blown up with no one in it. The Porsche we had now was two shades of red—and I could make out both, or at least one of them, sort of, no matter what Bernie says about me and red—painted personally by our car guy, Nixon Panero, best mechanic in the Valley and a real good buddy even though we'd put him away for a while. This Porsche also sported martini glass images on the front fenders, a last-minute addition by Nixon that had led to us getting pulled over more often than you might want. But we know most of the highway patrol dudes, and a lot of them have a treat or two somewhere in the cruiser, even a stale old biscuit under the seat, maybe news to you. I'm not fussy.

We zoomed up a ramp, got on the freeway, zipped over to the fast lane. Faster, Bernie, faster! He glanced over at me. "You're in a good mood," he said.

No doubt about it! And why not? I stuck my head out into the wind, picked up so many smells I didn't know what to do with them!

"Home is the hunter, huh, big guy?"

Wow! We were going hunting? At last, at last, at last! I'd seen hunting on TV many times, been a little envious of those members of the nation within who got to chase after all those ducks and elk and animals I didn't even know the names of, so envious that more than once I might have tried to get in the TV and . . . and do things I'd have regretted later. But the point is we'd never been hunting. Why not? Bernie could shoot dimes out of the air. I'd seen him do it out in the desert, just the two of us. We'd done a lot of that in those strange days after the divorce when Charlie went away to live with Leda. So much fun to watch those dimes spinning in the sunshine and then *ping! ping! ping!* and they'd spark out into the blue. There's all kinds of beauty in life. Was that why we shot dimes out of the air, for beauty? I didn't know. One day it just stopped, stopped with a last dime still spinning in the air, untouched and unfired on, and Bernie tucking the .38 Special in his belt and turning away. Maybe not the happiest of days, totally unlike today because today we were finally going hunting! At last, at last, at last!

"Chet! What's getting into you? Knock it off!"

Getting into me? Hunting, of course.

"I mean it—back on your own seat or you're not coming. I can't see a damn thing."

So what? We could find our way by my nose alone! Whoa, Chet. Not a good thought. We were a team, me and Bernie, meaning Bernie needed to see, if that's what he thought best. I got back on my own seat pronto, sat up tall and absolutely silent, silent to you, anyway. It takes real good hearing to pick up the sound of my heart, thump thump thumping in my chest.

Quiet and silent, but so much was going on in my mind, all of it about hunting, of course. Were mountain lions a possibility? I'd had an encounter with a mountain lion once, not good. Bears? I'd dealt with one of them, too. That was the fastest I'd ever run. Had Bernie laughed and laughed at the sight? Oh, yeah, but only when we were making our getaway, burning rubber for miles. Mother bears have a thing about their cubs, something I wouldn't be forgetting anytime soon.

We got off the freeway, drove through a neighborhood with lots of construction going on, slowed down. What sort of hunting ground was this? I started to ramp down my expectations— pretty much the hardest thing to do in life—from mountain lions and bears to squirrels and chipmunks. Would I be able to get excited at hunting chipmunks? Squirrels, maybe. Then it hit me we weren't even carrying! Bernie must have left our stopper behind. I can smell a gun even if it hasn't been fired or cleaned in a long time, and we were gunless, end of story. I know my job, amigo. But how could we hunt without a weapon?

Worries had pretty much taken over my mind by the time we came to a construction site at the end of a street, one of those big holes in the ground surrounded by a chain-link fence. Bernie parked and we hopped out, me actually hopping, and Bernie not, maybe on account of his bad leg, the one that got wounded in the war. But he doesn't talk about it, so I really don't know. And once when we were visiting Suzie after not seeing her for some time, he did hop out, possibly meaning he could do it if he wanted. But why would anyone choose not to? That was confusing.

I forgot all about it just like that and followed Bernie to an opening in the fence, followed from in front, just one of my tricks. A dusty pickup stood by the opening, passenger side window cracked open, but not enough for Shooter to squeeze through, which is what he tried doing the moment he spotted us. He barked at me. I barked at him. He barked at me. I—

"Chet!"

We walked along a curving path that led down the hole in the ground, me and Bernie, and there at the bottom stood Ellie Newburg, still dressed in her khaki uniform, now kind of muddy. She wore gloves, and in one of her gloved hands she was holding a frog, kind of greenish with black stripes. At her feet was a small, empty cage. We were hunting frogs? And Ellie had beaten us to it? That was as far as I could go on my own.

"What you got there?" Bernie said.

Ellie glanced at Bernie. Did her eyes—pretty icy, as I recalled—warm up a bit? That was my impression, but I've been wrong before. Take the time a perp name of Ticface Fescue jumped off the Rio Arroyo Bridge rather than let me take him gently by the pant leg and close the case. I hadn't had a clue that was coming. And the next thing I'd known there I was in midair myself! Lucky for me we had water down below, it being monsoon season at the time. I'd ended up grabbing a soggy pant leg, no harm done.

Meanwhile, Ellie, in answer to I had no idea what, was saying, "Chiricahua leopard frog, Bernie. A mature male of the species."

"Cute little critter," Bernie said, leaning in closer.

The frog looked at me. I looked at him. I would never attack a little froggy or harm one in any way, certainly not by biting or anything of that nature. Was pawing at him another story? Could pawing even be called attacking? I thought not. One of my front paws got this feeling that sometimes comes over it where it just has to paw. Just has to! Paws paw! And then my other paw got it, even worse. While they tried to make up their minds who was going to do the actual pawing—uh-oh, we had more than two minds involved here all of a sudden?—I shifted my position a bit, sort of narrowing in. And what was this? Bernie shifted his position, too, kind of blocking me off? Not on purpose, of course: the thought didn't even occur to me.

"The question is," Ellie said, "what's it doing here?"

Bernie glanced down at a small puddle at the very bottom of the hole we stood in. Hey! Was it growing a bit? I went over, the mud feeling nice and cool on my foot pads, and licked up some of the water. It looked kind of muddy but tasted terrific.

"Don't frogs like water?" Bernie said.

Ellie nodded. "And these leopard frogs also like excavations. But this one's a good twenty miles from the nearest known leopard frog habitat. The kicker, of course, being that they're on the endangered list."

"Didn't know that was part of your job," Bernie said.

"There's overlap," said Ellie. "And a lot of calls seem to come my way, who knows why."

"Maybe because . . ." Bernie stopped himself.

"Because what?" said Ellie. They exchanged a look, kind of complicated on both sides.

"I mean this in a nice way."

"Uh-oh."

Bernie smiled. "You get calls because people can see you're a bulldog."

What a stunner! I know bulldogs, of course. Take Tyke, for example, not a tyke at all but a massive dude with rippling muscles and drool pretty much always streaming from his mouth, a mouth constantly open, maybe on account of the size of his teeth. We'd had some interesting encounters, me and Tyke, and finally worked out an arrangement, although he needed reminding about that arrangement every time we met. But that's not the point. The point is that no matter how closely I looked, I found no similarities between Tyke and Ellie Newburg. No drool, teeth on the small side, even for a human, although very white, and while she looked in decent shape, I'm afraid you couldn't call her massive, not a rippling muscle in view.

I watched Bernie carefully. He's hardly ever wrong about anything, and if he is it's because he's tired or we hadn't had water in too long—like one time out in the desert, when Bernie had wanted to go one way, but I could clearly hear a highway in the other. Was that it? Dehydration? I took a few noisy sips from the puddle, hoping he'd get the idea.

Which he did not. But it ended up not mattering, because Ellie said, "I'll take that as a compliment."

"Whew," said Bernie. And I thought the same. Often happens: We're a lot alike in some ways, me and Bernie. Don't forget.

Meanwhile, Ellie's gaze had swung over to me. "Chet seems to like that water. Probably tastes extra good."

Hey! How did she know? The next moment—and this kind of thing doesn't happen often—I'd figured it out all on my own. She must have lapped up some herself, probably just finishing when we showed up! Wow! I was on fire.

"Why would that be?" Bernie said.

Ellie pointed to puddle with her chin, second time I'd seen her point like that. We do some pointing in our world, too, but never with our chins. One of the best human moves out there, in my opinion. Ellie was doing all right in my book, although I had no books at the moment, and had really only possessed one in my life, much too briefly: namely an extremely tasty leather-bound volume that I'd sniffed out at the home of a—judge, was it?—where Bernie and I'd been invited to a big, noisy party. I myself spent a quiet evening, curled up behind a couch with my book. A very pleasant memory to this day! And if things had gone down-hill later—some back-and-forth about first editions and Mark Twain autographs, whatever those happened to be—why let it spoil things? That's one of my core beliefs.

Meanwhile, Ellie was saying, ". . . because it's as fresh as fresh can be—coming straight from the aquifer."

Bernie's eyes got very bright, a sign that he was on fire, too. Both of us on fire at the same time? Look out!

"The aquifer's this close to the surface?" he said.

"In a few places east of the arroyo, here being one, evidently," said Ellie. "Another problem with this development. I'm shutting it down."

Back up. This was the aquifer? The aquifer I'd heard so much about? Bernie's biggest worry? There was only one, he always said, and when it was gone, game over. I studied the puddle. Getting bigger since our arrival, but basically pretty puny. Bernie was too late. Game over. I sat beside him, pressed against his leg.

"That's funny," Ellie said. "Shooter does that exact same thing when he thinks I'm upset about something."

"What thing?" said Bernie.

"Like Chet's doing now—pressing against your leg."

Bernie glanced down at me. "Yeah?"

One of Ellie's eyebrows rose in a way that reminded me of Bernie when he was about to have some fun. "Upset about some-thing, Bernie?" she said.

"No," said Bernie. Which was just Bernie being brave. They

don't come any braver than Bernie, goes without mentioning. Good luck getting anything out of him, Special Investigator Newburg. But then came a surprise. "Actually," Bernie went on, "there is something I'm—maybe not upset, but concerned about."

"And that is?"

"Daniel Parsons," Bernie said. "The old man with the—"

"What about him?"

"He's completely innocent."

"You know that for a fact?"

"I do."

"What else do you know?"

"Just that he's in no shape to get squeezed right now. You won't find what you want, and he'll be damaged."

"But you got what I want from him, didn't you?"

Bernie said nothing.

"So why don't you tell me," Ellie went on, "and leave the old man out of it while I do my job?"

Bernie stayed silent.

"Because," she said, bending down and popping the frog into the little cage, "I'm going to do my job."

"Give me twenty-four hours," Bernie said.

"You tried that already."

"I'm trying again," Bernie said. "Now that we know each other better. We're practically related."

Sometimes you get this strange kind of pause between humans where just about anything can happen. Including—maybe even especially—gunplay. But Ellie wasn't carrying. Was that why she laughed instead? I had no idea. "You're talking about Shooter and Chet?" she said.

"I am."

That sounded interesting. I waited for more, but no more

came. Instead, Ellie straightened and looked Bernie in the eye. "You married?" she said.

"Divorced."

"Seeing anybody?"

"Yes."

"We're in the exact same position," Ellie said. She gazed down at the frog. The frog's throat made some strange bulging motions. "You've got"—Ellie checked her watch—"twenty-three hours, fifty-eight minutes."

SIX

N ot a whole lot of time, Chet," Bernie said as we drove away from the construction site. "And traffic's going to be . . ." He went silent, although I could almost hear his voice continuing inside him. "How about we take a short cut through High Chaparral Estates?"

Sounded good to me, High Chaparral Estates being maybe the fanciest part of the whole Valley, meaning it had the fanciest smells. Also it was where Leda lived with her husband, Malcolm. And Charlie, of course, except for some weekends and holidays when he was with us. Those times were the best. Charlie likes everything I like, such as running around crazily. Hadn't seen him in way too long!

Then, all of a sudden, wouldn't you know? We rounded a corner and drew up behind a school bus. A kid in the backseat had turned around so he could see out the window.

"Hey!" said Bernie. "That looks like—"

Charlie! No doubt about it. There was Charlie's round little face in the window, although maybe not as round or as little as before. Also he had a new thing going on with his hair, a kind of sticking-up clump toward the back, a bit like an Indian feather. He looked great! Bernie leaned on the horn, kept leaning on it until finally Charlie lowered his gaze down to us. And then came an expression on his face that I can't even begin to describe, so I'll leave it like this: it was all about humans at their very best. Don't see it every day, but when you do . . . well, you remember, and maybe cut them a little slack next time around the circuit. And I'm sure Charlie was happy about seeing Bernie, too. Let's not leave that out.

Soon Charlie was waving at us, and then a bunch of kids were crowding around him, all of them waving their little hands. Bernie beeped the horn—*beep beep beep*. I did this high-pitched thing I can do, not a howl, really, more like a faraway train whistle, or maybe not that far away. The fun we were having! But then the bus pulled over, stopped by the side of the road. We stopped behind it. A gray-haired woman in a baseball cap appeared at the back of the bus, sunlight glaring off the lenses of her glasses. Her lips moved, and all the kids except Charlie instantly disappeared from view. Charlie whipped around and faced front. The woman—had to be the driver, right? I was catching on fast—gave us a look, the corners of her mouth pointing straight down, and then strode back to the front of the bus.

We followed at a distance, Bernie and I at our very quietest, heads down. You wouldn't have noticed us. Soon the bus turned onto a street I knew and stopped in front of a house I knew, too, namely Leda's. Charlie got out and the bus drove away. Bernie hopped—yes!—hopped out of the Porsche and ran over to Charlie. He scooped him right up—kind of scooping me up in the process, at least momentarily, since I'd reached Charlie first, as I'm sure you've figured out already. Next came hugging and kissing and laughing, and during all that I happened to glance over at the

house, not just Leda's, of course, but Malcolm's as well and Charlie's most of the time—and there was Malcolm watching from an
upstairs window, his long, narrow face reminding me of the bus
driver on account of the downturned corners of his lips.

"Dad! Ms. Peoples is so mad at you!"

"The bus driver?"

"She didn't even believe you were my dad!"

"Oh?"

"'Cause dads are more mature."

"Um."

The front door of Leda's house opened and Leda stepped out,
dressed for tennis, with a tennis racket over her shoulder and a
pink visor on her head. How tan she was, her skin like mahogany,
maybe the best of all woods in terms of gnawing, which I know
from our one and only visit to the bar at the Ritz. She walked over
to us, gave Bernie not the friendliest look.

"Not more about the stupid key?" she said.

"No, no, we're all set on that."

"Small mercies," said Leda. She turned to Charlie and gave
him a smile. Leda has one of the biggest smiles you'll ever see,
lights up the whole world, except for wherever Bernie happens
to be. Whoa! Where did that thought even come from? I had no
idea what it meant.

"Hey, there," she said, licking her fingers and trying to flatten
the Indian feather thing Charlie's hair had going on, "how was
school?"

"Ms. Peoples is mad at Dad."

Leda's smile started to disappear. That takes time, what with
there being so much of it. "Ms. Peoples, the bus driver?"

"She has a cat named Agatha."

"Why is she mad at da—at your father?"

Charlie's mouth opened like he was about to say something. Then he glanced at Bernie—who actually wasn't even watching, his gaze having turned to the window, where Malcolm was just stepping back, out of view—and that little mouth closed right up.

"Charlie?" Leda said.

"Ms. Peoples thinks I'm immature," Bernie told her.

Leda's smile was now entirely gone. "What did you do? Forget it—I don't even want to know."

"He stirred the kids up!" Charlie said. Blurted: Could that be the expression?

"Is that how Ms. Peoples put it?"

Charlie nodded. "She doesn't like when we get stirred up. She likes when we sit still and think quiet thoughts."

"Quiet thoughts?" Bernie said. "What the hell are—"

Leda gave Bernie a look I remembered from the old days, and he went silent. At that moment a shiny new car drove up, a woman also in a tennis dress and pink visor at the wheel. "So if it's not about the key," Leda said, "to what do we owe this visit?"

"Well," Bernie said. "Uh, it's Friday, right? Meaning tomorrow's Saturday, when Charlie comes over. I was thinking, you know—hey, why not now? Since you're playing tennis and all? If Charlie wants to, of course."

"I do," said Charlie.

But maybe not loud enough. "Now you know my tennis schedule?" Leda said. "What a detective you are!"

She was dead-on right about that. But even I knew her tennis schedule: she was carrying her racket! Leda was making me real nervous, hard to explain how, exactly, and unless she was planning to spill more info on Agatha the cat, I wanted her en route to the tennis court, and pronto.

Meanwhile, we'd fallen into one of those strange silences you sometimes get, and no one seemed to be in a good mood all of a sudden, except for me. Yes, Agatha was a bothersome new development, but other than that I was tip-top.

The woman in the car looked over, caught Leda's eye, and pointed to her watch. Leda adjusted her racket on her shoulder, her eyes going to Bernie, then Charlie—and finally me, for some reason. "All right." She leaned down and gave Charlie a kiss on the forehead. "You'll have to be the mature one."

This was living! Me, Bernie, and Charlie zooming through open country in the Porsche. Yes, Charlie had the shotgun seat, and I was on the horrible shelf in back, but it was never as horrible when Charlie was the one up front. Also the sun was shining, but not too hot, and the cooler was loaded with picnic supplies. You can't ask for more.

"Where are we going, Dad?" Charlie said.

"We're on a case," said Bernie.

"Wow! You're taking me on a real case?"

"Well, yeah, sort of."

"Are we gonna catch a bad guy?"

"Oh, no, nothing like that. I just want to take a look at something out in the desert."

"What kind of something?"

"A hole in the ground."

"With a body in it?"

Bernie laughed, tousled Charlie's hair, somehow making the Indian feather thing stand up taller and wackier than before. "Just an empty hole," Bernie said. "But can you guess what was in it?"

"Treasure!"

Bernie laughed some more. It was great to see him so happy. "Easy, big guy."

That was me, or at least the front part of me, somehow in the front seat, sort of wedged in between Bernie and Charlie? What a nice surprise! But maybe not now, was that the point? I drew back to the horrible little shelf, tried to make myself comfortable. Sometimes pawing at a seat back makes you more comfortable.

"Chet!"

I got a grip.

"Treasure's not a bad guess," Bernie was saying when I tuned back in. "In this case, the treasure was in the form of a cactus."

"A cactus, Dad?"

"Saguaro," Bernie said. "Like that one over at three o'clock, only not quite as big. Wonder if it has a chip inside."

"Huh?"

"Some of them do."

"Chips—like to eat?"

Bernie laughed again, went into a long explanation about chips, and GPS, and the whole history of mapmaking, which I'm sure was fascinating. When he was done, Charlie said, "Are there chips in the cooler?"

"Barbecue flavored."

"Can I have some?"

"Now?"

"Yeah."

"Why not?"

"Mom hates that."

"Hates what?"

"Me saying 'why not.' She says I say it too much."

"Why?"

Silence. Then all of a sudden Charlie was laughing and laughing. Human laughter is just about the best thing they do, and kid laughter is the best of the best. We pulled over—two-lane blacktop, no traffic, picnic spots out the yingyang—popped open the cooler, and found the chips.

"And maybe Chet wants a treat," Charlie said.

Charlie: had to love him, and I did.

My treat turned out to be a bone from Orlando the butcher. I've met a number of butchers, but Orlando is the best. He's got a place down in South Pedroia, near our self-storage unit, packed to the roof with Hawaiian pants, none having sold so far, one of the reasons our finances are such a mess. People love Hawaiian shirts—today Bernie wore the one with mermaids, actually a bit scary to my way of thinking—so why not Hawaiian pants? That was how the whole business got started, Bernie knocking back a bourbon or two and suddenly asking that very question. I had no answer at the time and still don't. All I know is that Bernie has never worn a pair of the Hawaiian pants himself. But back to Orlando, a little guy with huge arms and an apron that smells like you wouldn't believe. "Hey, Chet, how about I saw off something real special for you?" That's the kind of thing he says whenever we drop by. Why don't we drop by more often? Why?

"How come Chet just barked like that?" Charlie said. Or something close: hard to tell with his mouth so busy with potato chips.

"That muffled kind of bark?" said Bernie, reaching into the potato chip bag. "It's because he's so busy gnawing on that enormous bone."

"But what was he barking about?"

They gazed at me. I gazed back at them.

"Hard to tell," Bernie said.

"It sounded kind of impatient, Dad."

"What's he got to be impatient about?"

Try not dropping by Orlando's often enough. But who wants to sound impatient? Not me. I concentrated on my bone and forgot everything else. Was there some talk about saguaros and their red fruit and the drinks the Indians made from it? And about not calling them Indians, Dad? And all the ones I know actually do call themselves Indians, Charlie? And so how about coming to school and telling that to the class, Dad? And more back-and-forth like that? I couldn't tell you. But if you're interested in the bone: heaven.

Next thing I knew we were back in the car. We drove deeper into the desert, smells of sage and mesquite and greasewood drifting by, the sky its very bluest. No complaints, amigo. Do you ever think: What if time stopped right now? I never do, but Bernie does. He's mentioned it more than once. I kind of hope he doesn't again. It makes me a bit nervous.

"Porsches are expensive, huh, Dad?" Charlie said after a while.

"Who told you that?"

"Daddy Mal."

"Daddy Mal?"

"That's what they—um."

"That's what you call Malcolm?"

"Uh-huh. He's Daddy Mal and you're, like, just plain Dad." I caught Charlie shoot Bernie a quick glance. Bernie was looking straight ahead, eyes on the road.

"Sounds good to me," he said.

Not long after that, we turned onto a narrow, unpaved track.

Bernie slowed down, checked the screen of his phone. "Getting close." We rounded a hill and rode down to a dry wash lined with trees, where the track ended.

"Are we there?" Charlie said.

"Not yet," said Bernie. "But it's as far as we can go in the Porsche."

"'Cause it's so expensive?"

Bernie laughed. "This is a real old one, Charlie. Got it dirt cheap. But it's not meant for open country like this." We got out of the car. Bernie stuffed some water bottles and my portable bowl in a backpack, and we crossed the wash and climbed up the far side.

"But someone's been driving here, Dad," Charlie said. "See these tracks?"

Bernie smiled. "A natural."

"What's that mean?" said Charlie.

"Nothing," said Bernie. He got down on one knee, took a close look at the tracks. Charlie did the exact same thing. "At least five different sets here, some coming in, some going out. See how this one's crumbled the tread marks of the others?"

"Yeah."

"That's the latest. But it's hard to say exactly when. Never rains out here, so marks can last a long time."

We followed the tracks across easy ground, not too rough or steep, even for a kid. This particular kid marched on ahead of us, but I had him in sight every moment, no worries about that. There was a little rise not far distant, with some saguaros growing on its slope. It was nice and quiet, not a trace of the whole big world of human noise.

"What if this was olden days and we were the Spanish?" Charlie said.

"Be pretty exciting."

"Did the Native—did the Indians have dogs?"

"Yup."

"But not horses."

"Nope."

"What if some of them came over that hill with their bows and arrows?"

"And we were the conquistadors?"

"Yeah."

"I'd say, 'Hi, Native Americans or Indians or whatever you want us to call you. Now we're getting back on our boats and going home. Nice meeting you.'"

Charlie laughed.

We crossed the little plain and started up the slope.

"See that hole in the ground, up near the top?" Bernie said. "Means we've come to the right place."

"Where someone dug up the saguaro?" said Charlie.

"Yeah."

It got steeper. All at once this was going way too slow for me. I ran on ahead—"Wow—look at him go!"—and came to the hole. A pretty big hole, about the size of the one left in the Parsonses' yard after they'd taken the saguaro away. I scrambled over the dug-up rocks and dirt around the hole and looked down into it. Then I went still.

"Chet?" Bernie called up to me.

Right away I knew what to do. I turned and ran down the slope, barking my head off.

"Chet. Sit."

I sat.

"Charlie, I want you to stay right here with Chet. Don't move. I'll be right back. Okay, son?"

Charlie nodded. His eyes were open real wide. I could hear his little heart. Nothing to be afraid of. Chet's beside you.

Bernie scrambled up the hill, reached the hole, gazed down. He went still, just like me. Ellie Newburg was down at the bottom of that hole, all twisted up, a round red hole in her forehead. As for holes in the earth, there were more of them on the next slope over. I picked up Shooter's scent, but he wasn't around.

SEVEN

"You took him on a case?" Leda said. "What the hell is wrong with you?"

We were back in Leda's front yard, same people as before, except Malcolm was down here with her, and the face in the upstairs window was Charlie's. Maybe just a small switch up, but it made me uneasy, hard to say why. And what was this? My tail starting to droop? I got it right back up there, stiff and straight, the tail of a total pro. As for Leda's question, wasn't the answer pretty clear? Nothing was wrong with Bernie, not a damn thing. Not now, not yesterday, not tomorrow. I got ready for the satisfaction of hearing him say all that to Leda, and in no uncertain terms, whatever those might be.

But that's not what Bernie did. He took a deep breath and said, "It wasn't really taking him on a case. Well, sort of, except it was more or less an excuse for a nice drive in the desert. Um, a little picnic."

"A little picnic?" Leda said. "Toasting marshmallows around a dead body?"

Bernie stopped shuffling around. Not that he'd been shuffling—that could never happen—but he hadn't looked Leda in the eye. Now he did. A little muscle jumped in the side of his jaw. You didn't see that often. "The case was about a stolen cactus. Do you think I had the slightest inkling of what we'd find out there?"

Leda started to say something, but Malcolm beat her to it. He was a tall dude—taller than Bernie, although a lot thinner, more like an enormous skinny weed. Now he leaned forward in a weedy way and said, "Which simply indicates that your competence matches your judgment."

What did that even mean? Don't ask me. But it made Bernie boil up inside. I could feel the heat! Next would come that lightning jab to the chin and then the cracking hook right off it: *BAM BAM BAM*, the last *BAM* being the sound of Malcolm hitting the ground.

But no. Instead . . . Bernie backed away? Yes. I saw it with my own eyes. First, he glanced at that upstairs window, where Charlie was still looking out. Then he stuffed his hands in his pockets. And backed away. We walked toward the car, like . . . like we'd lost. Some dudes, when they win, keep their mouths shut. I heard Malcolm say, ". . . grounds for revisiting the whole custody arrangement." As we got in the car, I looked back, saw Leda and Malcolm heading toward the front door, hand in hand. There was no face in the upstairs window. Not glancing back even for a moment, Bernie missed all that.

Valley PD headquarters are downtown, standing on one side of a little park, the college being on the other. Love college kids, myself, and it was nice to catch a glimpse of them doing college things—like working hard on their suntans and throwing Frisbees and smoking all kinds of smokables, a dense smoky cloud hanging over the park all year except for summer, when the kids were gone and the street people took over, the street people being into smokables in a smaller way but other stuff in a bigger way. We climbed the steps to headquarters, said hi to people we knew, got patted a few times—me, not Bernie—and ended up in the office of our buddy Captain Stine.

Our buddy, yes, although not a human of the friendly-looking type. Captain Stine had a sharp-shaped kind of face and all his looks were dark. But he'd only made captain because of a case we'd cleared for the mayor, me and Bernie, details pretty much forgotten except for a cat name of Brando. Why couldn't I forget Brando and remember all the rest instead? You tell me. Actually, don't. What I want you to hang on to is the fact that Captain Stine—a tough cop who liked to lean on everybody and owed nobody nothing—did owe us.

"Ah, Chet," Stine said. "And Bernie. Want you to meet Ms. Newburg's boss, Carl Conte, director, Special Investigations, Department of Agriculture."

The only other person in the room was a dude in a suit, sitting on a chair to one side of Stine's desk, so it had to be him. This dude was smaller than Captain Stine but also had a sharp-shaped face, and although I didn't know about all his looks, the one he'd locked on Bernie at the moment was dark. Then a strange thought came to me: the dude—Conte, was that it?—owed us zip.

"My condolences," Bernie said.

Conte nodded. No handshaking took place. Bernie sat on the opposite side of the desk from Conte. I sat beside Bernie, kept my eye on Conte across the desk. He eyed me back.

"I think I've heard of this dog," he said.

"Everybody knows Chet," Stine said. "He's—"

"I have problems with dogs, ecologically speaking," Conte said. "But that's neither here nor there."

Whew. For a moment I'd worried we'd gone off the rails. But if something wasn't here nor there, it wasn't, so no worries.

"Uh, well then, Bernie," Stine said. "How about you walk us through it?"

"Starting where?" Bernie said.

"Starting," Conte said, before Stine could answer, "with how you got involved in my case."

"Instead," Bernie said, gazing across the desk at Conte, kind of just like me, "since you raised the subject of dogs, how about we start with Shooter? Where is he?"

"Who," said Conte, "is Shooter?"

"Ellie's dog," Bernie said. "She takes him everywhere."

"She does?" said Conte. "I specifically forbade that."

"Kind of moot, Carl, at this point," Stine said.

Conte's face swelled up a bit, got reddish. "I'll be the—"

"And where's her pickup?" Bernie said.

Stine looked at Conte. "Hasn't turned up yet," Conte said.

"Who's in charge of the investigation?" said Bernie.

"That's still being worked out," Stine said. "But it'd help, Bernie, if—"

"How about sending a chopper out there?" Bernie said.

"We did," said Stine. "Had to turn back—fuel pump crimped up or some damn thing."

"Send another one."

"All in the shop."

"Can we put a lid on this, for chrissake?" Conte said. "Whoever ends up running this case, it's sure as hell not gonna be this guy." He pointed at Bernie, even wagged his finger at him. Bernie hates that. A wagging finger is nothing like a wagging tail—took me some time to figure that out. "We need to know what you know, and stat."

His finger stopped wagging but remained pointed at Bernie. Bernie gazed at it. The finger folded back up, and Conte lowered his hand.

"I met Ellie at my neighbor's place," Bernie said. "She was investigating a saguaro theft that had turned up in your chip ID program. I guess she wanted to check the spot where it had been dug up. We did the same, which was how we found her."

"Why?" Conte said. "Why did you, quote, do the same?"

"Curiosity," said Bernie.

"You're a private investigator."

"Correct."

"Do you normally investigate on your own dime? Just out of 'curiosity?'"

"What are you trying to say?"

Conte leaned forward. "I looked into you. Some people around this town hate your guts. Others think you're the best thing since sliced bread. Somehow the mayor's one of that group, hard to believe. But I didn't get the impression you work on your own dime. Meaning there's a client. I want to know who."

Whoa! Slow down. There were Bernie haters? First I'd heard of it. Even most of the perps and gangbangers like Bernie, after they get to know him. Plus what was so great about sliced bread? I've had it both ways, and guess what, dude—dude meaning Conte, not you. Tastes the exact same, a not very interesting taste in my opinion.

"No one's paid me to work on this case," Bernie said.

Conte turned to Stine. "You always let him get away with this shit? We have a dead agent out there, murdered in the field, and this asshole is stonewalling."

I didn't know what was going on with anyone else's teeth, but my own were getting this sudden urge that sometimes comes over them, namely the urge to bite. Was now a good time? I went back and forth on that one, except there was no back, only forth. In short, yes! It was a good time! All at once, I felt Bernie's grip on my collar, not grasping it hard or anything like that, but just there. Why would that be?

Stine raised his hands, palms out in the stop sign. "Guys, can we lower the volume on this?"

"There's only one of us raising it," Bernie said.

Stine sighed. "Maybe. But you can understand why he's upset. And if that old man is in fact your client, then there's no point in stonewalling."

"Old man?" Bernie said, real quiet.

"What was it?" said Stine. "Partridge?"

"Parsons," Conte said.

"Right, Parsons," Stine went on. "We've got people over there questioning him right now, and—"

"You what?" Bernie said, starting to rise.

"Why is that surprising?" Stine said. "Normal procedure, straight out of—"

Bernie smacked Stine's desk, real hard, like a thunderclap. Stine had a nice gold pen set. It jumped right off the desk and was still airborne as we zipped on out of there, me and Bernie.

"Hey," Stine called after us. "Where the hell—"

"Arrest them!" Conte yelled.

Meaning me and Bernie? What a strange interview! Maybe the kind of thing to go over in my mind at some future time. Yeah, that was it.

We roared up Mesquite Road, hit the brakes in front of the Parsonses' house. Lots going on: We had a Valley PD cruiser, an ambulance, and—what was this?—an Animal Control truck? Yes, all parked on the street. The front door opened as we hurried up to the house and EMTs came hurrying the other way, rolling a stretcher. Humans rushing around in all directions: never a good sign. The stretcher flew right past us, Mr. Parsons on top, eyes closed, a breathing mask on his face. We followed the stretcher down to the ambulance where they threw open the back doors and slid Mr. Parsons inside. An EMT looked out as the doors were closing.

"What happened?" Bernie said.

The EMT shrugged. The doors closed and the ambulance took off. The driver hit the siren.

We turned toward the house. More action at the door? It was getting hard to keep up. Now we had a uniformed cop we didn't know followed by a Valley PD detective we did know, namely Brick Mickles. Was Bernie in the mood for Brick Mickles at the moment? I could see just from the way he stopped dead that he was not. Bernie and Brick Mickles went way back, back to the period between the end of Bernie's army days and the start of the Little Detective Agency. That was a time when Bernie himself had been with Valley PD. He never talked about it, so that was all I know, except that whenever we ran into Brick Mickles, things didn't go well.

Mickles saw us and also stopped dead. Then a smile spread across his face. He had a big face. Did I leave out that he was a huge guy, everything about him huge except for his tiny, round ears, actually quite beautifully shaped? Hardly anybody ever makes Bernie look small, but Brick Mickles was one.

"Well, well, well," he said. "I'll be doggone."

I'd never understood that one, just knew I myself wasn't going anywhere at the moment.

"What the hell are you doing here?" Bernie said.

Mickles shrugged his enormous shoulders. "Serving. Protecting. Et cetera."

"They sent you?"

"Just my luck. Missing saguaro, but I heard cigar, so I volunteered, thinking I could score a box or two." He glanced over at our place, then smacked his forehead. "That's your crib! Totally forgot. Now it's making sense."

"What are you talking about?"

"The old duffer," Mickles said, motioning down Mesquite Road in the direction the ambulance had taken. "Kept droning on about some goddamn neighbor. Neighbor was gonna sort everything out, if I'd just—how'd he put it?—be patient? But even a patient type such as myself gets a bit antsy in a murder case."

"What did you do to him?" Bernie said. He began moving toward the house, not quickly, but powerfully—a slow glide that reminded me of a mountain lion I'd once encountered, and maybe mentioned already. Wasn't a mountain lion just a very big cat? If so, was Bernie moving like a cat? That was disturbing. I moved along beside him, but not like a cat. We stopped within easy leaping range of Mickles. Easy leaping range for me, anyway, can't speak for any possible cat person on the scene.

"Took the thumbscrews to him, of course," Mickles said. "Only way to crack those tough old nuts."

When two dudes are right on the point of throwing down— meaning two human dudes, although a similar thing happens in my world—you can't miss a sudden smell that comes rising off both of them, and now we had it big-time. I could feel their muscles loading up—mine, too!—and could also feel their hate for each other, hate being something you hardly ever saw from Bernie. I made sure my weight was nicely balanced, all set for whatever needed doing.

Mickles smiled that big smile of his again. "Fixing to take

a swing at me, huh, Bernie? Remember what happened the last time?"

"Fondly," Bernie said.

"Fondly?" said Mickles. "You forget how it ended your golden-boy career? But maybe it makes sense psychologically. Taking pleasure in the beginning of your life as a nobody—defines the self-destructive type, doncha think?"

Bernie came oh, so close to throwing his jab. There was a kind of quick bunching in his shoulder, there and gone. Mickles saw it, too, and flinched—just the tiniest bit, but I caught it. Then came a pause, a long one that ended with the uniformed cop—who'd been watching from the road, hand on the butt of his gun—sliding behind the wheel of the cruiser. After that, Bernie seemed to step back, although he actually didn't, and he and Mickles both seemed to get smaller. The fighting smell—really kind of a stench, if you don't mind me pointing that out—faded away.

"As for your elderly buddy," Mickles said, stepping around us and heading toward the cruiser, "more likely a fainting spell than a heart attack, according to the EMTs. My bet's he faked the whole thing." He opened the car door, turned to us. "But there's no question he knows something, meaning I'll know, too, sooner rather than later."

He got in the cruiser. Bernie watched it drive off with a real hard look on his face, and was still watching when a yip-yip-yip-ping came from inside the house. We turned back to the door just in time to see Iggy emerge. He was on a leash, a leash held by a woman in a green uniform. I knew that uniform from the old days, before Bernie. It meant Animal Control. I remembered the Animal Control truck parked on the street and . . . and put one and one together! Wow! That was a first.

EIGHT

H ey!" Bernie said. "Where are you going with Iggy?"
The Animal Control woman paused. Iggy did not,
meaning he stretched out the leash to the max, came to a sudden
stop, and fell flat on the stoop. "Iggy?" she said. She checked her
clipboard. "Dispatch has it Izzy."

"It's Iggy," Bernie said.

"You sure?" The Animal Control woman looked down at
Iggy, still lying sprawled on the stoop, his stubby tail somehow
weirdly caught underneath him. "Iggy," she said. "Sit." Iggy didn't
move a muscle. "Izzy," she said. "Sit."

Iggy scrambled up immediately and sat straight and still, like
a total pro, which Iggy most definitely was not. But maybe . . .
maybe Izzy was a total pro? What a strange thought! I got confused. Sometimes strange thoughts come tumbling in on each
other's heels. Here was another: Why would the two of them, Iggy
and Izzy, smell exactly alike? That did not happen in the nation
within. I tried to shut my mind down, but totally. Meanwhile, the
Animal Control woman was giving Bernie one of those human
looks that means "I win."

"Let's not argue," Bernie said. "The point is we're neighbors and friends of the couple who live here. I'm taking him."

"Nothing wrong with that," said the woman. "Give little Izzy a day or two to get in the system and then you can start the adoption process."

Once in a while, Bernie's voice gets very soft, just when you'd think it would be going the other way. "Is he in the system now, at this moment?"

"Why, no, not at this very moment. But he will be as soon as I get to the truck and—"

Bernie put his hand on the leash, gently, but there. "You've got a tough job. How about today you let me make it a little easier?"

The Animal Control woman tightened her grip on the leash. "What if something goes wrong?"

"I'll take full responsibility."

She glanced around, appeared to see me for the first time. How come that took so long? "Is this your dog?"

"Chet's his name."

The Animal Control woman gazed at me for another moment or two, then let go of the leash.

After she left, we rounded up some of Iggy's things, locked up the Parsonses' house, and crossed over to our place, Iggy marking several spots along the way, starting with his own front door. I'd never even thought of marking our front door, but that was Iggy for you, every time.

Old man Heydrich, our neighbor on the other side, was out watering his lawn. We have a desert-style lawn, me and Bernie, and so do the Parsonses, but Heydrich has a golf-course-style lawn, or even greener. Bernie got a real annoyed look on his face. Now that I'd seen the aquifer with my own eyes, almost totally gone already, I was just as annoyed as Bernie. How hard would it be to snatch that hose right out of his hand? A piece of cake. Let's leave out my thoughts on actual cake for the time being.

Old man Heydrich glanced over at us, through a tiny rainbow that hovered in the spray. "Parsons kick the bucket?" he said.

"Excuse me?"

"Happened to see the ambulance." Heydrich turned the hose on a big flowerpot with one small yellow flower growing in the middle and watered it until it slumped over. "Happen to know he's been poorly. Added it up."

"There's one aquifer," Bernie said. "One and one only. Do the math on that."

We went inside the house. Bernie came close to slamming the door, reeled that impulse in at the last second. He unclipped Iggy, said, "Just want you to relax, little guy. Everything's going to be—" Which was when Iggy took off down the hall and darted into the office. We hurried after him, got there just in time to find him scratching at the wall under the waterfall painting.

"Iggy?" Bernie said. "What's up?"

Iggy did some more scratching of the wall. I gave him a low growl. If there were any walls that needed scratching in this house—a big no-no, by the way—they would be scratched by Chet the Jet, and Chet the Jet only.

"Chet! Knock it off! Can't hear myself think."

Me? Me knock it off! And how could a little low growling—possibly mixed in with a soft bark or two—disturb anyone's thoughts, especially the thoughts of someone as brainy as Bernie, meaning as brainy as they come?

Bernie took down the waterfall painting, exposing the hole in the wall where the safe used to be. Iggy stopped scratching, sat down, and began howling, his flattened snout raised up toward the hole in the wall. Bernie crouched beside him.

"Iggy? You trying to tell us something?"

I squeezed in between them. There's only so much you can take.

Iggy was still trying to squeeze me out, and I was still retrying to squeeze him back the other way, squeeze him but good, when the phone rang. The voice of old Mr. Parsons came over the speaker, sounding older than ever, a wispy sort of voice, more patches of blank air than of sound.

"Bernie? Bernie?"

"It's me, Daniel. How are you?"

"Bernie?"

"Yes, Bernie," said Bernie. "Are you all right?"

"Me? No. Well, physically, yes."

"You're all right physically?"

"Oh, I don't want—nurse!"

"Daniel? What's happening? Is the nurse with you?"

"I don't want any damn—"

Silence. Then came a sort of crash and a woman saying, "Now, now."

"Daniel?" Bernie said.

And suddenly Mr. Parsons was back. "Blood! Blood!" A shout, but so strange since it was mostly air.

"You're bleeding?"

"Me?" said Mr. Parsons, a very wispy "me." "Not . . . not so's you'd notice. But Bernie?"

"Yes, I'm here."

"They want my blood."

"Who does, Daniel?"

"The nurses, the docs. How much have I got to spare, answer me that?"

"I don't know," Bernie said. "Do they say—"

Then a woman was on the line. "Who's this?"

"Bernie Little—a friend of Mr. Parsons. You're the nurse?"

"I am. He's very agitated. Possible heart attack, but we need to get some blood work, and he's not making it easy."

"Put him on."

Then came some fumbling sounds, followed by Mr. Parsons's wispy voice. "Bernie?"

"I'm here."

"I don't like this place."

"Understood. But all they want to do is help you."

"Then why won't they take me to Edna? I want to see Edna."

"What hospital are you in?"

"The one with the . . . with the . . ."

The nurse spoke up in the background. "County."

"They've got you at County, Daniel," Bernie said. "Edna's at Valley General."

"I want to be at Valley General. Nurse? Please call me a taxi."

"Daniel," Bernie said. "First, let them take some blood. That's step one on getting you transferred over to General."

"It is?"

"Yes."

"You're a good friend, Bernie."

"I've got Iggy, so no need to worry about that."

"You've got Iggy? But . . . but . . . he's under my bed. Nurse? Isn't Iggy under my bed?"

"Iggy?" said the nurse.

More fumbling, and the line went dead.

Bernie stood at the desk, one hand resting on its top, almost like he was holding himself up. Which wasn't Bernie, and you can take that to the bank—although not our bank, where we were having problems with Ms. Oxley. You can count on Bernie to hold up his own self. You can count on Bernie for everything.

He looked over at Iggy, now curled up on the floor and trying to chew his tail.

"Easy, little guy, everything'll be—"

The phone buzzed again.

"Uh, Bernie Little? It's me, the nurse again. He's calmer now. Meds kicked in. He wants to talk to you."

"Bernie?"

"Feeling a bit better, Daniel?"

"I am," said Mr. Parsons, still sounding pretty wispy to me. "And thanks for asking. But—" He lowered his voice to a whisper: not so easy to hear, a wispy whisper, even for me. "—I'm ashamed to say I have to release you from your promise."

"Sorry, Daniel," Bernie said. "Didn't get that."

Mr. Parsons cleared his throat, a nasty metallic scraping that made my own throat hurt. "I said I have to release you from your promise."

"My promise about implicating Billy?"

"Yes, sir."

"Why? Has he been in touch? Have you talked to him?"

"Oh, no, nothing like that. The truth is I was a weakling."

"I don't understand."

"I caved, Bernie. I broke the promise myself."

"You implicated Billy?"

"To my disgrace. A detective came by my place. Not a detective like you, Bernie. More what you'd think of as a detective type, from Valley PD."

"Brick Mickles?"

"I missed the name. A very large man. I told him I was under no obligation to answer any questions—I know my rights, Bernie!—but he backed me into a corner."

"He laid hands on you?"

"Nothing like that. But worse in a way. He told me if I didn't confess all I knew about the cactus, he was going to have Edna brought downtown for questioning."

"For Christ sake, he can't do—" Bernie cut himself off suddenly.

"Edna might not understand her rights the way I do," Mr. Parsons said. "I—I had to choose between her and Billy. That was hateful, if you see what I mean."

"I do."

"Hatefulness filled me up to the brim," Mr. Parsons said. "I contemplated violence against him, I truly did. Then I heard a crack from inside like a twig, and I was on the floor."

Bernie said nothing. His face was grim and angry. I tried to think of something to amuse him. Fetch, for example. I sniffed around under the desk where tennis balls often lurked but came up empty.

"And now here I am," said Mr. Parsons. "Letting down the team."

"No more of that talk," Bernie said. "Your job is to get better. I'll drop by later. Meanwhile, if Mickles or anyone else tries to question you, tell them you've got nothing to say."

"You're a smart man, Bernie," Mr. Parsons said, his voice mostly air patches again. After some silence, Mr. Parsons added, "Who's Mickles?"

Bernie's eyes closed, real slow.

"All set, Iggy?" Bernie said, next morning. "Got everything you need?"

I should hope so: that was my only thought. Iggy had a big

bowl of kibble, a big bowl of water, a chew toy that looked like a bone, plus an actual bone from Orlando the butcher—

"Chet! That's not yours!"

—as well as a tennis ball and a lacrosse ball, both property of Chet the Jet. That'll do you, Iggy?

"Now we're just going to close this door, Iggy, keep you in the kitchen while we're gone, just in case you . . . just in case."

We left the kitchen. As Bernie closed the door, I glimpsed Iggy going right for the lacrosse ball in the most annoying way imaginable.

"Back real soon, little guy!"

And enough with the little guy stuff. Iggy was my best pal, no doubt about that, but . . . Let's just leave it there: but.

We drove into the parking lot at Donut Heaven. Whatever bad thoughts had been bubbling up in my mind vanished at once. Bernie parked us cop-style beside an unmarked sedan, driver's-side door to driver's-side door. The sedan's window slid down, and Captain Stine looked over at us.

"They're out of crullers," he said.

"No way."

"Baker got deported last night. But Chet likes bear claws, no?"

Yes! Yes! He does.

"How can they have bear claws and not crullers?" Bernie said.

"Assistant baker trains on the bear claws. You want them or not?"

We do! We do!

Stine handed over a paper bag and a coffee for Bernie. Bear claws sound scary, especially if, like me, you've come close to seeing real bear claws in action, but the bear claws at Donut Heaven, every bit as real, come to think of it . . . I lost the thread, and very soon was curled up in comfort, busy with breakfast.

Bernie sipped his coffee. "You don't look good," he said.

"Baby was up all night."

"What's fatherhood like?"

"Huh? You're a father. You know."

"I meant at your age."

"Fuck you, Bernie." Stine drained his coffee, crumpled the cup. "What do you want?"

"You put Mickles on the Ellie Newburg case."

"So?"

"Why him?"

"I don't have to explain to you. He's in the pool."

"So are good detectives."

"Maybe you have a history with him," Stine said. "I don't. Case closed."

I looked up from what I was doing. Case closed? Had we even started yet? Cases at the Little Detective Agency almost always closed with me grabbing the perp by the pant leg. The only pants wearers in the picture at the moment were Bernie and Captain Stine. This can be a tricky job. I went back to the bear claw.

"How about what he did to Daniel Parsons?" Bernie said. "That doesn't bother you?"

"Talking about the receiver of the stolen cactus?"

"If you want to put it that way. But he's just a sweet old guy. Maybe Mickles got what he wanted, but did he have to put him in the hospital to do it?"

"No clue what you're talking about." Stine took out a notebook, leafed through, shook his head. "Mickles knocked on the door and introduced himself, at which point the old man keeled over and Mickles called rescue." Stine looked across at Bernie. "He got zip, didn't even ask question one."

Bernie was sitting up real straight, his hands tight on the

wheel, even though we weren't moving. "Where are you getting that?"

"It's Mickles's report, for chrissake. He apologized and asked if I had suggestions."

"Apologized for what?"

"Being nowhere on the case."

"Nowhere on the case?"

"He's got no leads. It's like you don't remember how this is done, Bernie. What's wrong with you?"

NINE

"Here's a puzzle," Bernie said as we drove away from Donut Heaven. "Outside the Parsonses' house Mickles told us he suspected Daniel knew something and was going to get it out of him. Except according to Daniel, he'd already given him Billy's name. I can understand Mickles keeping us in the dark, but now in his official report to Stine he's claiming he has no leads. Mickles knows about Billy, but he's keeping it to himself? What's up?"

Uh-oh. Whatever that was, I'd missed the whole thing, hoped it wasn't important. Meanwhile, we were crossing the canyon on the Coronado Bridge. "Why name it after him?" Bernie said every single time we were on it, except for now. Now he said, "Do we want Mickles finding Billy before we do? No. So Billy's where we start."

We entered a quiet neighborhood somewhat like our own, except hillier, a neighborhood I recognized from a rather exciting night in my past.

"Question one. What's all the money for? Billy took twenty grand from his parents and almost certainly stole the watch. Adds up to a lot of green."

Or something like that: I was pretty much lost in memories of that exciting long-ago night. How pleasant memories can be!

"One thing for sure," Bernie said. "I smell a rat."

All at once Bernie had my full attention. He had never smelled a rat before, not in any back alley, Dumpster, or landfill we'd ever investigated, almost all of them as ratty as you could wish for. Once we'd even worked our way into a sewer system. Rats out the yingyang down there, my friends. Invisible, yes, on account of the darkness, but they'd smelled the place up in a way that couldn't be missed. But that was the point: Bernie had missed it. That was when I'd first been certain that his nose—really good-sized in human terms—was mostly for decoration. And now he was smelling a rat, when—trust me—there was no rat to smell? What was going on? I shifted my position a bit, keeping Bernie under close surveillance, waiting for some explanation.

But none came. After a while, he said, "We've got Billy's number—how about we just ask him?" He tapped at his phone. A voice spoke. "Number no longer in service." Bernie nodded as though that made sense. A moment or two later, he swung onto a cross street. "Wildheart Way—here we go." And soon we were parked in front of a small house with a desert-style front yard, just like ours. We got out, looked around. "Shooter?" Bernie called. "Shooter?"

Whoa! Now he thought he was smelling Shooter? I could actually detect a bit of Shooter scent, but not recent. What was happening to Bernie? I went closer, my go-to move when I'm worried about him.

"Hey, big guy, a little space."

I was already giving him space, more than he needed under these circumstances.

"Shooter!" he yelled. And maybe was fixing to do so again,

what with me blanking out on how to stop him—Bernie! No Shooter on the premises!—when the door to the small house opened and a woman looked out.

"Who are you?" she said. "What do you want?"

Her voice was all ragged, the way a woman's voice gets when she's angry. But also when she's been crying, and this woman had been crying: I could smell the telltale mixture of tears and snot. Why do women cry more than men? Is it because they also talk more? That was as far as I could take it, probably too far.

"I'm Bernie Little," Bernie said. "I was just, um, sort of checking to see if Shooter had turned up. That is, if this is where, uh, if this is the house . . ." He gazed at the woman, a gray-haired woman in jeans and a T-shirt, maybe overweight, but kind of strong-looking, too. "Are you Ellie's mother?"

The woman didn't nod or speak. A tear leaked out of one of her eyes and left a silvery track on her cheek.

"I'm sorry for your loss," Bernie said.

Now she nodded, a single brief nod. "I didn't get your name."

"Bernie Little," Bernie said. "I'm a private detective. I was working with her on the case that . . . on this last case. Chet and I—" He nodded toward me. "—are the ones who discovered—who found her."

"A saguaro?" the woman said.

"I'm sorry?"

She raised her voice. She'd been crying, yes, but she was angry, too. "The case. You're the one who brought it up."

"Sorry," Bernie said. "Yes, the case was—is about saguaros, illegally transplanted from the desert to—"

"Why the hell did she care so much about a goddamn cactus?" the woman said. Her voice rose and rose, ended up close to a scream. I heard a window open in some nearby house.

When Bernie answered, his voice was very soft. "Someone has to," he said.

The woman went still. "That's exactly what Ellie said, her very words. But I'll never understand."

"I think she meant that if no one—"

The woman waved her arm, like she was knocking Bernie aside. "Why her?"

"I don't know," Bernie said. "But we mean to find out."

"Who is 'we'?" the woman said.

"Valley PD, for starters. Plus Carl Conte from her department. And—"

"She hated him."

"Hated Conte? Why?"

"She said he was just another scumbag politician."

"Any other reason?"

"Why would there be any other reason? What are you getting at?"

"Nothing," Bernie said. "What I was trying to tell you is that Chet and I will also be working on this, full-time."

"Who is Chet?"

Bernie pointed at me. At the time I was licking at an unruly tuft of fur sticking up on one shoulder, but I soon got that taken care of.

"He looks so much like . . ." the woman said.

"Ellie and I were discussing that," Bernie said.

"I can imagine," the woman said, and then with no warning she fell apart completely, wailing and sobbing, tears streaming down her face. Bernie went to her, turned her around, walked her into the house, and closed the door. Being inside didn't keep me from hearing another window opening up in the neighborhood, and then one more.

• • •

"What's your name?" Bernie said, refilling the woman's water glass at the kitchen sink and handing it to her.

"Barb," she said. She took a sip, dabbed at her face with the back of her arm, gazed around in that unseeing way humans sometimes do. How interesting they are! Meanwhile, there wasn't much to see, just a lot of boxes, mostly empty, and stacks of kitchen things here and there. "Sorting through all the . . . all the . . ." Barb said.

"Is there any hurry on that?" Bernie said.

"I don't know. Her lease is up at the end of the end of next month. But she was going to renew. So . . . I just don't know."

"Maybe you can get someone to help you."

"Yeah." Barb took another sip, looked my way. "Where do you think he is?"

"Shooter?"

Barb nodded.

"No idea," Bernie said. "How about we call some of the shelters?"

"Now?"

"Why not?"

Soon they were sitting across from each other at the kitchen table, talking on their phones. About what? I wondered about that. Then I picked up an interesting scent, followed it to a gap between the fridge and the stove, and discovered a chewy shaped like a little baseball bat—a chewy, from the smell, clearly belonging to Shooter. So nice of him to share! I'm a big fan of baseball—especially the ball itself, full of surprises when you get inside—and also of chewies, hardly bears mentioning, meaning my life was about to enter one of those perfect interludes. Do you have them? With me, they come around pretty often. Yet I'm always surprised, which takes it to an even nicer level. Who can make sense of all these things? Not me, amigo.

The phone calls went on for some time, then came to an end. Bernie and Barb shook their heads.

"Doesn't mean he won't turn up," Bernie said. "And now if he does, they'll call you."

"She loved Shooter so much."

"I understand."

Barb gave Bernie a quick sideways look. "Maybe this sounds crazy, but I'd really like him found."

"Why is that crazy?"

"Because I can't keep him—I'm allergic."

That puzzler cropping up again? I didn't let it affect my mood.

"We'll do our best to find him," Bernie said. "Any thoughts on where he'd go if not here?"

"Such as . . . ?"

"Such as somewhere else he likes to go," Bernie said. "Shooter didn't start from here—I'm going on the assumption that he was with her when . . . that he rode along on the trip."

"I didn't think of that. But of course you're right." Barb's eyes shifted, a sign her mind had gotten busy on something. "Where's her truck?"

"Good question," Bernie said. "But back to Shooter, and where he might go."

"I just don't know."

"What about Ellie's boyfriend? Where does he live?"

"Her boyfriend? Ellie doesn't . . . there was no boyfriend, not recently."

"My mistake," Bernie said.

"There were boyfriends in the past," said Barb. "But none of them panned out, for one reason or another. You know how men are these . . . excuse me."

"No," Bernie said. "Go on. It's a teachable moment."

Barb laughed. A small laugh, and quickly done with, but nice to hear. "I've said too much already."

"I can take it."

"That's what they all say," Barb said.

Bernie smiled. "Lesson one," he said.

From the look on her face, I thought Barb was about to laugh again, but she did not. Instead she picked up a little silver trophy, dusted it off, and wrapped it in newspaper.

"How about Ellie's ex?" Bernie said. "Did Shooter know him?"

Barb put down the trophy. "Ex? There's no ex. Where are you getting your information?"

"Sorry," Bernie said. "I must have gotten things mixed up."

Barb gave him a careful look. "I hope you're a good detective," she said. "I don't have money to waste."

"Not following you."

"I'm paying you, of course. To find whoever killed my daughter. And to bring Shooter back home."

Bernie shook his head. "We're going to do those things," he said. "But we're not taking any money from you."

"I won't accept charity," said Barb.

"Nothing to do with charity," Bernie said. "We already have a client."

"Who?"

"That's confidential."

Confidential meaning he was going to say the name of the client or he wasn't? I was hoping he was, the existence of this client being news to me. Do I need to fill you in on our finances? I kept hoping for client news until we were back in the car, and for some time after.

"Remember how that went, big guy?" Bernie said as we crossed back over the canyon. "Didn't I tell Ellie I was divorced and seeing someone, and didn't she say 'same!' or something like that?"

I had no idea what he was talking about. That was bad. On the flip side, I still had Shooter's bat-shaped chewy. That was good, one bad and one good always leveling out to good, in my opinion.

"Why would she do that?" he went on. I waited to hear. My teeth felt tip-top, the way teeth do when working on a first-class chewy. "Is it possible she was laying the foundation for some sort of . . . some sort of something?" Bernie took a deep breath, let it out slow, accompanied by a small sound, not happy. "I'm not going to deny that I felt . . . what did I feel, exactly? A kind of beginning? I'm pretty sure I did. Do I have to beat myself up over that?"

I stopped in mid-chew. Bernie beating himself up? Had I ever in my whole career heard anything worse? Could he have forgotten about that lightning-quick jab and the damage it could do? Not to mention the hook that came pounding in right off the jab, both of them in the air at the same time, one coming, one going? He wouldn't stand a chance! I kept a close eye on Bernie's hands, was relieved to see they didn't square up into fists, but stayed on the steering wheel, nice and relaxed. I wondered about taking Bernie on a long run in the canyon, maybe work off some of his excess energy. You had to get out in front of problems, as Bernie says, and now I really understood it for the first time. A simple plan—find a tennis ball, drop it at Bernie's feet—was already forming in my mind as we turned into our driveway, but then the phone buzzed.

"Bernie?"

Hey! It was Suzie. Hadn't heard her voice in way too long. Not easy for us, me and Bernie, being so far away from her. Seeing her in Foggy Bottom—if that was where we'd seen her: what a great time! Gunplay on a boat at night—you don't forget fun like that. And Suzie had written up the whole case—the Barnum case as I called it to myself, on account of Barnum, a guinea pig who'd played a small role—for her paper, Bernie reading the whole thing aloud, although I'd fallen into dreamland soon after the Barnum part. Suzie had even ended up on TV! We'd watched her in a bar somewhere on our drive back home, except not all of it, what with the bartender changing the channel, which had led to a little rumpus best forgotten.

"Uh, hi, Suzie," Bernie said.

"You okay, Bernie?"

"Yeah, sure. Just working on a case."

"Is this a bad time?"

"No, no. I mean—for what?"

Suzie laughed. "Oh, Bernie, you're just so . . ."

"Go on."

"You. You're so you."

"That's it? I was hoping for some revelation."

"I'm no revelator," Suzie said. "Just a journalist. Which is actually the point of my call."

"Oh?"

"As well as hearing you being you, of course. Goes without saying." Then came a pause. I noticed old man Heydrich out on the sidewalk, sweeping dust from his side to ours. He saw me, flashed a quick glare, and headed back toward his house. "The thing is," Suzie went on, "they've offered me a promotion."

"So soon?"

"My first thought, too. Either they're in total disarray, or . . ."

"Or they really like you."

"They've offered me Europe," Suzie said.

"The whole of Europe, or just west of the Rhine?" Bernie said.

"Stop it. I mean the European desk. Head of it, Bernie!" She took a breath, reined herself in a bit. "Based in London. I want you to come."

TEN

L ike for a long weekend?" Bernie said.

Silence on the other end.

Bernie tried again. "Um, a week or so?"

What was this about? Europe? London? Both new to me, whatever they were. I worked on the remains of Shooter's chewy. Nothing lasts forever—you hear that all the time—and it was certainly true of chewies, in my experience. But just you wait and a fresh new chewy is bound to come along! The only hard part is the waiting. Waiting is the only thing that . . . lasts forever? Whoa! Where did that come from? Way too disturbing. Best forgotten. Done!

". . . sure, Bernie," Suzie was saying when I tuned back in. "For a visit, at first. That makes total sense."

"A visit," Bernie said. "As, uh, opposed to . . . ?"

"Sorry, Bernie," Suzie said. "I'm not doing this very well. Started in the wrong place, a common misstep in my profession. How about we back up a bit?"

"As far as you want," Bernie said. "But let me get my congratulations in. You're a star, Suzie. I . . . I couldn't be prouder of you."

"You mean that?"

"Of course. Why wouldn't I?"

"It's just nice to hear, that's all," Suzie said. "Lots of men might say it, but how many would mean it?"

"Why wouldn't they mean it?" Bernie said.

"See, right there—the very fact you could ask that question simply proves everything."

"Lost me," Bernie said.

Suzie laughed. "Don't you get it?"

"Maybe I do," Bernie said, "and just don't know it."

"That's exactly where I've been for way too long," Suzie said. "Then last night I was so restless, couldn't sleep, when suddenly it hit me. We should be together, you and I, period."

Suzie is one of my very favorite people in the world, so I knew she'd meant to say we should be together, you and Chet and I, period. Or possibly Chet and you and I, period. As for what she was talking about, it made no sense. Weren't we together already?

Bernie looked my way. The expression on his face was new to me. Not that I hadn't seen it on human faces before, and plenty of them: comes with the territory. But on Bernie's face? Never! The expression was . . . oh, but I don't want to say it! All right: fear. There. I won't be mentioning it again, so don't hold your breath. Or do. I was present at a breath-holding contest once at a bar in South Pedroia, and none of the dudes could last even long enough to make it interesting. Except for the drunkest one, and his girlfriend got him breathing again on the ride to the hospital. She took him there on the back of her Harley, strapped in tight with bungee cords, an unusual sight and the only reason I'm remembering any of this.

"Aren't we together now, sort of?" Bernie said, possibly thinking along the same lines as me. No surprise there: we're a lot alike in some ways, me and Bernie, as I may have mentioned before.

Have I also mentioned that even his scent has some similarity to mine? In a very small way, true, but no other human I've come across even gets on the board.

"Is 'sort of' what you want out of life, Bernie?"

"No."

"Then come with me to London."

"And live there?"

"You make it sound like Mars."

"But what would I do?"

"I knew you'd say that! So I made a few calls and I've got some leads already."

"Oh?" Bernie said.

"For example, have you heard of SecureX?"

"I know the name."

"They're all over Europe and the Middle East. I had coffee with one of the directors yesterday—he knows you!"

"What's his name?"

"Marv Lister."

"Yeah," Bernie said. "We crossed paths once or twice in the service."

"Well, you made a big impression. And they're hiring now— in London and Dubai, mostly."

"Hiring what?"

"Investigators, of course! We're not looking for bodyguard duty, are we?"

"No."

"I hear something in your voice," Suzie said. "Have I done wrong?"

"No."

"Been too pushy? I was actually meeting him about a story I'm working on and you came up by accident. Pretty much."

"It's all right," Bernie said. "I—"

A small car came slowly down the street. The driver—hey! Mr. Singh—caught sight of us and waved kind of wildly. He parked—not very well, one wheel sort of resting on the curb— and hurried up the driveway, if a quick sort of waddle can be called hurrying.

"Bernie?" Suzie said. "Still there? Did we get cut off?"

"Uh, no. No, it's just—can I call you back?"

"Call me back?"

"Just that I'm working on something now, and a potential witness has shown up, out of the blue kind of thing, wasn't even—"

"Yeah, sure," Suzie said. "Sure. Call me when it suits your schedule." Click.

"Damn it," Bernie said, why I wasn't sure. Wasn't he happy to see Mr. Singh? Mr. Singh was a buddy, unless I'd missed something. Too bad he wasn't carrying a paper bag. A snack-sized helping of curried goat would fit perfectly in a paper bag, but Mr. Singh's hands were empty. We got out of the car.

"Bernie, Bernie, one of my colleagues has seen your watch!"

"Yeah?" Bernie said. "What happened? Something that made you come in person?"

"Coming in person is no problem—I have business in your neighborhood. I am killing two birds with one stone!"

Oh, yeah? How many times had I heard that one? And was I still waiting for a human—any human, step right up—to kill even one single bird with a stone? Or even try? The only human who'd come close was Bernie, as you might have guessed, and he'd thrown a tire iron, not a stone, and the bird had turned out to be a machine, possibly called a drone. As for Mr. Singh, he had no stone, did not appear to be looking for one, and the only bird in sight was the buzzard perched in its usual spot next to old man Heydrich's chimney, far enough away so you'd need a cannon arm to knock it off, and Mr. Singh's arms were of the short and pudgy sort.

"Yeah," Bernie was saying. "Who's the—"

At that moment, old man Heydrich's door opened and out stepped old man Heydrich.

"Hey," he called. "Over here, for chrissake."

Mr. Singh raised a finger to the sky. "One moment, sir, one moment!"

Heydrich didn't like that—you could see from his face, although not liking things was pretty much his go-to expression—but he went back in his house and closed the door. Is this the time to mention a little puzzlement I have with human finger pointing? Pointing goes on with either that first finger, next to the thumb, like Mr. Singh had just done it, or with the big one in the middle. For some reason that big one in the middle gets humans stirred up—you see it on the highway all the time. But I'm still waiting to find out what's going on. A lot of humans—not Bernie, of course—seem to be in the grip of sudden mood changes. No offense.

"You know Heydrich?" Bernie said.

"In a purely business sense," said Mr. Singh.

"He pawns things?"

"No, no, Bernie—he has no use for my lending capability. The selling of memorabilia is his interest."

"Heydrich's into memorabilia? Like old Grateful Dead posters?"

"Ha ha, Bernie. All I know about the American sense of humor I have learned from you."

"Then you're in trouble," Bernie said.

Mr. Singh blinked. "Explain, please?"

"Doesn't matter," Bernie said. "What does Heydrich sell you?"

"Things of a military sort," said Mr. Singh.

"Weapons?"

"I do not deal in weapons," Mr. Singh said. "Other than a single World War Two M4 Sherman tank, which can be yours for a special price."

"Seventy-five or seventy-six millimeter gun?"

"The one-oh-five howitzer, Bernie! What a lot of wheely-deally to obtain it! But as for Mr. Heydrich, he is a provider of vintage uniforms, plus the occasional battle ribbon or medal."

"What era?" Bernie said.

"World War Two exclusively."

"Army? Navy? Marines?"

"Wehrmacht," said Mr. Singh. "Mostly army but with some Luftwaffe articles."

"He sells you Nazi uniforms?"

"And the occasional battle ribbon and medal, as I mentioned."

Bernie gazed over at Heydrich's house. The buzzard on the roof—one of those red-headed buzzards with a bone-colored beak—turned in our direction. It loosed a squawky cry, rose heavily into the air, and flapped away.

"So nice for you to have an interesting neighbor," Mr. Singh said. "My neighbor owns car washes in the west Valley, not so interesting. But the watch, Bernie! After your visit I notified some of my colleagues to be on the lookout. My instructions were to show keen interest, but make some palaver about further research, and invite the purveyor back at a specific time, when an excellent offer would most certainly be forthcoming."

"You should be in my business," Bernie said.

"But, forgive me, there's no money in it, is there, Bernie?" said Mr. Singh.

"No."

No? Just like that? No? Meaning our finances would always

be a mess? I refused to believe that. This must have been an example of Bernie playing what he called a deep game. The last deep game I recalled had involved crawling down an old mine shaft in the hills. And hadn't we found a real old Navajo blanket, which could have sold for big bucks if Bernie hadn't given it to the tribe? We could play deep games, Mr. Singh, and there was money in our business, better believe it.

"So," Mr. Singh said, handing Bernie a sheet of paper, "here is all the—four one one, is that how you put it?—on my colleague. The—perp? correct?—is scheduled to arrive in"—Mr. Singh checked his watch—"forty-five minutes."

"I owe you," Bernie said.

"Join the crowd!" Mr. Singh laughed and laughed. He walked across our lawn toward Heydrich's house. The door opened, although Heydrich did not step into view. Mr. Singh stopped laughing and went inside.

A bell tinkled as we entered a shop in a strip mall out beyond the Old Western Studios, almost where the last housing developments peter out and open country starts up at last. Love that tinkling sound! It sends a nice little charge down to the tip of my tail and partway back again.

"Deke Stargell?" Bernie said to the dude back of the counter.

"Yup."

No man looks good in a wife beater, in my opinion, and those who come off the worst are the ones with no muscles, just skin and bone. Deke Stargell was very much of that type. The bony knobs sticking up from each of his shoulders bothered me the most. Also he smelled like a smoker and Bernie had been doing so well lately. On the plus side he was one of those shopkeepers who supplied a bowl of water in case a member of the nation within should happen by. And wouldn't you know it? I was hit by a sudden thirst. Deke Stargell's water proved to be first rate, fresh and cool.

"Nice to meet you," Bernie said. "I'm Bernie Little, friend of Mr. Singh. He—"

"Friend of Pappy's is a friend of mine," Deke said.

"His first name is Pappy?" Bernie said. "Didn't know that."

"Course it isn't Pappy, for fuck sake," Deke said. "He's from India. His real name's some godawful gibberish but with lots of *P*s in it, so we all call him Pappy."

"We all being?"

"Everyone in the biz. We're big fans of Pappy. Honest as the day is long and sharp as a whip." Deke leaned across the counter. "Tell you something. I was totally against immigration till I met up with Pappy. Now I'm all for letting in the Indians willy-nilly. From India Indians. T'others is here already."

"Before us, actually," Bernie said.

Deke tilted his head sideways, squinted at Bernie. "Don't tell me you're a goddamn do-gooder."

"Definitely not."

Deke extended his hand. They shook. Deke looked my way. "Whoa! Your dog lapped up that whole bowl of water? Except what he splashed all over my floor?"

"Uh, this is Chet," Bernie said, kind of rubbing his foot in a windshield wiper pattern on the floor, for reasons of his own. "He . . . he gets thirsty in this climate."

Deke gazed at me. "Sizable fella."

"Hundred-plus-pounder," Bernie said. "Can't say exactly. Getting him on the scale's not so easy."

I remembered that game! One of my favorites, and we hadn't played it in way too long. I glanced around. No scale in sight. I didn't like my chances.

"What is he, anyways?" Deke said.

"Chet? What is he? Want the long answer or the short?"

Oh, the long, please.

"Huh?" said Deke. "I meant like German shepherd, border collie, what's the word?"

"Breed?"

"Yeah. What's the breed?"

Bernie gave me a look. "He's a mix, obviously."

"A mix of what?"

"I've wondered about that," Bernie said. "A combo you don't often see, whatever it is."

Deke thought for a moment or two. "I'm part Canadian myself, but you'd never guess."

"You're right about that."

"My mama's daddy was a lumberjack up in the Yukon." Deke checked his watch. "Two on the dot," he said. "Told him to be punctual."

"Thanks," Bernie said, glancing out the window. A car pulled in. A man got out, but he went into another store.

"This is a sting, right?" Deke said.

"Kind of," Bernie said.

"Expect any trouble?"

"I doubt it."

Deke reached under the counter, came up with a shotgun. "Better safe than sorry."

"How about we keep it out of sight until needed?" Bernie said.

Deke put the shotgun away, lit up a cigarette, saw how Bernie was looking at it. "Smoke?" he said.

"No," said Bernie. "Thanks. No thanks."

But some time later—this was after I woke from a pleasant

nap—Bernie and Deke were smoking together, Bernie on one side of the counter, Deke on the other.

"Looks like—what's his name again?" Deke said.

"Billy Parsons."

"Looks like little Billy ain't comin'. Think he got cold feet?"

"No idea," Bernie said, blowing out a long stream of smoke. "How little is he?"

"Wanna see a photo?"

"You've got a photo of him?"

"Hell, yeah. Everything here's on tape."

Bernie stubbed out his cigarette in an ashtray.

Not long after that, Deke had a monitor set up on the counter and we were watching a video. There was Billy, kind of the way he'd appeared in Mr. Parsons's photo: shoulder-length fair hair, vague sort of eyes, that snakehead tattoo on his cheek. Plus he turned out to have lots of ink on his arms as well. He stood at this very same counter, holding up a watch so that Deke could see. The Deke on the screen, is what I mean. The other Deke, Deke himself, right here, pressed a button, and the action on the screen froze. Then he pressed another button and we zoomed in on the watch.

"Yours?" Deke said.

"For sure," said Bernie.

"A knockout," Deke said.

Our watch, no doubt about it. A kind of wild idea—something about biting the screen—rose up in my mind. While I was getting that under control, Deke said, "Told me it was a family heirloom."

"True as far as it goes."

"Hear that all the time," Deke said.

They both glanced outside. Nothing doing.

"Happen to see what he was driving?" Bernie said.

"Got that on tape, too."

"I was hoping."

More tape went blurring by on the screen, then slowed down, and we were looking out the window, not in the here and now—how hard this is!—but in the here and then, if that makes any sense. A dusty and dented sedan was parked outside.

"Little shitbox," Deke said.

"Can you zoom in on the plate?" said Bernie.

Deke laughed to himself. "Sure thing, but hell of a lotta good it'll do you."

He zoomed in the plate.

"All mudded up?" Bernie said.

"The kind of trick pulled by the kind of guy who thinks he's smart," Deke said.

Bernie nodded.

"Which is a kind of guy that's always bugged me, know what I mean?"

"I do," Bernie said.

"So while I had little Mr. Billy in here, I texted to my buddy Esteban who runs the auto parts store two doors down."

Bernie smiled. I had no idea why and didn't care: Bernie's smiles are always a highlight of my day.

More blurring on the screen, and when it slowed down a man in denim bib overalls was moving toward the dusty sedan, a rag in hand. He knelt, wiped the license plate clean, and walked away. Deke zoomed in on the plate. Bernie grabbed a pen off the counter, wrote something on his hand. I loved when he did that.

"Did little Billy happen to notice on his way out?" Bernie said.

"The little Billys never do," said Deke. "They do all their noticing after the fat lady sings."

What was this? Now I had to be on the lookout for fat ladies? The case had taken an unexpected turn.

ELEVEN

B ack in the car, Bernie had a look on his face I always like to see, a strong-jawed look that means we know what we're doing and now we're going to do it, step aside, amigos! Maybe not all of that, but some. We took a crisp turn, then another, and were soon zooming toward the freeway ramp just past the big wooden cowboy who stood outside the Dry Gulch Steakhouse and Saloon—one of our favorite hangouts in the Valley, with a patio out back where they know how to take care of me and my kind, but no time to go on and on and on some more about their steak tips right now—when Bernie lightened his foot on the gas and eased into the slow lane.

He turned to me and said, "Iggy."

Iggy? What did Iggy have to do with anything? Weren't we on the job, me and Bernie? Me and Bernie, period?

"We better look in on him."

Look in on Iggy? What for? We'd never looked in on Iggy in the past. Why start now? Then I remembered where Iggy actually was at the moment, not at his place where he belonged but at our place where he was always welcome for a visit, of course, but in no way belonged. How had that happened, again? I took a swing at lining up all the facts in an orderly way. That was something Bernie often said, "Let's line up all the facts in an orderly way." Who wouldn't love Bernie? A surprising number of people, in fact. I fell into a fun little daydream of meeting up with each of them, one on one.

Soon after that, we rolled into our driveway and walked up to the house. Bernie opened the door. "Oh, Iggy," he said.

A long long time passed before we had everything all straightened out. We ended up pulling into the MVD just before closing, which was the only part of the day when the line wasn't out the door. In our business you need a contact at the MVD, and ours was Mrs. Trujillo. She spotted us in the waiting area and fluttered her fingers in the "come here" sign. We went past the counter where people were waiting to take a number and entered Mrs. Trujillo's corner office.

Mrs. Trujillo leaned back in her chair, stuck a pencil in her bun, if that's what you called the big round pile of graying hair on top of her head. "Well, well," she said. "Long time no see." Which made no sense to me, Mrs. Trujillo's eyes—pretty much the sharpest in the whole Valley—looking just the way they always did.

"How's Ramfis?" Bernie said, Ramfis being Mrs. Trujillo's kid, a grown-up kid we'd kept out of the slammer for reasons I couldn't remember, although I did recall that Ramfis was always nice to me. The same went for Mrs. Trujillo, who at that very moment was reaching into a desk drawer that contained biscuits, reasonably fresh and sniffed out by me as we'd come through the doorway. They were a fine family.

"He got a real job," Mrs. Trujillo said, offering a nice big biscuit. I went closer and sat, the way you do when a biscuit is on the way. Although not sitting completely, in this case: Mrs. Trujillo didn't care about little things like that. Ah. Delish.

"Doing what?" Bernie said.

"Bartending for a wedding caterer."

"Bartending?"

"It was either that or fracking in North Dakota, and Ramfis hates the cold."

"Makes sense, then," Bernie said. He held out his hand, the one with the writing on it.

Mrs. Trujillo glanced at the writing, then turned to her computer and started tapping away at the keyboard. "Here we go. Plate's registered to a Ms. Dee D. Branch, 2177 El Norte Highway, High Pines."

"High Pines?

"A one-stoplight town up in the Burro Mountains. Starting to lose it, Bernie? Never stumped you before."

"You haven't been trying," Bernie said. "Can you bring up her driver's license photo?"

"Ha! One day I'll be able to bring up her innermost thoughts."

"Stop scaring me."

Uh-oh. Mrs. Trujillo was scaring Bernie? How was that possible? Just in case, I sidled into the space between them, the biscuit secure between my teeth, but droppable at any moment, supposing my teeth were needed for something else.

Meanwhile, Mrs. Trujillo was tapping away again. A woman's face appeared on the screen—a woman with lots of blond hair, not as old as Mrs. Trujillo, not as young as Suzie.

"What's that look called?" Bernie said.

"Tramp," said Mrs. Trujillo.

. . .

The sun was low in the sky, a fiery blob quivering in our rearview mirror, as we left the last developments in the Valley behind and started climbing into the mountains.

"Did she hit on something?" Bernie said. "Am I losing it?" He rubbed his forehead.

What was this? Something totally beyond me. I curled up on the shotgun seat and thought about biscuits. Another one would have been nice. But you can't let little disappointments bring you down in this life. Forget all about them and get on with something else! For example: a nap.

"High Pines," Bernie said.

I opened my eyes.

"Elevation four thousand sixty-three feet, population three hundred eighty-two. Could maybe plot them on an x and y axis, express each in terms of . . ."

Imagine waking up to that! As though Bernie had gone completely incomprehensible in the space of my very brief—what does Bernie call it?

He turned to me. "Catch a little beauty sleep, Chet?"

Beauty sleep: that was it. Did I need beauty sleep? I couldn't think why. But not the point. Bernie was back to being comprehensible again, meaning we'd be at our best for whatever came next. Heads up, bad guys! And even some good guys who sometimes let their goodness slide.

We rounded a bend, the sky deep purple on one side, black with a few stars on the other, and huge in every direction. All at once, despite being a hundred-plus-pounder, I felt a bit smallish.

The fur on the back of my neck stood up. Feeling smallish? What was going on? Were we both losing it, me and Bernie?

"Hey! What are you barking about?"

That was me? I got a grip. But that bark, echoing and re-echoing through the hills, made me feel much better, in fact, pretty close to tip-top.

The land flattened out, and we rode down the main street of a little town, a few stores on either side, closed for the night, and a bar and a restaurant showing lights, dim figures inside. We came to the sole light in town, caught it on red. No traffic other than us. A quiet town—High Pines, was that it?—except for the wind, rising from the black part of the sky. The light made a clicking sound and turned green. Bernie peered at the cross-street sign. "El Norte."

We followed El Norte out of town. Full night lowered itself around us, all except for the yellow tunnel our headlights made. The road narrowed, zigzagged through some switchbacks, and straightened out. A mailbox came in sight. Bernie slowed down and read the number. "Two one seven seven." I saw a bullet hole or two in the mailbox, but that didn't mean anything out here. We turned onto a dirt track, bumped over a low rise, and stopped in front of a double-wide trailer up on blocks. The handlebars of a motorcycle gleamed at the entrance to a shed over on one side. No cars in sight, but lights shone in the windows of the double-wide. Bernie cut the engine, and we got out of the car. A woman called from inside.

"Billy? That you?"

Bernie put one finger across his lips. That was our signal for quiet. We have all kinds of signals. Take the trigger-pull signal. That means go-get-'im, one of my favorites. For a moment I forgot about quiet and thought only of go-get-'im.

"Billy?" the woman called. "What are you doing?"

Bernie gave me a surprised look and made the quiet sign again. Whatever low growling had been going on stopped on a dime, if that makes any sense, but still my tail drooped, as though it knew I'd done wrong. I got it back up nice and high. If by any chance there'd been some mess-up, it wouldn't happen again.

We walked around a kid's swing set, lying on its side, and stopped at the door. Bernie knocked.

"Use your key, Billy," the woman called again. "I just got out of the shower."

Bernie knocked.

"For chrissake!"

Then came approaching footsteps—the barefoot kind—and the door opened. A woman stood in the doorway. She had a towel wrapped around her head—the way women do after a shower, but not men, just another one of those man-woman mysteries—and was trying to get another one around her body, and fast. Meanwhile, her face was running through some expressions, surprise and fear being two. With her hair hidden under the towel, her face seemed so bare. And what was this? Practically no eyebrows at all?

"Ms. Dee Branch?" Bernie said.

At which point she lost her grip on the towel—not the one wrapped around her head, the other one—and it fell to the floor.

"Fucking hell," she said, sort of half-bending and half-twisting around to pick it up. Bernie sort of half-turned away. What exactly was going on? Was this an interview? Were we off to a good start?

The woman finally got the towel nicely around herself, from the neck to not much below her waist: I'd seen bigger towels.

"Dee Branch?" Bernie said.

The woman made a grab for the door and slammed it in our faces. But not quite: Bernie already had one foot in the doorway, just one of our techniques at the Little Detective Agency. The door ended up slamming against his foot. Have I mentioned Bernie was wearing flip-flops at the time?

"Ow!" Bernie said, kind of loudly, like . . . like a cry of pain. Whoa! I'd never once heard a cry of pain from Bernie, not even that time when he'd climbed the big tree in our yard with the chainsaw, something about a dead limb. I won't go into what happened after that. No cry of pain, that's the takeaway. This woman—Dee Branch, perhaps—turned out to be dangerous. I stepped inside.

She backed away.

"What's going on?" she said, her voice rising in an edgy and unpleasant combo of bad emotions. "Who the hell are you?"

"I'm Bernie Little, and this is Chet."

"Keep him away from me."

"No reason to be skittish around Chet. He likes people, especially the cooperative kind."

Hard to deny! I even like most of the perps and gangbangers we've rounded up.

"You're a cop," the woman said.

"Nope," said Bernie.

"You look like a cop."

"Private investigator from the Valley," Bernie said. He glanced around. "When's Billy supposed to turn up?"

The woman's eyes shifted. "Billy? Don't know any Billys."

Bernie turned to her. "How about the Billy who has a key to your abode?"

The woman's face, so bare, went pink, and she called Bernie some names I'm sure she didn't mean. While that was going on, we eased our way inside and closed the door, Bernie doing the actual closing with his heel, a small move maybe, but one of his best, in my opinion.

"Any idea what he's up to when he's driving around in your car, Dee?" Bernie said.

"Shows what you know," Dee said. "I don't have a car."

"Fifteen-year-old Corolla, Arizona plate FTT347?" Bernie said.

Dee backed up another step. "So what if I have a car? It's my constitutional right."

"It's also your constitutional right to strike up friendships with inmates," Bernie said.

"Huh?"

"Or did you meet Billy after he got out?"

"I don't know what you're talking about."

Bernie gazed at her. "Maybe you don't," Bernie said. "If not, you should know you're involved with a dangerous man."

"You on something?" Dee said. "You're not making sense."

"Billy Parsons did fifteen years for kidnapping. That's about as dangerous as it gets."

Dee's voice rose. "You're so full of shit. They railroaded him. He was totally inno—" She clapped a hand over her mouth.

"Go on," Bernie said.

Dee shook her head, kind of violently. The towel she'd wrapped around her hair slipped off, releasing a damp tangle, mostly blond but brown at the roots. Now her face didn't seem quite so bare; also it looked much more like the face in Mrs. Trujillo's photo. Ms. Dee Branch, no doubt about it, although much less friendly in person.

"I've got nothing more to say. Get the hell out of here. You're trespassing."

"Why don't you call the cops?"

What was this? Her eyes shifted, like maybe she was considering doing exactly that? When was the last time a perp had called the cops on us? Wasn't Dee a perp? Kind of confusing, and that wasn't the end of it.

Bernie nodded. "Okay," he said. "We're leaving. Here's our card if you ever want to talk." He held it out. This was our new card, designed by Suzie. It had a floral decoration we weren't happy about, me and Bernie. Maybe Dee didn't like it either, because she made no move to take the card. Bernie dropped it on an upside-down milk crate by the door. And then we were outside. Turning tail on account of some cops? That didn't sound like us.

We got into the Porsche. Bernie backed away, spun us around in a quick three-point turn—which I loved even though I don't go past two—and we headed onto the dirt track, past the mailbox with the bullet holes in it, and down the mountain road.

But not far down. Just past the first switchback, a big rock, square and reddish in the headlights, rose by the side of the road. Bernie pulled over, tucked us in behind it, killed the lights.

"Let's see if we stirred up some hornets, big guy," he said.

Silence fell, the deep nighttime desert silence you can feel, almost like there's a real big someone else out there with you. No missing the buzz of a hornet in a silence like that, but I listened my hardest anyway. Stirring up hornets? How could that strike Bernie as a good idea?

He looked over at me. "Chet? What are you doing with your paws?"

Nothing. Nothing at all, except for covering up my nose. My nose had a past with stirred-up hornets. You get a feeling when a case is going well. I did not have that feeling.

TWELVE

Sitting in the Porsche, out in the desert at night, me and Bernie: didn't get any better than this. I remembered the last time—some case involving parrots—when we'd been sitting in much the same way, nice and peaceable, until dudes with flamethrowers came barreling over the next ridge. What did that have to do with parrots? I never figured it out, but all those flame-throwing dudes are now over at Central State Correctional, breaking rocks in the hot sun.

"Hey," Bernie said, "see the shooting star?"

He pointed at the sky. Whatever it was, I missed it, but it was still pleasant to gaze at the night sky with Bernie.

"Not an actual star, of course. A meteor."

How interesting! Was there anything Bernie didn't know?

"I'll have to explain that to Charlie."

Then came a silence, pleasant until I felt Bernie's thoughts begin to darken. He actually smells different when that happens. Have I mentioned Bernie's smell—a very nice one, my second favorite, in fact, with hints of apples, bourbon, salt, and pepper overlaying your basic human male? When dark thoughts are happening, the whole thing gets toned down, like the smell is coming from a smaller Bernie. I edged up against him.

He looked my way, gave me a pat. "Leda's right," he said.

Wow! I'd never heard that before. Good or bad? I had no idea. In general I like new things, especially if they're nice. That was as far as I could take it.

"Should never have taken him on that little caper," Bernie said. "Things can go off the rails at any time in this job."

Couldn't be truer, in my experience! And all in all a plus, unless I was missing something—other than what Bernie was actually talking about. That I was missing, but totally.

"And then there's London."

Bernie started fishing under his seat. That meant he wanted a cigarette, didn't have any on account of never buying cigarettes anymore, part of his plan for quitting, and was hoping to score one somewhere or other. Which he was going to do, if he kept on searching—a faint and stale tobacco smell had been rising up from under his seat since we left Foggy Bottom.

"Hey!" he said. "My lucky day." And not long after that, he was lighting up and blowing a long, slow smoke stream, a tiny cloud rising in the night sky, hazing over a star or two. "What would we do in London, Chet?"

London? Wherever it was, why wouldn't we do what we were doing now, stirring up hornets out in the desert, keeping an eye out for shooting stars? I was about to edge still closer to him—not easy, since I'd pretty much completely closed the gap between us, but I'm not one to give up at the first sign of difficulty—when I heard a motorcycle cranking up somewhere higher on the mountain.

"A galoot," Bernie said. "Would I end up like some galoot sidekick of Suzie's? On the other hand, what about the idea that love conquers—Chet? Something up?"

Most definitely. A motorcycle was roaring toward us down the mountain. Bernie really didn't hear it? I couldn't believe—

"Hearing anything, big guy? I thought I might have . . ." Bernie cocked one ear toward the road. We do the same thing in the nation within, but way earlier in the game. "Yeah, for sure," Bernie said, turning the key. "Good boy."

Engine on, lights off—our usual technique in situations like this—we waited, both of us hunched forward, eyes on the road. Bernie's heartbeat changed a bit—not speeding up, just getting stronger. Mine was doing the exact same thing. Look out, world!

"Sounds more like a motorcycle than a car," Bernie said, his voice low. That had to be one of Bernie's jokes, since the bike was practically right on us. A moment later its headlight beam flashed down the road, and the bike blew into view, banked far over as it shot out of the switchback, ridden by someone who knew what she was doing. Her long blond hair streaming out in the night reminded me of the shooting star I'd missed seeing, no explaining that. But the point: the rider was Ms. Dee Branch.

"One Mississippi, two Mississippi, three Mississippi," Bernie said, losing me completely, and then pulled out from our spot by the big rock and onto the road. Bernie's the best wheelman in the Valley, can follow from up close, back far, many lanes over, and even going backward, which I'd seen once and was in no hurry to see again. But tailing Dee Branch didn't call for anything tricky. The beam of her headlight pointed our way through High Pines and down the mountain. We followed from quite close behind, our own lights out and the sound of our engine masked by the bike's loud vroom-vroom, at least to human ears.

Some time later, out of the mountains and on the freeway, Bernie dropped back into traffic and hit the lights. Dee took one of the first Valley exits and headed into South Pedroia. Bernie dropped back a little more, keeping a van between us and Dee. We went right past Orlando the butcher's place, closed for the night—but smelling as good as ever, or even better, what with how smells are stronger in the night air—and then our self-storage, where we keep our stock of Hawaiian pants. Our finances! But not now, big guy, not now.

Meanwhile, we'd entered one of the worst parts of South Pedroia—boarded-up buildings, broken streetlights, dudes slouching around with nothing good in mind. One or two looked up as Dee passed by and called out to her, but if she heard, she gave no sign. At a corner where the stop sign lay in the gutter, the van went one way and Dee another, leaving nothing between us. Bernie stopped there and waited, the sound of Dee's bike fading.

And fading. Maybe I got a little anxious, possibly putting a paw on Bernie's leg, specifically the leg we used for stepping on the gas. He stroked my head. "It's all right, Chet. It's a dead end, backs on to the canal. She's not going anywhere."

The smartest human in the world? There he was, right beside me!

Real slow, lights off, we drove down the dead-end street. I picked up the smell of the canal, which had nothing to do with water, by the way, the canal being empty except during monsoon season. Pee, mostly human, is the normal canal smell, in case you're interested. There are times the whole world pretty much smells of human pee. What a life!

Hardly any lights showed on the dead-end street, but the night sky in the Valley is a kind of deep, dark pink, making it easy to see the sights going by: a retread tire place, a blackened warehouse with all the windows blown out, an empty lot full of trash, a dark little low cement house, painted green, and another one just like it, except that it was yellow. Also a light glowed in the front window of the yellow house. Plus the yard had a chain-link fence around it, high but leapable, at least for me. What else? A motorcycle was parked in that yard, metal popping as it cooled down. Bernie cruised on to the end of the block, only two houses farther, came to the canal, and turned around. Then he drove back the way we'd come and parked across the street from the small yellow house. He reached into the glove box and took out the .45. We needed the stopper? It was that kind of case? I made a . . . what did Bernie call it? Mental note? Yes. I made a mental note to . . . to do whatever you did with mental notes.

We got out of the car, moving silently in the night, meaning silently for me and not too noisily for Bernie. Pink light glinted off those sharp twisties you find at the top of chain-link fences. Bernie checked the gate: padlocked. We walked around the house, down a nasty little path that separated it from the green one. The fence continued all the way around to the back, but here's something you need to know about humans: they can be careless, especially about the things that don't show. Look under just about any bed, for example. And here was another one: a hole in the fence, almost big enough for us to squeeze through side by side. But not quite, so I went first. The truth is I would have gone first no matter what. How did Bernie put it? Chet has certain preferences. Yes, that was it. You had to give him credit: Bernie notices every little thing.

We crept across a packed bare-dirt strip to the back of the yellow house. At that moment and for no reason I thought of Ellie Newburg and the round red hole in her forehead. Yes, it was that kind of case. I gave myself a shake of the very quickest sort. Set to go.

No lights shone in the back windows of the yellow house, and it was quiet inside. But humans were in there, more than one.

Here in the nation within we get good at sensing the human presence. Bernie approached the back door. If you'd been expecting one of those feeble screen doors, you'd have been disappointed. I hadn't been expecting anything, other than grabbing perps by the pant leg, and soon. But back to the door, an unpainted steel door, solid and heavy. Bernie was reaching for the handle when with no warning that I caught, the door banged open. Meaning it was the kind of door that opened out instead of in. That turned out to be important, because the door clipped Bernie's gun hand. The stopper got knocked loose and spun off to the side.

Two men on their way out the back door for a smoke—one was lighting up, the other had an unlit cigarette in his hand—saw us and froze. These were big dudes, bigger than Bernie. They looked like twins with their popping muscles, shaved heads, Fu Manchu mustaches—my least favorite of the possible mustaches, although there's no good type, in my opinion. As for their smells, they reeked identically. Hey! Maybe they were twins for real. That was the last moment for clear thinking, or even after the moment, if you get my meaning.

"What the fuck?" the reeking twins said as one, both of them reaching into their belts. And out came iron, glinting pink in the night. At the Little Detective Agency we don't dawdle at times like that.

"Chet!"

But I was already in midair, teeth bared, front paws out, eyes locked on the gun in the hand—tattooed hand, by the way—of Twin One. Then came a scream, possibly meaning I'd missed the gun, made contact—biting contact to be accurate—with the hand. The taste of human blood in my mouth backed up that interpretation. The gun went flying, and we hit the ground, first me on top and then him on top, kind of surprising. He turned out to be on the heavy side, as was the forearm he planted across my neck, pressing down so I couldn't breathe. Our faces were close—the main source of the reeking was his breath, that was clear right away—plenty close for me to see the murderous look in his eyes. They never stop on their own after that look appears—one of the most important things I'd learned in my career.

Twin One raised his free hand high, a hand that had somehow gotten hold of a big and jagged chunk of concrete. He didn't bring it down right away, wanted me to get a good long look at the thing. And while I was taking that good long look, I heard Bernie grunt nearby, like he'd been hit in the gut, and then grunt again. Once in a while something happens in life that makes you stronger. This was one of those once in a whiles. Just like that I was stronger!

Couldn't have come at a better time, what with me on my back, breathing cut off, and a muscle bulging in Twin One's shoulder as he brought that chunk of concrete bashing down for a real crusher. Into his eyes—small and close together, which I should have mentioned from the get-go—now came the added gleam of someone enjoying every moment. Maybe Twin One was too caught up in his own emotions to sense the surge of energy rippling through me, me this suddenly even stronger Chet. As that crusher came down, I wriggled in one snapping wriggle out from under him and his heavy forearm—

"What the hell?"

—and in a single motion twisted around and got him a good one, with all the power of my jaws, deep into the very shoulder that had just been bulging in that killer way.

That brought a cry of pain and fear, real harsh and ragged but somehow easy on the ears, which I know doesn't make sense, but it did at the time, especially the fear part. And the next thing I knew, Twin One was on the run, not toward the house, because I was blocking his way, but toward the fence, which he scrambled right over, a pretty nifty feat considering one arm was just dangling by his side. At the same time you had to wonder why he didn't simply use the hole in the fence, which I was about to do, my plan being to bring him down on the other side and . . . and take it from there. But then I heard another one of those grunts that comes from getting hit in the gut. Bernie!

I wheeled around. What was this? Bernie, still on his feet but doubling over? Twin Two squared up to hit him again. He was somehow getting the best of Bernie in a fistfight? I refused to let myself even think it, and the truth was Twin Two's nose—the squishy, flattened, saddleback kind you find on the faces of boxing's losers—was gushing blood. But he was standing straight and Bernie was not. As Twin Two cocked his fist to throw another punch, I spotted something not quite right: a metallic glint, barely visible in the night. Brass knuckles? Yes. The sight set off a sort of explosion in my mind. I felt rage—which hardly ever happens to me—and saw red, even though Bernie says I can't be trusted when it comes to the red end of the spectrum.

But the red end of the spectrum, whatever that might be, was now where we were. It turned out to be bloody and noisy at the red end of the spectrum, and also pretty exciting, and very soon Twin Two was also scrambling over the back fence, ignoring the hole just as Twin One had done. One difference was that Twin Two no longer wore pants, now in my possession for some reason. I let go of them, darted toward the hole in the fence, and—

"Chet!"

—made a quick U-turn and trotted over to Bernie. Bent over, one hand over his stomach, but still he had a smile for me. "Beyond good, Chet. What would I do without you?"

I didn't understand the question.

"C'mon, boy," he said, his voice not loud but full of strength and power. How I loved that! "Into the house. Let's go get 'em."

No time to figure out who he meant. What an evening this was turning out to be! I happened to notice the .45—first actually catching a whiff of it, to be accurate. It lay on the hard-packed dirt of the backyard. I picked it up and offered it to Bernie. He gave me a very nice pat.

THIRTEEN

The heavy steel back door hung open. We waltzed right in, me slightly in front, found ourselves in a darkened kitchen, a fridge humming away against the far wall, baloney and cheddar cheese inside it. I made another one of those mental notes—hey! I was starting to get it!—and headed for a narrow and dimly lit hall. Somewhere in the front of the house, a door slammed. The next moment we were both running. We charged down the hall and into a front room lit by a lamp with a naked bulb. What else? Two open beer bottles, not empty; two pizza boxes, also not empty, neither pizza including pepperoni, which made no sense to me; a TV on the wall, the biggest thing in the room by far, football on the screen, sound off. In short, a homey little scene, missing only the people.

Vroom vroom. A motorcycle engine started up. Of course! Dee's motorcycle in the front yard! I was fitting the pieces together like never before. Bernie threw open the door and we burst outside. And what a lot we had to take in, with not much time for doing it. For one thing, the gate was open. For another, the bike was already on the street, Dee up top. She was watching a little long-haired dude in jeans and a T-shirt—both arms pretty much totally inked up—who was . . . over by the Porsche? Kind of kneeling like he was . . . slashing the tires!

We raced toward the gate. Dee glanced in our direction and yelled, "Billy!" Then she spun the bike around and rumbled right up next to him.

"Billy!" Bernie shouted. "Stop! Think! Your parents!"

Billy turned toward Bernie, his mouth—a soft sort of mouth—opening, his look confused, the lines of the snakehead on his cheek hard and clear. "My parents? What about them?"

Dee shouted, too, almost louder than Bernie, and way higher. "Get on the goddamn bike!"

Billy took one last glance at Bernie, then hopped up behind Dee. The next moment I was in midair, but Dee spun the bike again, tires smoking, and I flew right over the top. Dee gunned the engine, the front wheel rising off the pavement. Bernie dove, grabbed hold of Billy's wrist, and started getting dragged away from me. I caught the look in his eyes: he was never letting go, no matter what. But then Dee swerved, grazing a fire hydrant by the side of the road, and rubbing Bernie right off. He lost his grip on Billy and rolled into the gutter. The bike zoomed to the crossroads, made another one of Dee's low-leaning turns, and vanished from sight. I ran over to Bernie.

He was already sitting up, looking not too bad, except for torn clothing and some scrapes here and there. Bernie is a tough man, and don't you forget it. The worst scrapes were on his arm. I gave that arm a lick. He opened his fist: and there was his grandfather's watch, our most valuable possession! Any more questions about Bernie? Just when you think he's done amazing you, he amazes you again. We had the watch! Did that mean the case was closed? For a moment or two I thought so. Then I remembered that we hadn't actually collared any perps. Plus one of the front tires on the Porsche did not look good. Meaning we were in a real bad part of South Pedroia with no ride. At that point I spotted the stopper, once more lying on the ground all on its lonesome. I went over and got it. This case was not closed. Maybe it wasn't even going that well.

Bernie took the gun, rose, went over to the Porsche, checked out the tires. Two were just fine. The other two had deep slashes across the sidewalls. Bernie took out his phone.

"Nixon?" he said, the only Nixon I knew being Nixon Panero, our buddy and the best mechanic it the Valley. "Need a favor."

Then I heard Nixon's voice, tiny over the phone. "The paying kind?" he said. Bernie laughed, so maybe some joking had been going on. If so, I'd missed it.

We went back in the house, searched it from top to bottom, although since there was only one floor we just had to do the bottom. Sometimes you catch a break in this job. And of course it's always interesting to watch a pro like Bernie conducting a search, looking under pillows, overturning furniture, tapping walls. After a while, I got a little less interested, wandered into the kitchen, nosed up the lids of the pizza boxes, made extra sure they were pepperoniless. Do things right, as Bernie always says. Only one slice left in each box, and no pepperoni, just as I'd thought. I tried the chicken and mushrooms first and then the plain cheese and tomato. The truth is I'd had better, but no complaints. I was trying to lick off a long and sticky string of cheese that had gotten stuck to my muzzle, when I heard Bernie in the front room.

"About time," he said.

I trotted into the front room. He was looking out the window, one of those high windows, which meant I had to stand up on my back legs, front paws on the glass. We looked out the window side by side, me and Bernie, our heads at the same height, which was always nice.

A black-and-white came down the street. "No sense of urgency at all," Bernie said. "Even kind of cynical, if you can say that about driving." I had no idea, but if Bernie said it, then it had to be right. "I understand why Valley PD assumes the worst in a neighborhood like this, but we'll never change things without—what's this?"

The cruiser slowed down, pulled over next to the Porsche. A cop got out, the kind of cop you sometimes see who's rocking the belly hanging over gun belt look. He walked around the cruiser, fished his ticket pad out of his shirt pocket, and . . . started writing us up?

"What the hell?" Bernie said.

We hurried outside, not quietly, but the cop didn't appear to have heard us. He was chewing gum—cinnamon flavor.

"Hey!" Bernie called. "Hold it."

The cop's head turned slightly toward us but he didn't stop writing.

"What are you doing?" Bernie said as we came up to him.

The cop chomped on his gum once or twice—a pretty big glob of it, to judge by how hard his jaws were working. "What's it look like?" He tore the ticket off the pad and stuck it under our wiper blade. "Parking in a delivery zone, fifty bucks. You got twenty-one days to pay, then it's a hunnert."

"That's your priority?"

"Huh?"

Bernie motioned toward the yellow house. "What about your goddamn call?"

The cop cracked his gum, normally a sound I like a lot, but not now. "That's how your mama taught you to address an officer of the law?" he said.

Without actually moving, Bernie somehow closed the distance between him and the cop. I tried to do the same thing, but maybe cheated a little. The cop seemed to notice me for the first time. He backed up a step, hand on the butt of his gun.

"Leave my mother out of this," Bernie said, in this certain quiet tone he has that makes the fur on my neck stand up, which it now did. I felt like . . . like grabbing somebody by the pant leg, this cop, for example. Was he a perp? I got a little confused. As for Bernie's mom, a real piece of work—she calls him Kiddo!—I agreed with him: we had enough complications at the moment. Was she coming again for Thanksgiving? Maybe it was far off.

Sometimes a physical fight can happen without any actual punches getting thrown. This was one of those times. "Suit yourself," the cop said, turning his head and spitting out his gum. Bernie won.

"Let's back up a bit," he said. "How come East Arroyo sent you by yourself?"

"East Arroyo?" said the cop.

"The precinct we happen to be standing in. Why just you?"

The cop shrugged. "It's a one-man patrol car."

Bernie glanced at the house. "Must have been pretty noisy here for a bit, reason it got called in in the first place. Sending one lone car seems reckless."

The cop squinted at Bernie. Sometimes humans squint when they've forgotten their glasses. Sometimes it's when they're facing the sun. Or when they're trying to understand something. Or just being a jerk. This cop's squint—never a good look on any human in my opinion—was one of those last two.

"Call?" he said. "Don't know about any call."

"Then what are you doing here?" Bernie said.

"My job. I'm on patrol."

"You just happened by?"

"I'm on patrol," the cop said again. I got the feeling he liked saying it.

"Very conscientious," Bernie said. "What's your name?"

"It's on the ticket," the cop said. He got in the cruiser, moving kind of quickly like he was all of a sudden running late, and drove away.

Bernie slid the ticket out from under the wiper blade, held it up to the light. With no streetlights working, that meant the light of the dark-pink sky. "Totally illegible," he said. "But guess what, big guy?" Uh-oh. I had to guess something? I guessed that we were planning to end the evening with steak tips at the Dry Gulch Steakhouse and Saloon. "I caught the number on his badge— eighteen sixty-three." I liked my guess better. Bernie reached into the Porsche, grabbed a pen, and started writing on the palm of his hand. A lot of that going on lately: I took it as a good sign. Meanwhile, Bernie paused, his brow furrowing a bit. Those forehead lines should have made him seem older; in fact, he now looked more like Charlie. Life's full of surprises, big and little. "Or was it eighteen thirty-six?" he said. Sounded like more than two. I couldn't help him.

Then we were just standing there on the street, Bernie gazing at the yellow house, me gazing at Bernie. "Couldn't even remember the goddamn number," he said in this voice he has just for talking to himself. "Everybody loses it eventually. I just didn't think . . ." He rubbed his forehead.

Whatever this was, I didn't like it.

Bernie looked at me in surprise. "What are you growling about?"

Growling? I stiffened my ears for hard listening. Yes, growling for sure. And it had to be me, no other members of the nation within nearby.

"Annoyed they got away, huh?" Bernie said.

No! That wasn't it! Although, thinking it over, I was annoyed they'd gotten away. So maybe that was it after all. I growled again. Bernie gave me a pat.

"Don't worry. We're not done yet. We got the watch back, didn't we?"

My tail started up. A successful evening so far? I couldn't think of any reason why not. Then Nixon came driving down the street at the wheel of a big wrecker with flashing lights all over the place and painted dancing girls on the fenders. Would I trade places with anyone on this earth? You tell me.

We drove to the East Arroyo precinct HQ, not far away. Hadn't been there in some time. I've got buddies at most of the precinct houses, but one of my favorites is Munchy Ford, and wouldn't you know it? There was ol' Munchy on desk duty when we walked in.

"Hey, Chet!" he said. "And Bernie. How ya doin'?"

"No complaints," Bernie said. "You?"

"Gotta lose fifty pounds," Munchy said. "Doc won't replace my hip until I do. Talk about blaming the victim, huh?"

"Uh . . ."

"But what can you do? Bastard's got me by the balls."

Oh, no. Had I ever heard anything so horrible? At the same time, I saw no one crouched under Munchy's desk, and he didn't seem to be in pain. Some things are hard to understand.

"Which is how come I didn't finish my supper," Munchy went on, opening a drawer. "Self-discipline. But it's been talkin' to me nonstop. Think Chet would be up for half a roast beef sandwich?"

"He just had pizza," Bernie said. How did he know? But no time to figure it out, because I was already over by Munchy's drawer. If half a roast beef sandwich could talk, I wanted to see it up close.

The half sandwich remained silent, reminding me of some of the very toughest perps we'd come across. Munchy held it out for me. I didn't take it. Speak, sandwich!

"Don't want it, Chet?" Munchy moved like he was going to put the sandwich back in the drawer. I snapped out of whatever I'd snapped into and grabbed it out of Munchy's hand. He laughed. "What was that all about?"

"Couldn't tell you," Bernie said. He gave me a careful look. I gave him a careful look back, chewing a juicy bite of roast beef at the same time.

"Tell you one thing about Chet," Munchy said. "He's the take-no-prisoners type."

Bernie nodded. As I may have mentioned, Bernie has many nods, meaning all kinds of things. This particular nod had to mean no, because Bernie knew I was very much the taking-lots-of-prisoners type, having rounded up too many to count in my career, even for a good counter like him.

"Any calls come in for ninety-seven Velez Street tonight?" Bernie said.

"That anywhere near Orlando's?" said Munchy.

"Four or five blocks east."

"His lamb chops are off the charts," Munchy said. He glanced at his computer screen. "Nope. No calls. Been a quiet night, so far. Couple of nightclub stabbings, assault with intent, suspected arson at the chemical plant—nothing to write home about."

"Name Dee Branch mean anything to you?"

"Nope."

"Ever come across identical twins, six four, two thirty or so, shaved heads, Fu Manchu mustaches?"

"Nope," said Munchy. "And I hope it stays that way."

Bernie checked the palm of his hand. "Who's eighteen sixty-three?"

"Here at the precinct? We got no one with that number."

"Might be eighteen thirty-six."

Munchy shook his head. "No one under two triple zero in this building. Not since the reshuffle."

"Can you find him anyway?"

"Sure," said Munchy, turning to his keyboard. "Is this kosher?"

"Don't see why not," Bernie said, which was great news, kosher chicken being the best of all possible chickens. True, I hadn't quite polished off the roast beef sandwich, but isn't it nice to have something to look forward to?

"Here we go," Munchy said, tapping the screen with his soft, plump finger. "Officer up at Indian Hills."

"Name?"

"Mickles."

"Mickles?" Bernie said, leaning closer to the screen.

"First name Garwood, eight years on the force. Some relation to Brick Mickles, detective captain up there, as I recall. Nephew, maybe?" He turned to Bernie. "You know Brick?" Then something changed in Munchy's eyes, like they kind of went private, and he looked away.

FOURTEEN

ny ideas?" Bernie said as we drove away from the East Arroyo
precinct house.

Ideas? Since when were ideas my department? I brought other things to the table, such as grabbing perps by the pant leg. Did I expect Bernie to do the pant leg grabbing? No. But if he wanted ideas, then I'd get cracking on that, and pronto. I got cracking. No ideas came. I tried harder, tried so hard I felt this pressure in my head, right at the top part, quite unpleasant. I put a stop to that, tried to think of some other way to come up with ideas. Even that—trying to think of how to come up with ideas—brought the unpleasant pressure.

"What are you doing?" Bernie said, glancing over.

Me? Not a thing.

"Showing a lot of upper front gum line there, big guy. And your nose is all wrinkled up."

Oh, no! How embarrassing! A real good shake was the only way to get out of this, not so easy in the shotgun seat, but I gave it my best shot. We swerved across the yellow line and over to the wrong side of the road, not sure why. Bernie was normally the best wheelman in the Valley.

"Christ Almighty!" he jerked the wheel, got us back where we belonged. He gave me a look—couldn't call it annoyed; no way Bernie could ever be annoyed with me—so it had to be something else, like maybe he was tired. Bernie needs his sleep.

"Let's go home," he said. "Sleep on it."

Whoa! I was right about Bernie being tired, of course, but this particular sleep was going to be a first, and maybe even not that safe, on account of the roof of our house being the slanting kind. Why couldn't we just sleep inside, like normal? I came very close to giving myself another shake, thought better of it, curled up on the seat.

We went home, walked through the house and out onto the patio. And there was Iggy, just where we'd left him, although you couldn't say things were right, exactly.

"Oh, Iggy!"

At which point I had an idea after all, zooming in from out of the blue. No effort on my part, no unpleasant head pressure, just a big and simple idea: I wanted Iggy back at his place, and fast. My best pal, yes, but living together? A bad idea: I never would have guessed how bad. Now I knew.

Some time later, we all lay down for the night—Bernie in his bed; me lying in the hall by the front door, the sounds and smells of the night leaking in through the crack underneath; and Iggy right beside me, for some reason. Whenever I tried to roll away, he rolled away with me. The difference was he slept more deeply than any member of the nation within I'd ever known, while I was up practically the whole night. At least we weren't on the roof. All in all, no complaints.

• • •

"Well, well," Bernie said first thing next morning, Iggy bounding toward him across the hall, "who's looking chipper?"

And next he was giving Iggy a nice pat. As I got my paws under me and slowly rose—also trying not to yawn, which never works—I thought of wood chippers, no telling why. Iggy and I go way back, if I haven't mentioned that already.

I was on my way to Bernie and Iggy, all set to make some space between them, enough for me and no one else, when there was a knock at the door. A knock at the door and I hadn't heard anyone coming? What with security being part of my job? I whirled around and barked at the door, yes, savagely, like I was going to take it apart, and then take apart whoever was out there, and then—

"Chet! What the hell!" Bernie said. "Someone woke up on the wrong side of the bed today, huh, Iggy?"

Oh, boy. Just oh, boy. Let's leave it at that.

Knock knock.

"Chet! Sit!"

Things were coming at me from every direction. This was impossible. I felt like I was about to—

"Chet?"

I sat. And felt quite a lot better right away. Even well rested! Don't ask me to explain.

Bernie opened the front door. Without warning, Iggy took off and darted out—but no. Just when you might have thought that it was too late and the little bugger was gone, possibly for good, Bernie—without even looking!—reached down and grabbed his collar. Iggy's stubby legs kept churning, but he went nowhere, a very pleasant sight I could have watched all day.

But meanwhile we had a visitor: a woman of what Bernie calls the no-nonsense type, wearing a white nurse's outfit. Bernie scooped up Iggy and—and held him in one arm, like a baby. Iggy wriggled wildly. Bernie held him with two arms.

"Yes?" he said.

"Mr. Little?" said the nurse.

"Call me Bernie," Bernie said.

"I'm from Valley General. Mrs. Parsons has come home and I'm getting her settled."

"She's well enough to come home?" Bernie said. "That's good news."

"I'm with the hospice department."

"Oh."

"Apparently there's a dog named Iggy?"

Bernie—how to put it? Brandished, maybe? Bernie brandished the little guy.

"Not the other one?" the nurse said, looking past Iggy to me.

"Nope," Bernie said. "That's Chet." I sat up nice and straight, a total pro.

The nurse's gaze returned to the little wriggler. "I see," she said. "In any case, Mrs. Parsons would like him to come home."

Chet the Jet catches a break!

"Is she able to take care of him?" Bernie said.

Bernie! Don't argue!

The Parsonses had a little room at the back of the house they called a den. "A time machine back to 1956," Bernie called it, not sure why. But that was where we found Mrs. Parsons, sitting in an armchair, feet up on a stool, a big smile on her face at the sight of Iggy. Let's not go into their reunion, and all that tail wagging and slobbering, and the nurse cleaning up a bit of broken bric-a-brac before she left, and get right to when things had calmed down, Iggy fast asleep on the footstool, Mrs. Parsons sipping tea Bernie made her, Bernie on the little couch opposite the easy chair, and me beside Bernie, working on a special chewy Mrs. Parsons might or might not have bought for Iggy at the hospital gift shop.

"Any news on Daniel?" Bernie said.

Mrs. Parsons smiled. A big smile, although it sagged to one side in an odd kind of way. "He's coming home, too! Maybe as soon as next week."

"Wonderful," said Bernie.

"We're very lucky," said Mrs. Parsons. "From appearances, would you take us for the type to afford hospice-at-home privileges? I'll say not! But Daniel was always a big believer in insurance. We have the best." Mrs. Parsons took a sip of tea, her pinky finger sticking out to the side, a sight I never tire of. She studied Bernie over the rim of her cup. "I trust you're well set up in that regard," she said. "What with your line of work and all."

"Um," Bernie said, followed by, "uh."

He glanced over at me this way he sometimes does, like he wanted a little input on my part. I shifted the chewy to the other side of my mouth, all the input I could come up with on short notice. I hoped it was helpful.

"Speaking of my work," Bernie said, "I wonder if you're up to talking a bit about Billy?"

Mrs. Parsons's pinky finger folded back up. "Our son Billy?"

"Yes. But not if you're . . ."

"Oh, that's all right," said Mrs. Parsons. "Did you know he gave us a saguaro? A truly grand one. The stately kind, if you know what I mean."

"I do."

Mrs. Parsons twisted around to the side table, tried to place the cup on the saucer. The saucer and cup tilted, and almost went over the side, then righted themselves, a little tea slopping over the side of the cup, unnoticed by Mrs. Parsons. "But now it's gone for some reason. I never got to see it, except on his phone."

"He showed you a picture when he came to the hospital?"

"That's right. You're easy to talk to, Bernie. Like a river flowing right along. Has anyone told you that?"

"Never."

"Of course, all talents can be used for good or evil," Mrs. Parsons said.

Bernie nodded one of his nods.

"But I had a lovely visit with Billy," Mrs. Parsons said. "That's the main thing. All those parental clichés—like he's still my little baby—are true. All the more so since he's our only child." She smiled that lopsided smile again, although at no one in particular. "He remembers the polka-dot socks."

"Are you a grandparent as well as a parent?" Bernie said.

Mrs. Parsons's smile sagged at both ends and then vanished. "Didn't Dan tell you? Billy's been . . . away for some time. He . . . wasn't in a position to enjoy the normal things in life."

"I didn't get many details," Bernie said. "Does the name Dee Branch mean anything to you?"

"I—I'd have to think," said Mrs. Parsons. One of her hands reached over for the teacup, felt around, didn't find it. The human hand has a mind of its own, kind of like the tail in the nation within. At that moment, I was struck by maybe the most amazing thought of my whole life: What if I had two tails? Wow! That stopped me in my tracks, even though I wasn't going anywhere. I even forgot about my chewy, perhaps just letting it dangle out the side of my mouth. "Should it?" Mrs. Parsons went on.

"Not necessarily," Bernie said.

"I hear a 'but.'"

Funny. I did not, and there was no way Mrs. Parsons had better hearing than me. For one thing, she was human. Second, she was old. Old humans say, "What? What?" and cup their ears with their hands, making other humans repeat things—like "a little ground pepper on that?"—over and over and over, reminding me of certain bad dreams I've had. And what's with pepper? But forget all that. There were no buts: that's the point.

"No buts," Bernie said. No surprise there. "It's just that I'm concerned about Billy."

"Oh?" said Mrs. Parsons. "In what way?"

"It starts with the saguaro," Bernie said. "Turns out it was illegally transplanted from a protected area near Rincon City. That's why the state came and took it away."

Mrs. Parsons's eyes got all faraway. Normally, the eyes of old people look just as old as the rest of them, but not always, and Mrs. Parsons belonged to this second group. Her eyes, if you just concentrated on them and screened out the rest of her face, looked kind of young. "Are you saying he dealt with a dishonest landscaper?" Mrs. Parsons said.

"That's one possibility," Bernie said.

"There are others?"

"None that I know of."

Her gaze went to Bernie, sharp and quick. "But you implied there were."

Bernie smiled. "My mistake. Let's put it like this. Daniel did mention that Billy's on parole, and I've seen it revoked for some real Mickey Mouse stuff."

Now we had mice in the picture? If so, they weren't close by, making the Parsonses' house unusual, in my experience. I've caught a few mice in my career, but it's never easy. And here's something odd: it's a snap for cats. Why would that be? Even more amazing is the fact that cats can also catch birds. How I'd love to catch a bird, just once! Cats do it by pouncing. I can pounce, too, not that it's one of my best moves. But it is in my repertoire. So maybe one day it will happen for me. You can always hope, and I always do.

"You can't mean they'd send him back to prison," Mrs. Parsons was saying.

"I'd need more facts to answer that," Bernie said.

"But it wouldn't be just!" said Mrs. Parsons. "Locking someone up for buying the wrong cactus? What country are we in?"

A tough question. The Valley was in Arizona, a fact I'd picked up fairly recently. Also we were Americans, me and Bernie. That was as far as I could take it. Maybe not far, but farther than Iggy. He wriggled around on the footstool, getting more comfortable, and began to snore.

"The same one," Bernie said, "that put Billy away the first time."

"What do you mean by that?"

"Justice can be rough. Daniel also said that Billy wasn't aware that a kidnapping was planned."

Mrs. Parsons gazed down at her lap. "What else did he say?"

"That Billy's crime, more or less, was to fall in with the wrong people."

"He's a kind man," Mrs. Parsons said.

"You're speaking of Billy?"

Mrs. Parsons's head snapped up. "Oh, no—Daniel. I'm speaking of Daniel."

"Uh," Bernie said, "are you suggesting that—"

Whatever it was, Mrs. Parsons interrupted before Bernie could get there, meaning I didn't get there, either. "Certainly not!" she said. Her hand again felt around for the teacup with no success.

"Can I get you some more tea?" Bernie said.

"No, thank you," she said. Then she said it again, more softly. "In fact," she went on, "I'm getting a little tired."

Bernie rose. I rose, too, not forgetting my chew strip. "Do you need any help getting upstairs or anything?" he said.

"I'll just nap right here with Iggy," Mrs. Parsons said. Sounded like a plan to me. Couldn't ask for a better napping buddy than Iggy. He was world-class.

"Just call if you need anything," Bernie said.

"That's very nice, Bernie. I'm sure I can manage. The hospice people come three times a day."

"Good to hear," said Bernie. He took a step toward the door. I did, too. "Meanwhile, I'll be looking for Billy."

"Why?"

"Aren't you worried about him?"

Mrs. Parsons's eyes filled with tears. "It's just a stupid plant," she said.

Bernie nodded. I was pretty sure this nod meant it was not just a stupid plant. Not that the plant was smart or anything like that. But before I could nail it down completely, Bernie said, "Daniel asked me to."

"To find Billy?"

"To clear up the saguaro matter in general," Bernie said. "But that's going to mean finding Billy. I hope it won't cause trouble between the two of you."

Mrs. Parsons's eyes cleared. "It might," she said. "But nothing we can't handle."

Bernie opened the door to the hall, paused again. "Do you remember the names of any of those wrong people Billy fell in with?"

Mrs. Parsons's eyes had closed. She said nothing. Iggy whimpered in his sleep.

FIFTEEN

S hould I feel bad?" Bernie said, when we were outside the Parsonses' house.

Not for any reason I could see. Bernie should feel tip-top, now and forever.

"To let Edna go on thinking it's a cactus case, is what I mean. When it's actually murder."

Murder? This was interesting. I concentrated my very hardest.

"Suppose," Bernie went on, "that Billy dug up the cactus himself. And then Ellie Newburg tracked him down. Stealing a saguaro would be a clear parole violation, meaning he'd be on his way back to prison and facing new charges. Did Billy snap? Does he have it in him to kill? Don't forget that the weak can kill, too, Chet."

I made another mental note! Something or other about the weak, was it? I was in brand-new territory.

"And if Billy doesn't have it in him, those 'roided-up twins sure as hell do," Bernie said. "We know that for a fact."

The twins? I could practically still taste the blood of Twin One. I was in the picture, but totally.

Bernie went quiet for a moment or two, and then his face darkened. "Is it also a fact that Brick Mickles knows about the twins? And that he knew Billy's whereabouts? See where this leads?"

I waited to find out.

"Mickles is working the case and he didn't bring Billy in, Chet. Why not?"

I searched my mind for answers, but it was my bad luck that at that same moment it was failing to hang on to the question. Does that ever happen to you?

"Here's a crazy thought—maybe Mickles knows Billy isn't the killer," Bernie said. "But if that's the case, then . . ." He gave his head a quick little shake, maybe to change things up inside. I do the same thing. "One thing for sure, we need to learn a lot more about Billy Parsons." He turned toward the Porsche, parked in our driveway. "Maybe time to pay a visit to Northern State Correctional. How does that sound?"

It sounded better than anything I'd ever heard. Hadn't been to Northern State Correctional in way too long. I missed my pals up there, too many to mention. To get to Northern State Correctional you drive out of the Valley and head for the middle of nowhere, nowhere being lovely open country with nothing human in sight until you come to a gate in the road. We stopped. A guard stepped out of the guardhouse, came over.

"Hey, it's Chet!" She turned to the guardhouse. "Chet's here. And Bernie."

"Hi," Bernie said.

"Looks like he's grown," the guard said.

"We're both still the same size," Bernie said, which I didn't get, and perhaps the guard didn't either, because she showed no reaction. Meanwhile, another guard came hurrying over from the guardhouse, a nice surprise in his hand, the kind of surprise I'd actually been counting on.

"Chet still partial to Slim Jims?" he said.

Bernie grunted. His mood wasn't tip-top all of a sudden. Was he tired from the drive? Poor Bernie, I thought, and then got busy with the Slim Jim. The answer to the Slim Jim question is that I'm as partial as they come.

"Sure appreciates his food," said one of the guards.

"A real pleasure to watch him eat," said the other. "No . . . what's the expression?"

"Food issues," said the first one.

"Exactly," the second one said. "No food issues. We've lost the simple—"

"Excuse me," Bernie said. "Can we get through?"

The guards turned to him, both of them blinking in a where'd-he-come-from sort of way. "Uh, sure, Bernie," one said. "Here on business?"

Bernie opened his mouth, closed it, opened it again, a complicated move you didn't see often from him. It meant he'd had something all set to say—maybe a real zinger, with fistfighting coming next—and changed his mind. "Yeah," he said. "Business. Name Billy Parsons mean anything to you?"

"Billy Parsons? Rings a bell."

"Wasn't he the one—"

"—running the meth lab out of his cell? You're thinking of Bob Carson. Billy Parsons was that little dude—"

"—finishing up his sentence over at the farm?"

"Yeah, but—"

"The farm?" Bernie said. "That the minimum security annex?"

"Even less than minimum."

"But the guy you're looking for—"

"—got released a few weeks ago."

"That's all right," Bernie said. "I'd like to talk to people who knew him."

"Need permission from the boss up there."

"Who's that?"

"Assistant Warden Stackhouse—new guy."

"Transferred up from Central."

"Want us to call?"

"That'd be nice," Bernie said.

The guards went into the guardhouse. One talked on the phone. The other yawned. Pretty soon the yawner came back with visitor passes to wear around our necks, one for Bernie and one for me. "Stackhouse says if he knew you were coming, he'd have turned down the job."

The gate swung open. We drove on through, rounded a curve, and there in a wide field was a wonderful sight: a whole big gang of dudes in orange jumpsuits, breaking rocks in the hot sun! As we got closer I saw that they weren't actually breaking rocks—leaning on shovels and rakes was more like it. Also it wasn't particularly hot. But the sun was out, no doubt about that. I wouldn't trade this job for anything.

Assistant Warden Stackhouse turned out to be one of those short, thick guys, maybe the thickest I'd seen, not the popping-muscle type, more like he was all one big muscle. Also he was pretty much neckless. He and Bernie pounded each other on the back, Bernie wincing a bit.

"And this must be Chet," Stackhouse said. "Heard a lot about him. C'mon over here, pal." He squatted down like a baseball catcher. I like when people do that. Plus he had nation within smells all over him. He gave me a nice pat, ran his hands along my sides. "A real specimen, huh? I've got a Malinois bitch at home just going on three. Ever thought of putting him out to stud?"

Whatever that was, it sounded interesting, but Bernie said, "We're taking a little break from that at the moment."

"Meaning?"

"Nothing. What can you tell me about Billy Parsons?"

"Billy Parsons?" Stackhouse shrugged, his shoulders like two hillsides going up and down. "Had him for six months, normal pre-parole step-down from Max. Quiet, no trouble, kept his nose clean."

Good to hear. Some humans—more than you might think— have problems with that. Why is it so hard, their noses generally being on the smallish side?

"I'd like to see his paperwork," Bernie said.

"Sure thing," said Stackhouse, turning to his computer. "He screwed up already?"

"Looks that way," Bernie said.

"The record is eight minutes," Stackhouse said.

"Someone hijacked a car right outside the gate?"

"A bus, actually, but close enough." A printer whirred in one corner of Stackhouse's office. Did I forget to mention we were in his office, inside the main building at the farm, which looked like the kind of low office complex you might see in any business park? No high walls, no guard towers, no barbed wire, and really nothing interesting to describe, except for the distant view of Max through the window—distant but still huge, and all about those things I just mentioned: walls, towers, wire.

Stackhouse went over to the printer, brought back some sheets of paper. Bernie looked through them, his eyes going back and forth, back and forth, like they were vacuuming up stuff real fast, if that makes any sense.

"Nothing here about the original crime?" he said.

Stackhouse leaned over Bernie's shoulder and pointed. "Kidnapping in the first degree—says right there."

"But no police report," Bernie said. "No trial transcript."

"They don't send those up," Stackhouse told him. "I can get the police report."

"Thanks."

Now Stackhouse's eyes were doing the back-and-forth thing, just about as fast as Bernie's but not in the same rhythm. I felt a little pukey, hard to say why.

"But here's something, top of the page," Stackhouse said. "See this guy, also sent up, same case, same sentence?"

"Travis Baca."

"He's still here."

"Here at the farm?"

"His release day is tomorrow, in fact. Want to talk to him?"

"I'm Bernie Little and this is Chet," Bernie said. "We live next door to Billy Parsons's parents."

"Yeah?" said Travis Baca, a wiry guy with sunken cheeks. He sat on a bench watching dudes shooting hoops on an outdoor basketball court, a paperback book on his lap. "I never knew my old man and my ma died two years ago."

"Sorry for your loss," Bernie said. "Billy's parents are worried about him. I'd like to ease their minds."

Travis Baca gave Bernie a quick look; then his gaze shifted to me. Some humans shower less often than others. Travis was in that first group. He was also the jittery type, one foot tapping away nonstop. "Your dog dangerous?"

"Only when threatened," Bernie said.

Travis sat back a little farther on the bench. One of the basketball players—skinny, with real long arms—shot us a look as he ran down the court.

"What you reading?" Bernie said.

Travis held up the book.

"The biography of Pablo Escobar?"

"That's all I read—biographies of successful men. Pick up a few tips."

"Word is you're getting out tomorrow."

"Yeah."

"Any plans?"

"Kind of sick of hearing that question."

Bernie nodded. "What did you do before this?" he said.

"Before what?"

"The kidnapping."

"I didn't do no kidnapping."

"No?"

"I fell in with bad people. That's not the same as kidnapping."

"Word is Billy says the exact same thing about you."

With no warning, Travis's hands tensed up into claws, claws that shifted slightly toward Bernie and then put on the brakes. And just in time: I was that close to being airborne. His voice got loud and harsh. "He says that, he's a fucking liar." The long-armed basketball player pulled down a rebound, passed off, and gave us another look, more careful this time.

"You're saying Billy Parsons led you astray?" Bernie said.

"Goddamn right," said Travis, calmer and quieter, although his foot tapping speed ramped up.

"Tell me the whole story."

"What story?"

"About the kidnapping."

"I don't know," Travis said. "Like . . ."

"Like a Pablo Escobar drug deal," Bernie said, pointing to Travis's book with his chin. "Beginning, middle, end."

"Beginning first?"

"Yeah," said Bernie. "Whose idea was it? Who was the victim? That kind of thing."

Travis's voice rose again. He had a way of taking you by surprise that I was starting not to like. "There was no victim!"

The long-armed player stepped to the far sidelines, tapped the shoulder of another guy who took his place, then just stood there watching us.

"No victim?" Bernie said.

Travis's eyes shifted. He looked down. "Just, ah, sayin' we were all victims. Like in the end."

"Who got kidnapped?" Bernie said.

"This girl," said Travis, gaze still on the ground.

"What was her name?"

"Uh, I never got the name."

"That's hard to believe."

"Believe what you want. I didn't know nothin' about nothin'. I was just the driver, end of story."

"You were the driver?"

"What I just said."

"So Billy was the brains?"

"What sense would that make?" Travis looked up. "He's a moron."

"Then who was the brains?"

Travis stared at Bernie, his eyes narrowing. Then he turned away. "No one. That's clear from how it ended."

"Which was?"

"With me and Billy doing fifteen years, what the hell do you think?"

"Did anyone else do time?"

"Anyone else, like who?"

"Like the brains behind the kidnapping, Travis. You were the driver and Billy was the moron. Was anyone else arrested? Was anyone else charged?"

"Know something?" Travis said. "You sound like a cop." He stared at Bernie again, this time held the look. "I don't trust cops. Cops stab you in the back. That's what happened to me fifteen years ago—stabbed in the goddamn back."

"By who?" Bernie said.

"Told you—a cop," Travis said. "Are you even listening? The cop who collared me and Billy."

"Remember his name?"

"That I won't forget. It was Mickles."

SIXTEEN

After that, we had a long silence—silence in this case meaning no more back-and-forth between Bernie and Travis
Baca. Otherwise, there was plenty to hear, starting with Bernie's
heart, suddenly pounding like a drum in his chest. And he's got
a big strong chest, like a drum to begin with, so . . . I got no
further with that one. But hey! Pretty far, to my way of thinking!
Another sound was the bounce bounce of the basketball on the
court, actually somewhat like Bernie's heartbeat. The two of them
together made a kind of music. Wow! What a thought! Was I on
fire or what? Here's a funny thing about being on fire: it can happen in just part of you. Another part can be doing its job at the
same time, if that makes any sense. And if it doesn't, let's leave it
at this: the other part of me, not the on-fire part, happened to
notice that Travis was gazing across the court, a gaze that fell on
the long-armed basketball player. The long-armed player gazed
back, then—what was this? Pulled out a cell phone from down in
his pants? The perps at Northern State had cell phones? You never
stopped learning in this business. Travis turned away.

"How did Mickles stab you in the back?" Bernie said.

Travis looked at Bernie, cocking his head to one side, like he was seeing him differently. "Know what?" he said, standing up. "We're done."

"Not so fast," Bernie said. "If you got dealt a bad deal, maybe I can help make it right, make it right for Billy, too. Are you planning to meet up with him?"

"What for?"

"You tell me."

Travis's eyes narrowed. "Dream on." He started walking away, stopped, turned. "One more thing—don't come back."

"How'd it go?" said Assistant Warden Stackhouse, back in his office. "Seem rehabilitated to you?"

"Need more time to evaluate him," Bernie said. "Which is kind of what I'd like to do."

"Meaning?"

"When does he walk out?"

"Why do I get the feeling you're fixing to tail him?"

Bernie spread his hands. "Beats me."

"Front gate at zero eight thirty," Stackhouse said. "Anything else I can do for you?"

"Just that police report."

Stackhouse shook his head. "Not available—some screwup downtown."

"What kind of screwup?"

"They're scanning all the files, decade by decade, converting to digital. You'll be able to access anything you want on your phone in real time. Can't argue with that."

"Wouldn't even try," Bernie said.

"But right now Valley PD's a madhouse. They can't find shit."

That sounded bad. Was there anything easier to find? Not

that I could think of. Valley PD was in big trouble—that was my takeaway.

"This is my day off," Captain Stine said.

"No such thing in a job like yours," said Bernie.

"Maybe," said Stine, "but that's for me to say, not you."

He rocked the baby carriage back and forth. Inside was the baby, all covered up except for his fat little face. His eyes were closed. He smelled great. Was this a good time to lean in and give him a quick lick? I wasn't sure. We were in a park between the last of the downtown towers and the zoo. I'd been to the zoo once, would probably not be returning. But from right where I was, the zoo not even in sight, I could easily smell the tigers, as well as the chimps. The chimps smelled a lot like humans—more so, in fact. The smell of chimps helped me understand the human smell even better, if that makes sense.

The baby stirred in his sleep, made a little groaning sound.

"Uh-oh," Stine said. "Mona wants him to sleep till supper time."

"Ease off on the rocking a bit," Bernie said.

"This is too hard?"

"When they almost catapult out is a clue."

Stine eased off on the rocking. The baby settled down. "I'll be sixty-eight when he graduates from high school."

"Maybe he'll drop out," Bernie said. He gazed in at the baby. "Got his looks from Mona—you lucked out there. What's his name?"

"Kyle."

"Nice."

Stine glanced across the carriage at Bernie. "And his middle name's Bernard."

"Yeah?" said Bernie.

"Mona wouldn't hear of it as a first name," Stine said. "Not esthetically pleasing, she says."

"She's right about that," said Bernie. His face was a little flushed, for reasons unclear to me. I knew for a fact he hadn't had even a sip of bourbon yet today.

Now they were both looking at the baby. The baby lay there, eyes shut tight. He wasn't bringing much to the table, in my opinion.

"Maybe it's crazy," Stine said, "even pathetic. But I wanted to be a captain in the worst way. And it wouldn't have happened except for you."

"Uh," Bernie said.

Stine turned to him. "So what's so important it couldn't wait?"

"The original file on an old case that may be connected to the Ellie Newburg murder."

"What about it?"

"Unavailable, ostensibly on account of digitizing. I need it anyway."

"Email me the details."

"Thanks," Bernie said.

"But records are a mess right now, no ostensibly about it."

"A file has to be somewhere," Bernie said. "Where are you on the Newburg case?"

"Nothing but dead ends so far."

"Is that according to Mickles?"

"Don't start."

"Why him?" Bernie said.

"We went through this already," Stine said, "but because I know there's no one more bullheaded than you, meaning I was going to be condemned to go over the whole thing till the cows come home, I checked with the chief of D's. The call went in in the normal way and Mickles was next up, as per their system. That's that."

"As per their system? What's that mean?"

"Organizations rely on systems, Bernie—in this case, parameters of district, seniority, fitness reports, other metrics like that. Mickles came up. Finito."

Bernie looked at Stine like he was going to say more, but he did not.

"What?" said Stine. "Spit it out."

Which Bernie didn't do. Bernie—a man, yes, but not the spitting kind. I was glad of that. Hard to explain why, and besides I was otherwise engaged in a careful examination of Bernie's head. Not a delicate sort of head, yet bullish? I wouldn't have gone that far. But did cows find him bullish? Was that why they were coming home? I was lost.

"Just get me that file," Bernie said.

The baby groaned again. Bernard was his name? That's Bernie's name, sort of, although the only person I've ever heard call him that was his old kindergarten teacher who we ran into once, I forget where. "Learn how to behave in all these years, Bernard?" she'd said. Still, you couldn't ask for a finer name. Stine eased off on the rocking.

Bright and early the next morning—and how I love bright and early, sharpens you up like nothing else, although there's also a lot to be said for dark and late—we were parked on a little rise off the highway to Northern State Correctional, in easy viewing sight of the front gate, closed at the moment, nothing happening. Bernie sipped coffee from a paper cup. I sat up nice and tall, just breathing. The smell of coffee mixed with the smell of greasewood in a very interesting way. I sniffed at that mix from several angles, if you get what I mean.

Bernie glanced over. "Something caught in your nose, big guy?"

Which had to be Bernie's sense of humor. He can be quite the joker, as I'm sure I've mentioned.

"Or is it something else?" he went on. "I've read that you have over twenty million—"

A banged-up old van appeared on the highway, rounded the curve below us, and stopped near the gate, pulling over to the side of the road. We had vans like that out the yingyang in these parts. No reason to stop talking, Bernie, especially when you were clearly gearing up for something big. I had twenty million what, exactly? It sounded like way more than two. But what? And where?

"Easy, big guy, easy," Bernie said, taking the binoculars out of the glove box. "Gotta get that plate number, just in case. Need to pee, maybe?"

No! I did not need to pee! I needed my twenty million—but then, funnily enough, I did need to pee. I hopped out of the car— "Knew it," said Bernie—and marked the biggest greasewood bush I could find, marked it up, down, and sideways so it would stay marked, amigo. That brought something new to the coffee and greasewood smell, spicing it up nicely. I was just getting down to the last few drops—although I always hold on to a little something because you never know—when an ambulance came roaring up the highway, lights flashing, siren blaring. The gate swung open, and the ambulance barreled through, disappearing around the bend that led to the prison.

After that, things got quiet. Bernie checked his watch a few times. "Any minute now," he said. That had to mean soon, but nothing happened soon. Some time later, the ambulance came back the other way, no lights this time, no siren. The gate opened and the ambulance drove through—not fast—and headed up the highway. I preferred it the first way, meaning zooming with lights and siren, no telling why.

I got comfortable on the shotgun seat, the most comfortable seat I know to begin with. Hard to beat this, Bernie and I side by side in the Porsche, time passing. Why were we here, by the way? Did it matter?

Bernie checked his watch one more time, got on the phone. "Assistant Warden Stackhouse, please."

"Unavailable," said a woman at the other end. "Would you like his voicemail?"

Bernie clicked off. "I would hate his voicemail. I would also hate—"

The driver's-side door of the beat-up van opened and a woman got out. Bernie watched her through the binoculars. I don't know what he saw—and I'm no fan of binoculars, which make humans seem even more like machines than they already do—but I saw that she was wearing a baseball cap with a ponytail sticking out the back, a very nice look, to my way of thinking, plus a light blue sweat suit, and sneakers. She walked up to the guardhouse, knocked on the door. It opened and a guard stepped out, a woman, but lighter-skinned than the guard from yesterday. They seemed to talk for a bit, and then with no warning, the ponytail woman slumped to the ground like she'd lost all her strength in an instant and lay still.

We were on the move before she hit the ground, the Porsche fishtailing as we ripped down the dirt track that led from the lookout to the highway. The other guard—the male from yesterday, in the know about me and Slim Jims—hurried out of the guardhouse, bent over the ponytail woman. By the time we'd driven up and jumped out of the car, the guards had her on her feet. One patted her on the shoulder. The other held a bottle of water to her mouth, tilted it up, but she shook her head wildly, knocking the bottle to the ground.

The female guard saw us and raised her hand in the stop sign. "Hey, just a minute."

"It's all right," the other guard told her. "They're friends."

"What's going on?" Bernie said.

"Uh, the lady's here to pick up a released inmate," the male guard said. "Unfortunately, he seems to have met with an accident this morning."

The lady turned to us. Hard to tell human ages sometimes. From her ponytail and the way she moved I'd have thought she was around the same age as Bernie, but her face had more lines and creases, something you saw on people who were living hard lives. At the moment she also looked real weak, her face all washed out.

"He's dead," she said. She kicked the water bottle away. Her voice rose. "Fifteen years and now he's dead. Dead, dead, dead! How is that possible?"

"Something in the weight room, ma'am," the male guard said.

"Something in the weight room, something in the weight room. You told me that already. I'm asking how is it possible?"

"We don't have the details yet," said the female guard, "but as soon as we do—"

"I don't give a shit about the details! How is it possible? I need to know how it's possible!"

The guards looked at Bernie. He bent down, picked the water bottle up off the road. Most of the water had spilled out, but there was still some at the bottom. He handed the bottle to the ponytail woman and said, "Drink this." His voice wasn't gentle, in fact, harsh and demanding. The ponytail woman looked a bit startled. She put the bottle to her lips and drank it down. After that, she straightened up and stood under her own power, some color returning to her face. Then she handed the bottle back to Bernie.

Bernie has a lot of nods, as I may have mentioned, and now he showed me a new one, more of a bow, almost like he was grateful that the woman had given him back the empty bottle. No idea what was going on, but her gaze settled on him in a new way.

"And the name of your friend?" Bernie said.

"My brother," the woman said. "My kid brother."

"I'm sorry for your loss," Bernie said.

A silence fell over all of us outside the guardhouse of Northern State Correctional. Then the wind rose, soft and rustling in the hills.

The female guard nodded, like she'd been waiting for the go-ahead. "The inmate's name was Travis Baca," she said.

The ponytail woman spoke softly, maybe too softly for anyone to hear but me. "A free man, not an inmate," she said. "As of today."

SEVENTEEN

"S ure you want to do this?" said Assistant Warden Stackhouse.

The ponytail woman—whose name turned out to be Trish, if I'd understood the conversation on the way into the building, not something you'd want to put a lot of money on—nodded her head in a forceful way. "Got to," she said.

Stackhouse opened a door. "The weight room."

We went inside—me, Bernie, Trish, Stackhouse. I'd been in weight rooms before, especially around the time of the Roidman Rafferty case. Roidman! He'd flipped the Porsche—this was several Porsches ago, all newer and less dinged than the one we had now—right over with his bare hands! But he ended up getting grabbed by the pant leg in the usual way. Back to the weight room here at the farm, which was on the small side, with a few benches, bars and plates, rigs and racks, plus a heavy scent of human male sweat on everything, some of it fairly fresh, some going way back. Everything was tidy except for one little area against the far wall, where a bench lay on its side, the front part resting on a barbell with big plates on both ends. The two stands for racking the bar also lay on the floor in a scattered kind of way. We stood around the messy area. Stackhouse pointed to the barbell.

"Benching two fifty," he said. "Someone reported hearing noise. A CO looked in and found him lying on his back with the bar across his throat. He freed him up and started CPR, but it was too late. Sorry to say, ma'am. Death by asphyxiation. It's a risk that comes with the bench-press exercise, which is why we encourage the use of spotters."

Trish covered her mouth with both hands, but still a high little cry escaped. Her eyes filled with tears, although they didn't flow, sort of like she'd bottled them up, too.

"He was alone?" Bernie was saying.

Stackhouse nodded. At the same time, he touched Trish's shoulder in a comforting way. She didn't exactly shrug him off; more like she just drifted back a step or two and leaned against the wall.

"What time was this?" Bernie said.

"CO made it zero six forty-five," said Stackhouse.

"So less than two hours before his release from a fifteen-year stretch he was in here pumping iron?" Bernie said.

"You know gym rats," Stackhouse said.

This conversation was hard to follow. For one thing, there were no rats anywhere nearby. For another, Bernie knew no rats of any kind. I began to suspect that Stackhouse might not be on top of things.

"The inmates are locked up at night?" Bernie said.

"Yup," said Stackhouse. "Cell doors open at zero five thirty, breakfast at six. After that, there's some free time till work assignments. This is minimum security, Bernie, pretty much everyone here for less than six months. Even the morons don't screw up."

Bernie went over to the fallen bar, half-squatted, picked it up, hefted it, seemed to feel the weight. "Two fifty his normal load?"

Stackhouse shrugged. "A decent amount, but nothing special, right?"

"No, nothing special," Bernie said, gently lowering the bar to the floor.

Trish turned toward us. "Travis was captain of the freshman football team in high school," she said with an edge to her voice, like they'd offended her.

"That's, uh, a nice accomplishment," Stackhouse said.

Meanwhile, Bernie was looking around the room. "Had time to check the video?" he said.

Stackhouse rubbed his chin, a human thing—mostly male—that means some problem is on the way. Stackhouse not on top of things? For sure! Had I nailed it or what? And so early in the game! Chet the Jet, ahead of the curve—which had actually happened once in the Porsche when we went into a sudden spin, but no time for that now. "We're in a transitional phase when it comes to video," Stackhouse said.

"You're telling me this is a prison with no video surveillance?" Bernie said.

Trish frowned, the lines in her face, already deepish, deepening more. Stackhouse glanced at her, then took Bernie by the elbow and led him aside, which only works if Bernie wants to be led aside. He lowered his voice and said, "We've got video, but no longer comprehensive."

"Huh?"

"You must have read about the budget cuts, Bernie. I had to prioritize the video coverage."

Bernie took a deep breath, let it out slow. Trish moved toward them. "What are you two whispering about?"

"Nothing," said Stackhouse.

She didn't seem to hear. "What are you hiding from me?"

"Not a thing, ma'am." He gestured toward the tipped-over bench. "I'm sorry."

Trish shook her head. "Don't want to hear it," she said. "Don't want to hear anything." She strode across the weight room and out the door. We followed. Trish was moving fast, already rounding a corner, so we moved fast, too. But then for no reason I knew, I stopped and looked back, down the hall the other way. And there, leaning on a mop, was the long-armed dude with the cell phone down his pants, watching us. I like most of the humans I've met, but I did not like the long-armed dude. Was there any reason not to let him know? None occurred to me, at least not right away, and right away is my comfort zone when it comes to time.

Bernie spun around. "Chet! What are you barking at?"

The long-armed dude, of course. And now he had a little grin on his face that made me bark all the more.

"Chet! Cool it!"

Certainly, but not now. Cooling it later? No objection to that, at least none I could think of at the—

"CHET!"

I cooled it. Bernie took one quick glance at the long-armed dude, now busy with his mop, head down, and then we turned and followed Stackhouse and Trish out of the building.

Trish's van was parked next to the Porsche. Bernie and I trailed after her across the lot. She paid no attention to us, but you can always tell if someone knows you're behind them and she knew. We stopped beside the Porsche.

"Uh, Trish?" Bernie said.

Trish opened the passenger door of the van. On the seat lay a paper bag with burgers and fries inside and a six-pack of beer, which was more than two. Trish grabbed the fast-food bag and the six-pack and turned to Bernie.

"Here," she said.

"I don't want that," Bernie said. "It's yours."

"No," Trish said. "It's for Travis. Burgers and beer. He couldn't wait." She held out the bag and the six-pack.

Bernie shook his head. "I can understand why you maybe wouldn't want to consume—" He cut himself off, but maybe too late. Trish let go of the bag and the six-pack, which fell on the pavement, glass shattering. Then, her hands just dangling empty in the air, she started to wail, a piercing high-pitched wail that went on and on. I crouched down, as though a storm had sprung up, had no idea what to do. That was when Bernie stepped forward, sort of hugged Trish without getting too close, and patted her back. She sobbed on his shoulder, gradually went still.

"The world's a goddamn filthy mess," she said.

"Let's try to clean up one little corner," said Bernie.

That brightened things up, at least for me. I began to take an interest in my surroundings, and what do you know? The bag of burgers had split open in a convenient way and lay practically at my feet.

We took Trish out for coffee at a little roadside place on the way to town. It had a patio out back overlooking an empty swimming pool and a trailer park. There's all kinds of beauty in life. Bernie had coffee black, Trish had hers with cream and sugar, and I had water. You can't beat water, in my opinion. Don't know about your insides, but mine are like a well. Wells need water.

Trish held her cup in both hands—as women sometimes do, but men hardly ever—and took a sip. The sun shone on her face, so rough from too much sun already. "You're a detective?" she said.

"Private," Bernie said. "Right now we're working for the parents of Billy Parsons."

Trish put down her cup. "Weak men are the ones who screw you up."

"How so?" Bernie said.

"In my life, anyhow. The strong ones just screw you, period."

"And Billy's a weak one?"

"I don't know about now," she said. "I haven't seen him in a long time."

"Fifteen years?" Bernie said.

"Longer than that," said Trish.

"He got out a few weeks ago," Bernie said.

"Figures," said Trish.

"What do you mean?"

Trish didn't answer. She tore open another sugar packet, emptied it into her cup, stirred with her finger. What a nice sight that was! Also the smell of sugar is very pleasant, and licking sugar bowls—the chance coming along all too rarely, in my experience—is a fun activity. I decided this interview was going well. Trish took another sip. Bernie waited, in this very still way he has, like we had forever. It's one of his best techniques.

"Do you know how Travis and Billy met?" Trish said at last. "In high school detention—this was at Mesa City High, their junior year. They walked out of detention together and never went back." Trish did one of those little nose laughs, a kind of snort. I was starting to like her a lot. "That's the buddy thing you see in a place like Mesa City—two idiots who think they have life by the balls."

Bernie nodded. "When it's really the other way around."

"Exactly." She leaned forward. "They weren't bad guys, not inside, more just that they did stupid things."

"Like kidnapping?" Bernie said.

Trish narrowed her eyes. "Are you turning out to be an asshole? That never surprises me."

"If disapproval of kidnapping makes me an asshole, then guilty as charged," Bernie said.

Wow! He was copping to the very crime we were investigating? A brand-new technique. But that was Bernie: just when you think he's done amazing you, he amazes you again.

"You don't understand," Trish said.

"Then explain."

She checked her watch. "I've got to be getting back."

"Back to where?"

"Texas," Trish said. "I'm living in Texas now. Didn't you see my license plate? What kind of detective are you?"

What was this? Bernie flinching slightly? I must have imagined it.

"I need a little more of your time," he said.

"How about paying for it?" said Trish.

Bernie's face hardened. Much better than flinching, in my opinion. "I don't like to do that," he said.

"No one likes to pay for anything," said Trish. "If I've learned one goddamn thing in life, it's that."

"You're misinterpreting," Bernie said. "The reason I don't like to pay is that it changes the information I get."

"Huh?"

"People tend to say what they think I want to hear."

"Yeah?" said Trish. "Well, I don't have the first clue what you want to hear."

Then came a bit of a surprise: Bernie laughed. What a beautiful sound! I could listen to it all day. Once—this was on a case we worked at a strippers' convention, too complicated to go into now—one of the ladies started laughing in just that way, like it would last all day. Then with no warning, laughter changed to tears. One of the scariest moments in my career, so I was glad when Bernie put a lid on it. He took out his wallet.

"How's fifty?" he said.

"Halfway there."

Bernie smiled, not what you'd call the happiest type of smile, and handed over some money, I hoped not a lot. Trish tucked it down her front, something men never do. Once you start noticing the differences between men and women it never ends, but where does it lead? Nowhere I've ever gotten, amigo.

"Where do you want me to start?" Trish said. "It's your dime."

"See?" said Bernie. "That's the problem, right there."

Trish stared at Bernie for a moment, then nodded. "Okay," she said. "How about Billy's nature, which was kind of sweet inside?"

"Sure," said Bernie.

"I'm two years older," Trish said. "I was working when Travis and Billy dropped out, had my own apartment. My stepdad could never stand Travis, and especially couldn't stand him just hanging out all day, which is what my stepdad did, by the way, so he kicked him out, and Travis came to live with me. Billy moved in soon after. Both of them paying rent, by the way. It was like I was mom, all of a sudden, a good mom who cracks the whip. Then one night I let Billy into my bed, and things started to slide."

Trish reached into her pocket, took out a pack of cigarettes, lit one up. She squinted through smoke, caught Bernie's expression, offered the pack.

"No, thanks," said Bernie. "No. No, thanks."

She laid the pack on the table, not far from Bernie's hand. His hand sort of shrank back, like it was afraid. Trish took a deep drag, held it in for what seemed like a long time, and then let it out in a smoky kind of sigh.

"By the time I . . . got back to the light, it was three years later and I'd kicked myself out, kicked myself all the way to Louisiana. Got married, made some new mistakes, got divorced, ended up in Texas with a good job."

"What's that?"

"I'm a service tech at an auto repair shop," Trish said. "Unemployed at the moment."

Bernie gazed at his hand, then at the pack of cigarettes.

"Help yourself," Trish said.

Poor Bernie! You could see how much he loved smoking from the little ceremony that happened next: unlit cigarette dangling from the corner of his mouth, striking of the match, hand cupping the flame, that first inhale. I'd been in a church once—briefly—and this reminded me of things I'd seen there; in rapid passing, it's true.

And now when he looked at Trish he seemed friendlier, as though he'd known her for a long time. "Tell me about the sweet side of Billy."

Trish thought for a moment or two. "He brought me coffee in bed. And . . . things like that. But the drugs wrecked everything, like always. And the two of them started up on their stupid life of crime."

"What kind of crimes?"

"Like the Three Stooges, missing one."

"Meaning they always went wrong."

"Pretty much."

"In a violent way?"

Trish shook her head. "At least they were smart enough to know they weren't cut out for that. If there was violence, they ended up on the receiving end."

"Kidnapping is a violent crime by definition," Bernie said.

"By definition, huh?" Trish said. "I can see that. But they never could of."

"What went down?" Bernie said.

"Don't know too much about the details—not firsthand. I was already in Lafayette by that time. Travis and Billy had a connection down in Sonora, and they were dealing out of a recording studio in South Pedroia."

"Do you remember the name?" Bernie said.

"Yeah," said Trish. "Cactus Sound."

"Cactus?" Bernie said.

Trish nodded. "Naturally, they started getting big dreams about the music business. Not that they had any musical talent. I waitressed one winter in a joint in Houma, Louisiana. I've seen musical talent up close." She stubbed out her cigarette. "Way too close."

"How did they go from dealing to kidnapping?" Bernie said.

"No idea."

"What kind of kidnapping was it?"

"Doomed to fail. I thought that was clear by now."

"I'm after the motive—revenge, human trafficking, ransom—"

"Yeah, ransom."

"How much?"

"A lot. Half a mill? Something like that."

"Who was the victim?"

"A girl. Pretty. I remember seeing her picture in the paper. I didn't go back for the trial. I was done. And even though the girl came home unharmed, the judge threw the book at Travis and Billy."

"The girl came home unharmed?"

"Within days, wasn't it? Tire blew out on the old Highway Six—this was maybe an hour after they'd taken her—and some passing motorist snapped a picture with all three of them in it. So the case was open and shut."

"Who paid the ransom?"

"The girl's parents, if I remember right."

"And it was recovered?"

"Actually, not. Which is the stoogiest part of the whole thing, because if the boys coughed up the money, the judge woulda cut them a break."

"So why didn't they?"

"Couldn't tell you. I visited Travis once or twice in the early days—when he was still in max—and he wouldn't talk about it. But I can give you my best guess."

"I'm listening," Bernie said.

Me, too, but to tell the truth I was no further ahead on the case, in fact had that worrisome feeling of slipping backward.

"They stashed the money out in the desert somewheres," Trish said. "It made them feel like winners after all, if you get what I mean." She reached for another cigarette. "You say you're looking for Billy?"

Bernie nodded.

"If you find him, he'll be livin' large."

EIGHTEEN

"M issed the Texas plates, big guy," Bernie said, when we were back in the car, headed toward the sun, now halfway down the sky. I preferred the sun high above, but really low was good, too, when it got all strange and blobby. Just not halfway down the sky, which is right in my face. No one gets in my face, amigo.

"How is that possible? It doesn't get more basic."

I tried to remember what this was about, came up with zip.

He glanced in the rearview mirror, his gaze not on the traffic behind us—an endless many-colored sort of bumper-to-bumper snake—but on his own face, the best face going, in case that's not clear by now. "Am I losing it?"

That again? Maybe this was one of Bernie's jokes. Soon would come the funny part. I couldn't wait.

"Alzheimer's?" he went on. "Too young, right? Plus no family history. Concussion? Sure, I've had my bell rung once or twice— who hasn't? What else is there?"

He went silent, rubbing his forehead a bit. Had I somehow missed the funny part? We crossed the Rio Arroyo Bridge. Down below I spotted the tiniest trickle of blue. No surprise, now that I'd

seen the aquifer with my own eyes—just that one puddle Ellie Newburg had showed us at the construction sight. And soon after she'd
had a round, red hole in her head and smelled of the no-longer-living.
Was there some connection between the aquifer and what happened
to her? Connections were a big part of our business, an important
fact I'd picked up during the course of my career. Lucky for us, Bernie
was great at connections. I pitched in when I could.

He glanced over at me. "Something on your mind?"

Me? No. Not that I knew of.

"Have you already solved the whole case? And now you just
sit back and watch me bumble around? Has that been our MO
the whole time?"

The funny part at last! I'd known it was coming, of course.
Who wouldn't love Bernie? A surprising number of characters,
actually, but not me. I gave him a nice lick.

He laughed, and even though we perhaps swerved across a
lane or two—what was with all the honking?—he looked happier.

"What would I do without you?" he said.

I didn't understand the question. But so what?

Sometime later, we were on Central Street, the main drag in South
Pedroia. Headed to our self-storage, maybe, to check out our supply of Hawaiian pants? A big supply and never getting smaller, not
even by one measly pair. Our visits, infrequent and yet too often,
in my opinion, were always the same: Bernie stood in the doorway, just eyeing all those pants, on hangers and hooks and racks,
in stacks and piles and mounds, golden dust motes hanging in the
still air, nothing moving. I always got very uneasy, so I was glad
we rolled right past the road with all the self-storages and kept on
going.

Bernie made a phone call. "Captain Stine, please."

"One moment."

"Hey, Bernie. What's up?"

"Got that file yet?"

"Still working on it."

"The expected male life span is currently eighty-seven years, six months."

"You think you're funny, Bernie."

Of course! Didn't everybody?

"What do you know about the kidnapping?" Bernie said.

"What kidnapping?"

"The case in the file."

"How would I know anything? We don't have the file. Aren't you listening?"

"You know nothing at all? Never discussed it with anybody?"

"Here's some free advice," Stine said. "You're starting to sound paranoid. It's not attractive."

Click.

Bernie glanced at me. Had that conversation gone well? Wouldn't have been my takeaway, but Bernie didn't seem upset. His eyes had that lovely inner light thing going on. Maybe paranoid was something nice. Humans could be complicated, sometimes too complicated for their own good, no offense.

"Funny thing about our business, Chet. Sometimes you can't see a single way. Sometimes you can see one single way—doesn't make it right, though. And then there are those times—always the hardest, for some reason, where you can see more than one way. Take now, for example."

I sat very still, eyes on Bernie, listening my very best. This was not easy to understand, and now there was going to be more? And then, listening my very best, I picked up the sound of distant barking, very faint—but not so faint that I wouldn't have bet dollars to doughnuts, if that means you end up with doughnuts, on it being distant barking of the she-barking kind. Which made concentrating on what Bernie had to say even more of a challenge.

"We could go back out to the desert, hunt for more missing cactuses, get a bead on who's digging them up. Or we could talk to some biker pals, take a swing at seeing where Dee Branch might be hanging out. Then there's the obvious route of hitting all the muscle-head gyms for leads on the Fu Manchu twins. People tend to remember twins, especially twins who look like those two. There's also Garwood Mickles, the nephew, over at the Indian Hills precinct. We could even take a chance, try a direct route, get into a pissing contest with Brick himself. Or . . ."

But don't rely on me for what came after that. Because . . . because . . . pissing contest! There were pissing contests in this life? How was it possible that I'd reached my age—whatever it happened to be, exactly—without knowing about them? I knew about all kinds of competition, like baseball, football, basketball, lacrosse—great balls, each and every one, lacrosse balls being my favorite, just a wonderful springy resistance when you're chewing on them—as well as boxing, wrestling, and even hockey, where I'd gotten onto the ice once, the slipperiness of ice being the biggest surprise in a night of surprises, and actually tasted puck, very odd, kind of like tires, but forget all that. What I'm getting at is that I'd never once encountered a pissing contest. How crazy was that, especially since—and this is the whole point—who was going to beat me in a pissing contest? Go ahead. Name anybody, and I'll take him on. Two at a time! More than two! I was born for pissing contests. Pissing contests were my . . . how would you put it? Calling? Yes, that was it. Pissing contests were my calling. So why had I been kept away from them? I had a thought I'd never had before and hope I never have again: life was unfair.

Bernie looked over at me in surprise. "Growling?" he said. "What's that about? You mad at me?"

Whoa! Mad at Bernie? What could that possibly mean? I was mad because . . . because . . . nothing came to mind. Meaning I was mad at nothing, which had to mean I wasn't mad. There! All better. I rested my paw on Bernie's leg, just to let him know we were cool. The Porsche lurched forward for some reason, but Bernie soon had it under control. Best wheelman in the Valley, as I'm sure you know by now.

"Entry points is what I'm talking about, big guy, entry points to a trail that's fifteen years old, maybe more." For no reason at all, I had a nice big yawn. "A little—tedious from where you sit?" He kind of lost me there: I was sitting in the shotgun seat as usual. "But here's something I've learned. To find someone, you often have to understand them first. So what I think we should do is poke around at Cactus Sound, see if we can pick up Billy's trail from way back when."

Fine with me. Trails meant tracking. Tracking was my . . . how would you put it? Calling? Yes, tracking was my calling, except wasn't there some other calling that had come up quite recently? I took a swing at remembering what that was, and whiffed. Tracking was my calling and that was that.

We went down a street lined with warehouses, some boarded up, and parked in front of an unpainted steel door with a sign in the shape of a saguaro hanging over it. " 'Cactus Sound,' " Bernie said. " 'Tomorrow's Tunes Today.' " We got out of the car, and he pressed a button by the door. "What if you happen to like the sounds of yesterday?" he said.

"Then you're fucked." A shadowy man peeled himself off a brick wall a few steps up the block and came our way, staggering a bit. His breath—just about pure alcohol—reached us first, which was how it always went down with winos. He held out his hand, a shaky, bony hand. "Spare some change? Preferably the paper kind."

Bernie gave him a greenback, actually two.

"Bless you, friend." The wino noticed me. "Nice pooch," he said. "Looks kind of familiar."

Bernie was about to say something when a man's voice came through a speaker grille over the door. "Etley?"

The wino frowned and retreated back into the darkness. Bernie grunted into the speaker grille. A buzzer went *bzzz* and something clicked inside the steel door. Bernie turned the handle, pushed the door open, and we went into a little waiting room with nobody in it. Behind the reception desk was another door, also steel. Bernie tried the handle. It opened and out came the sound of a man singing. "Too much to ask / Is all I'm askin' / Why can't you love / A selfish guy?"

We followed the sound down a hall and into a dark room lit up mostly by the lights of a long, flat control panel. A man in a funny little hat—porkpie, maybe, although there were no pig or pie smells around, mainly just stale pot—sat at the panel with his back to us. "Etley?" he said without turning. "Take a seat."

Hey! And not only stale pot, come to think of it. What else did we have? Cocaine? Heroin? Even a whiff of meth? Yes to all. I . . . I made a mental note!

Bernie sat in a chair beside the porkpie man, but a little behind. I sat beside Bernie. From there I had a good view through a glass wall beyond the control panel and into a room where a man sat on a stool, playing a guitar and singing into a microphone that hung from the ceiling.

"I made you smile / Last night in bed / So how come . . ."

Over his shoulder, porkpie man handed Bernie a packet of paper. "We're just tinkering with the bridge, but here's your charts, you want to look them over."

Bernie took the charts, whatever they happened to be, and looked them over, his eyes going back and forth, back and forth. Meanwhile, on the other side of the glass, the singer had stopped singing and was now muttering, "'So how come now,/ I'm better off dead,' or 'So how come now / You wish me dead.' Mr. Winners? Any thoughts?"

The porkpie dude—Winners, if I was following this right—pressed a button. "Nope." He turned to Bernie. Winners had a short-trimmed white beard, not gray, but white as the puffy clouds. His teeth were also very white, especially for an older guy, older guy teeth usually being yellowish. The same thing goes on in the nation within, although the difference between what we've got and what you've got in the teeth department isn't worth discussing. No offense.

"Any thoughts?" Winners said.

Bernie shrugged. "Don't like 'wish me dead.' Kind of melodramatic."

Winners pressed the button. "'Wish me dead' is kind of melodramatic."

The singer frowned, stroked his stubbly chin. "Maybe the whole goddamn song's melodramatic. Even the chord progression. What if . . ." He pulled a scrap of paper from his pocket, started scribbling away.

Winners looked at me. "You brought a dog?"

"Any problem with that?"

"Guess not," Winners said. "Long as he don't have fleas. Van Morrison's dog had fleas. I itched like a bastard for a month."

"No fleas on Chet," Bernie said.

Totally true, not since I'd been on the drops. But here's a funny thing: all of a sudden I was itchy all over! How do you like that? I raised a paw, started in on the side of my neck.

Meanwhile, Winners was saying, "Charts okay?"

"Look fine to me."

Winners glanced around. "Where's your ax?"

"Ax?" said Bernie.

Our ax was in the garage, hanging on a wall bracket. We never took it on the road. The case had taken a bad turn.

"The bass. We don't supply instruments."

"I don't play the bass," Bernie said.

"Huh?" said Winners. "What do you play?"

"Ukulele."

"No goddamn ukulele part in this session. What the hell's going on?"

"Plus a bit of trumpet," Bernie went on, "although I haven't touched it since high school marching band. Fact is I'm looking for someone."

"You're not"—Winners flipped through a notebook—"Etley, bass player out of LA?"

Bernie shook his head.

"Then what the hell was all the chart bullshit?"

"I can read music."

Read music? Not just listen like everybody else, but read it, too? Maybe the most amazing thing I'd ever heard. My Bernie.

From a speaker came the voice of the singer. "How about we go to the next number, come back to this one later?"

Winners pressed a button. "Your dime." He swiveled toward Bernie. "Didn't catch your name."

"Bernie Little."

Winners, with his porkpie hat and his trimmed white beard, looked like a friendly older guy, but what stood out, and what I was just noticing now, were his eyes. They were the darkest I'd seen, even darker than Suzie's. They didn't sparkle like polished countertops, the way Suzie's did; instead they were flat and damp. Now they seemed to darken a little more, in fact, a lot.

"You're looking for someone here?" Winners said.

"More likely in the past," Bernie said. "Were you around fifteen years ago?"

"Affirmative."

"Do you remember Billy Parsons?"

"Billy Parsons," Winners said. He licked his lips. What a very damp tongue for a human! "There was a Bubba Parsons, played drums. Couldn't lay off the goddamn high hat."

"Billy wasn't a musician," Bernie said.

"Then why'd he be hanging out here?"

"That's one of the things I'm interested in."

"Why?"

"He's gone missing, for reasons that may go back fifteen years or more. I've been hired to find him."

Did that mean we were getting paid? Somehow I'd missed that.

"Well, well. You're a private eye?"

"We say private investigators in the trade, but yeah."

"A private eye who can read music."

"We all have our pasts."

That brought a big white smile from Winners, just the mouth kind. His eyes stayed out of it. "That we do. Sorry I can't help you."

"What about Travis Baca?" Bernie said. "Ring a bell?"

"Nope."

"What's your association with the studio?" Bernie said.

Winners laughed. "What kind of investigator are you? I'm the goddamn founder."

A buzzer buzzed. Winners pressed a different button. A voice sounded. "Etley."

"You're late," Winners said.

"Yeah?" said Etley.

"Musicians," Winners said, buzzing him in.

"One last thing," Bernie said. "Any possibility there were drug dealers operating out of here back then?"

Winners turned those damp, dark eyes full on Bernie. "Zero chance," he said. "Drugs have always been totally forbidden here. Won't have them on the premises."

Premises meant what again? I didn't know. All I knew was that the place reeked of drugs, as I mentioned already. Even a hint of those sickening 'shrooms. Weren't 'shrooms so last year? And whoa! What was this? The scent, fairly fresh, of a member of the nation within, and not just any member of the nation within, but one who smelled a lot like me.

"Chet?" Bernie said. "What's up?"

"Probably hungry," said Winners.

"He never barks for food."

"Might have a treat here." Winners reached under the control panel, found a box of bone-shaped biscuits, tossed me one. I wasn't hungry, never barked for food, in fact was barking about . . . something else, which would possibly come to me later. Meanwhile, I got busy with the bone-shaped biscuit, one of the tastiest I'd had in some time.

"See?" said Winners.

Bernie gave me a thoughtful look. I gave him one back. Then a tall thin dude came in from down the hall, a big, hard guitar-shaped case on his back. "Ric Etley," he said, pot on his breath, but big-time.

"Here's the charts," said Winners.

"Don't read music," Etley said. "I'll pick it up real quick soon's I hear the tune."

Over the speaker came the singer's voice. "Thought of a work-around on 'Selfish Guy,'" he said. "Kind of open ended, let the music do the talking." He peered at the glass wall, like maybe the control room was too dark for him to see in, and strummed his guitar. "I made you smile / Last night in bed / So how come now, oh, baby, how come now?"

"Cool," said Etley, unpacking his instrument.

NINETEEN

L et the music do the talking?" Bernie said, back on the street
at Cactus Sound and on our way to the car. "Then what's the
point of . . ."

And maybe he went on about whatever it was, but at that
moment I'd picked up a scent—the same scent I'd sniffed inside
the studio but somehow forgotten all about! Funny how the mind
works. There's you and then there's your mind, side by side. A
bit tricky, probably not worth thinking about, plus there was no
time, because this scent I mentioned, so like mine, was the scent
of my little buddy Shooter. Shooter: who rode shotgun with Ellie
Newburg, and wasn't Ellie a big part of this case? Wow! Nothing
was getting past me! Already I had no complaints in life and now
things were getting better? I couldn't begin to figure that out.

Instead, I followed Shooter's scent. It led me to a narrow alley
that ran alongside the Cactus Sound building and—

"Hey, Chet!"

—through what you might call a sea of pee smells, typical
of alleys, and around to the back, ending at a pickup dusty with
desert dust, desert dust so often carrying the smell of greasewood.

And not only greasewood in this case, but also the scent of saguaros, hard to describe but slightly reminiscent of the smell of
tequila, a drink that Bernie stays away from. So: we had desert,
saguaro, and Shooter. I barked this low rumbly bark I have, sending a message.

"What?" said Bernie, coming up behind me. "What?" He
eyed the pickup, then knelt and rubbed the dusty layer off a bumper sticker. " 'Cactus Man Festival—Wild in the Wilderness.' " He
gazed at the bumper sticker, which seemed to be all about a saguaro
with a human face, sporting a porkpie hat. Meanwhile, I heard a
faint clink from above, the sound made by metal rings sliding on
a curtain rod, for example. I looked up at the back of the Cactus
Sound building. From a window up there Winners was staring
down at us. He wasn't wearing the porkpie hat—turned out to
have closely trimmed hair, pure white like his beard—which was
why I didn't recognize him at first. I barked, not loud, but sharp
and urgent.

"Trying to tell me something, huh, Chet? Let me guess." And
in the act of thinking up his guess he—finally!—raised his eyes to
that upstairs window. The curtain was now closed. "Pot, right?"
Bernie said. "You smell pot all over this pickup, meaning that the
verboten line is pure cock and bull."

No! Well, yes. But no! And cock and bull? What was Bernie
thinking? Those were barnyard smells, well known to me from
cases we'd worked in ranch country, but totally absent here. Plus
neither cocks nor bulls were favorites of mine—in fact, placed far
down my list. I've had run-ins with both, enough said. Although
never both at the same time, which would be a nightmare. But
back to Bernie. This wasn't about pot. It was about—

"Good work, big guy." He gave me a pat, quick but very nice.
"Got an idea. Let's hit the road."

I liked pats. I liked doing good work. I liked hitting the road. But this wasn't about pot. That wasn't what I was smelling by the dusty pickup. Well, I could if I wanted to: the whole Valley smelled of pot, from the meanest streets of Vista City to the fanciest mansions in High Chaparral Estates, but not every tool is a hammer, as Bernie says, or something like that. Also there was don't take a spoon to a fork fight. And others. I felt a big yawn coming on. No fighting that, as I'm sure you know. The big yawn took over, leaving me with nothing to do but sort of wait on the sidelines, and while I was waiting, my gaze happened to rise once more to the upstairs window, the curtain again open, revealing Winners in his porkpie hat, now with another man beside him. This other dude had one of those real big shaved heads with a very broad face, although the features—nose, chin, eyes—were kind of small. Not the ears, though, which were sizable and had gold hoops in the lobes. I got ready to bark my head off, but the yawn wouldn't let me. Winners pointed out Bernie—now checking out his phone— to the big-headed dude and closed the curtain. The yawn finally came to an end. I barked, a kind of bark I have when the horse is out of the barn. Better to have them in the barn than on the loose, no question.

"You want me to make a drug buy?" said Smoky Cabot.

"Basically," said Bernie.

"What do you take me for?"

"A habitual smoker of illegal substances."

"And proud of it," said Smoky.

We were in the front room of Smoky's Tattoo Emporium, no customers around at the moment, which suited me just fine. Those needles going in and out, in and out? I don't like to watch. But I can't stop!

"But," Smoky went on, "I don't make drug buys for cops."

"I'm not a cop."

"Private eyes aren't cops?"

"No."

"I never knew that." Smoky scratched his nose, pretty much the only untattooed part of him. Tattoos were some sort of decoration, unless I was missing something. For decoration, I myself rocked only a collar, black leather for formal occasions—I'd once been Exhibit A down at the courthouse, where the judge slipped me a biscuit from under his robe and sent a real bad dude up the river, even though it had no water in it—and my gator-skin collar for everyday. No time for the gator story now, the point being a collar was plenty of decoration for me. "If I say yes," Smoky went on, "what do I get out of it?"

"You can keep the product," Bernie said.

"How much?"

"Whatever a C-note will buy."

"Count me in," Smoky said. "Where and when?"

"Know Cactus Sound in South Pedroia?" said Bernie.

"Heard of it—the festival dude. I know the festival. Cactus Man—Wild in the Wilderness. Next week, actually. I've got a concession."

"Lost me," Bernie said.

Whoa! Bernie lost in a back-and-forth with—let's admit it—one of those dudes who's not completely here? That never happened. I didn't know what to do. Then I caught sight of the huge tiger head on Smoky's chest—he was only wearing shorts and boots—and I didn't know what to do even more, if that makes sense. A tiger that smelled like Smoky: I suddenly wanted to sort of bite it. Very bad, you don't need to tell me. I backed away, got a grip.

"At the festival," Smoky said. "Set up my tent, run the needles off a generator, business is pretty much nonstop day and night."

"It's a music festival?" Bernie said.

"Kinda," said Smoky. "They got music but it's more like an event. People are starting to come from all over—LA, Las Vegas."

"These are kids?"

"You'd be surprised."

"In what way?"

"I mean kids, sure, plus bikers and hipsters, what you'd expect, but also corporate types, getting in touch with . . . you know, their inner whatever the hell it is. Corporate types from LA, I'm talking about."

"I get the LA part," Bernie said.

"You should check it out."

"I might."

"Chet would be a big hit."

"Why is that?"

Smoky pointed at me with his chin. "Just look at him."

Smoky: maybe not completely here, but that could be a good thing. Bernie handed over some cash. I hoped it wasn't much.

"What's the dude's name?" Smoky said.

"Winners."

"How come you think he deals drugs?"

"I don't think that yet," Bernie said. "It's what I'm trying to establish."

"Gotcha."

"How about we sniff around the World Wide Web?" Bernie said.

What was this? Hadn't we just gotten home? I was still at my water bowl, topping up that well inside me. But sniffing always sounded like a good move—although the "we" part was a little mysterious, sniffing not being Bernie's best thing—and sniffing around the whole world sounded even better. I trotted to the front door and stood there, eyes on the knob, waiting for Bernie. Why wait, when in fact I can turn most knobs myself? I thought about that. Meanwhile, Bernie didn't seem to be coming. I waited some more, standing completely still, eyes on that knob. Time passed. I thought about how to slide bolts open, something Bernie and I had been working on. You slide the bolt open with your paw and then get a steak tip: that's all there is to it. Give it a try sometime. When I'd thought all there was to think about bolts, I thought about nothing at all. Time slowed down in a very pleasant way. After a while I grew aware of keyboard sounds, Bernie tapping away. I gave myself a quick shake, always the right move after a period of standing completely still, trotted down the hall and looked into the office.

Bernie sat at the desk, peering at the computer screen. He glanced up. "What's that look mean?"

My look? It meant let's go. Let's start sniffing the wide world. What was the holdup? And why was he even asking me? Wasn't it his idea in the first place?

"How come you're sniffing like that?"

Because! Just because!

"Hey! You're clawing the door?"

Clawing the door? I most certainly was not. All I was trying to do was simply and without fuss . . . I paused, one paw in midair, actually quite close to the door. Then I walked around in a circle for a few times and lay down with a sigh. Bernie was as close as they come, but nobody's perfect.

Tap tap tap. I watched him tapping away through eyes half closed. A nice changeup when it comes to watching things. I recommend it. In this case, I saw how lovable Bernie was in a brand-new way.

"Bingo," he said, leaning a little closer to the screen. Then he paused, rubbed his head, and looked my way. "Why didn't I think of this before? What's wrong with me these days?"

Wrong with Bernie? Nada. My tail started up, sending him the right sort of message. Bernie gave me a quick almost-smile and turned back to the screen.

"Archived in the *Valley Tribune* from almost sixteen years ago. 'Kidnapped Teen Home Safe, Two in Custody. Summer Ann Ronich, daughter of Samuel and Marlene Ronich of Cottonwood Hills, was found unharmed last night in an abandoned service station on old Highway Six. Two men, William "Billy" Parsons and Travis Baca, both of South Pedroia, have been taken into custody. Detective Sergeant Brick Mickles of Valley PD, who found Ms. Ronich and later made the arrests, was unable to confirm reports that a ransom was paid. "This is an ongoing investigation," Mickles said. When asked if more arrests were expected, Mickles had no comment. Ms. Ronich disappeared last Friday while—'"

The phone rang. Bernie gave it a look that changed from un-friendly to real pleased. He hit the speaker button.

"Hi, Suzie."

"Hello, Bernie."

"Was just thinking of you this very moment," he said.

"In what context?"

Bernie laughed. "How come you're so goddamn quick?"

"These things are relative."

He laughed again, but in a doubtful sort of way. "Been look-ing at an archived *Tribune* piece. By . . ." He checked the com-puter. ". . . Rance Perth. Know him?"

"Rance was before my time," Suzie said. "He took a PR job in Singapore. But that's what got you thinking about me? Something in the *Trib*?"

"Uh, yeah, actually."

"Meaning the context was peripheral."

"Well, I wouldn't—"

"By definition."

"Uh-oh," Bernie said. "Suzie? Is something wrong?"

Her voice changed, hard to say how. It didn't get loud or harsh or even edgy. More like cooler, maybe. "I'm not sure how to answer," she said. "You can't have forgotten our last conversation."

Bernie looked my way, as if for help of some sort. But what could I do? "Uh, of course I haven't."

Then came a pause, before Suzie, her voice even less warm than before, but puzzled, too, said, "Were you planning to respond?"

Bernie shot me another *help me!* look. Maybe a long walk in the canyon was the answer? That was my only thought. "I was," Bernie said. "I am. It's just that I've been so busy with this case and—"

"Who isn't busy?" Suzie said.

Another pause, longer than the last. Finally Bernie said, "You're right. I should have . . . no excuses."

"I'm in London right now," Suzie said. "Marv Lister just left me a message. He said something's come up at the London office of SecureX that's right in your wheelhouse. He wants to fly you over for a meeting. What should I tell him?"

Now came the longest pause of all. Bernie was looking my way again, but this time didn't appear to be seeing me, as if he was looking at something far away, even thought there was nothing behind me but the hall and the closed door to Charlie's room.

"I wouldn't do well in London," Bernie said.

"What does that even mean?" said Suzie.

"I'm not suited."

"How do you know? It's changed a lot. When was the last time you were here?"

"Never."

"Excuse me?"

"I've never been to London."

"I see," said Suzie. "Then this conversation is really about something else, isn't it?"

Bernie shook his head. But he didn't say anything. You see that same combo from Charlie sometimes, and Bernie looked a lot like him just then. "My tongue-tied little boy," Leda says. Meaning Charlie, not Bernie, in case I'm unclear. Meanwhile, over on Suzie's end: *Click.* That was when Bernie finally got his tongue free, perhaps too late, if I was following this right. "Does she think I don't love her?" He looked at me. This was a bad moment of some sort, no doubt about that. My tail started up in an encouraging sort of way. Bernie didn't seem to notice.

"We're like historians," Bernie said, topping up his glass. "Or maybe anthropologists, even archaeologists." Did you know bourbon can talk? This is what it sounds like. We were still in the office, the bourbon coming out not long after the phone call. Bernie was back at work, tapping at the keyboard, making a call or two, writing notes on scraps of paper, sipping bourbon from his favorite glass, the one with the trumpets on the side. Trumpets had come up in this case already; it was possible I'd remember the details later. I loved the sound of trumpets, especially when Roy Eldridge starts up at the end of "If You Were Mine," one of our favorites. The fur on my neck stands right up! I lay on the office floor, trying to think of some way to get Bernie to play the song, and came up empty.

Shadows moved across the floor, inching toward me. I shifted away, more than once. Ice clinked, also more than once. Then Bernie was on his feet, sheets of paper in one hand, empty glass in the other. "Dig around long enough, big guy, and sometimes you hit pay dirt."

Digging had gone on? Had I fallen asleep, somehow missed it? I smelled no dirt on Bernie, fresh or otherwise. Bernie digging without me was at the top of the list of things that make no sense. This had to be the bourbon, still talking.

"Turns out," he said, leafing through the pages, "that Summer Ann Ronich got married five years ago, lives on a ranch east of the aircraft boneyard." He looked up. "Old Highway Six would actually be a shortcut."

Boneyard? I was at the door, bourbon, London, and even trumpets, all forgotten.

TWENTY

Two-lane blacktop, open country, cottonwoods growing tall in the deepest parts of the dry washes: old Highway Six was our kind of road. "Right there is where the old gas station must have been," Bernie said, pointing out a foundation slab so overgrown it was almost invisible. "Killed off by the interstates." The interstates? Brand new to me, but they sounded dangerous. I made another mental note, although I wasn't sure what to put in it. We rounded a curve at the top of a long rise, and there caught an unusual sight, rows and rows of airplanes stretching across the desert as far as I could see, the sun glinting off their wings in a dull way, like their wings had no shine on them at all.

"Had an English prof at West Point," Bernie said. "He wrote a poem about this, kind of an 'Ozymandias' thing." He went silent. Ozzie Mendoza? Had I heard that right? I was fond of Ozzie, now sporting an orange jumpsuit at Central State on account of an ATM scam involving peanut butter, but he didn't seem like the writing type to me, not with the puzzled way his mouth hung open all the time. Meanwhile, Bernie gazed at the airplanes, dusty and droopy-winged, going no place. "The class had to write a poem on the same subject," he said. "I took a different approach—more an Arlington National Cemetery comparison. C minus."

Not easy to follow, any of that, always the case when poems came up. But C minus had to be pretty good, almost certainly top of the class and possibly best ever at West Point. That was my takeaway. A lone vulture glided down from the sky in that heavy way they do and landed on the nose of the nearest airplane. It stood there, spreading its wings wide and facing in our direction. I could smell the .45 in the glove box.

We drove through an open gate, one of those ranch gates with a wrought-iron sign overhead. "Moonlight Ranch," Bernie said. "What's the point of naming a ranch if it's not a brand? And no one's going to brand Moonlight on the sides of their cattle." I sure hoped not: it sounded horrible.

A grove of trees rose on one side, shading a big glass house backed into a hillside. "An *Architectural Digest*-style ranch house," Bernie said. "Look out for an *Architectural Digest*-style herd."

I sat up my straightest, understanding nothing, meaning you had to be ready for anything, a mind-set that had actually served me well in the past. No herds seemed to be in sight, but the track split, and off to one side stood a corral with a woman inside it. She seemed to be talking to some small creature I couldn't quite make out. We drove to the corral, parked, and got out. The gun stayed in the glove box. Why was it on my mind all of a sudden? I didn't know.

The woman was saying, "Who's the prettiest little princess in the whole wide world?" But not, I didn't think, to us, although she must have heard the car. Put it this way: I'd have heard the car in her place. At that very moment, I happened to be hearing a snake slithering through some bushes beyond the far side of the corral, plus a phone ringing in the ranch house, invisible from where we were. But forget all that. The woman heard us now for sure, and turned our way.

"Summer Ronich?" Bernie said.

Summer Ronich, if this was her, looked like the kind of woman who has an effect on Bernie. She had glossy hair, smooth, tan skin, big blue eyes, and wore a riding outfit with red cowboy boots and a red cowboy hat that hung down her back. But here's the strange thing: that look on Bernie's face when a certain kind of woman is having an effect on him wasn't there. All that was kind of interesting but got blown away by an amazing sight in the corral, namely the creature who was supposedly the prettiest little princess in the whole wide world. This creature stood facing the woman, eyes on nothing, tail swishing around in a lazy way you could almost call sloppy. I can't say I'd never seen a creature like this in my entire life because I had. This creature looked exactly like a horse, except smaller. A lot smaller. Smaller that me? Oh, yeah. About the size of Iggy. Hard to believe, but true. A horse—in this case a creamy-white horse with a golden mane and a golden tail, and smelling very horsey—the size of Iggy! I hunched down and pawed at the ground a bit, all I could think of to do.

"Ronich was my maiden name," the woman said. "It's De-Witt now."

"Bernie Little," said Bernie. "And this is Chet."

Summer turned my way for the first time. "What's he up to?"

"Chet? Nothing." He shot me a glance that turned into a closer look. "Um, you mean that pawing thing? Not sure what that's about."

"He's going to attack Lovely," Summer said. "That's what it's about."

"Oh, Chet would never do a thing like that. He's actually very gen—"

And something or other that I didn't catch. Several moments of what you might call unawareness followed, and the next thing I knew I was sort of poised over Lovely, if I'd caught the name of this tiny object, one of my paws raised somewhat highishly. Not to do it—or her, as seemed to be the case—any harm: more just to . . . just to . . . I wasn't sure what. Before I could find out whatever I was up to, I felt Bernie's hand on my collar, not gripping hard, just there. I backed away, with some help from Bernie, always there for me, and sat up still and straight. You wouldn't have even noticed me.

"Uh, Lovely, huh?" Bernie said. "Perfect name for such a . . . decorative little thing."

"There's nothing decorative about her," Summer said. "Lovely's a therapy companion in training."

"Ah," said Bernie.

"That's what I do—raise therapy minis." Her gaze went to me—still doing the Little Detective Agency proud—and back to Bernie. "You don't look like a customer."

"True. But he is a cute little critter, just the same." Bernie reached down to give Lovely a pat. Lovely backed away. Horse eyes usually show fear or nothing at all, but I was pretty sure I saw annoyance in Lovely's eyes at that moment.

"She," Summer said.

"Sorry," said Bernie. "Of course—whoever heard of a boy named Lovely?" He laughed like something funny had just gone by. From Summer's face you'd think that just the opposite had happened.

"So if you're not a customer," Summer said, maybe leaving the end unspoken, which humans do sometimes. You can feel those unspoken ends hanging in the air, usually not a pleasant sensation, like a dust storm on the way.

Bernie handed her our card. In the old days we'd had a card with a picture of a magnifying glass on it; now we had Suzie's redesign, featuring a flower. We weren't happy about it, me and Bernie.

Summer gazed at the card, then handed it back. She said nothing. Lovely flicked at a passing fly with her tail, missed by plenty.

"I want to talk about the kidnapping," Bernie said.

Summer blinked. "My kidnapping?"

"Yes."

"Why?" Summer said. "It was such a long time ago I've practically forgotten about it. And there's nothing to investigate—I wasn't harmed." Her eyes narrowed. "Are you working for a malpractice lawyer or something? I don't have PTSD, if that's what you're thinking."

"I'm glad of that," Bernie said. "I'm not working for any lawyer. And it was a long time ago, as you say, but in my job the past has a way of coming back."

Summer glanced around. There was no one to see besides us, nice open country all around. "Coming back?" she said, her voice gone quiet.

"I'm afraid so," Bernie said. "How much do you remember about the trial?" Bernie said.

"The trial of the kidnappers?" Summer said. She shrugged. "Not much."

"You must have testified," Bernie said.

"Briefly," said Summer. "Then we went to Cabo."

"I'm sorry?"

"During the trial. My parents took me to Cabo for a vacation. I recall it ending while we were down there."

"With guilty verdicts."

Summer nodded.

"What can you tell me about the kidnappers?"

She shook her head. "It's like another lifetime."

"How about their names?"

Summer shook her head again.

Bernie smiled a smile that looked a lot like his friendly one. "How about taking me through the whole thing?"

Summer checked her watch. "I've got a customer coming."

"Just the CliffsNotes version, then," Bernie said.

Summer laughed, just a little laugh, here and gone, and regarded Bernie in a new way. That "regarding Bernie in a new way" routine often happens during our interviews, and then come good things, like me grabbing the perp by the pant leg. Summer was wearing a dress and red cowboy boots, as I may have mentioned, a bit of a challenge. Also, I wasn't sure this was the right moment. While I was thinking things over, Lovely snorted a surprisingly loud snort and went prancing off toward the corral fence. I trotted after her. Prancing's not my thing. She poked her head through the rails and started eating grass, a sure sign of an upset stomach, where I come from. Poor little lady. I gave her a friendly nudge. She got right back up and returned to eating grass. I watched over her, not so far from Bernie and Summer that I couldn't hear them easily.

"Your dog's all right," she said. "Some dogs can't deal with minis at all."

"Chet's been around," Bernie said. So true! My whole MO, right there. Bernie never missed a thing. "Why don't you start with the kidnapping itself? Where were you when it happened?"

"At a club downtown," Summer said. "The Black Rose."

"I remember it," Bernie said. "But weren't you eighteen?"

"My dad owned the place."

"It had a reputation."

"I know that. But I wasn't into the drinking and drugs part. I just loved to dance."

"So you were dancing and then . . . ?"

"I went outside to catch a breath of fresh air."

"Outside on Olive Street?"

"No. The alley out back. You got there through the kitchen. I was just standing by the door when a van drove up and two guys jumped out and grabbed me. They wore ski masks—with the Boston Bruins logo, that sticks in my mind—but it all went down so fast. Then I was in the back of the van with my wrists tied up in those plastic cuffs and a hood over my head. One of them drove and the other stayed in the back with me. He said I wasn't going to get hurt, and it would all be over as soon as my dad paid up."

"Half a million dollars?"

Summer nodded.

"Did your family have that kind of money?"

She nodded again.

"Those nightclubs must be pretty lucrative."

She nodded once more, just a very slight motion this time.

"Can you describe the voice of the kidnapper?" Bernie said.

"It was actually sort of gentle."

"But you still must have been scared."

"Who wouldn't be?"

"Any chance you recognized that voice?"

"Why—how . . . how would that be possible?" Summer said.

"If you'd known one or both of them from before," said Bernie.

Summer's voice rose. "Of course I didn't. Where would you even get an idea like that?"

"I'm not pushing any ideas," Bernie said. "These are just the questions you ask in a case like this."

"What case? How can there be a case? The case was all done with practically twenty years ago."

"Fifteen is more like it," Bernie said. "Which happened to be the sentence the judge handed down. So time's up."

Summer licked her lips. That sent a tiny whiff of her lipstick my way, lipstick that smelled of those little purple flowers you see in some gardens, including old man Heydrich's in the days before an unfortunate incident. "Time's up meaning . . . ?"

"The prison sentences are over," Bernie said. "Billy Parsons is no longer in prison." Then his eyes locked right on Summer's in a way I wouldn't want them locking on mine, as of course they never would. Bernie loves me, simple as that. "Neither is Travis Baca."

Was he looking for something in those big blue eyes? Did he find it? I had no idea. A fly came idling past. Lovely flicked at it with her fluffy golden tail, missed again, and went on munching grass. The sound annoyed me, hard to say why. Hurry up and puke, was my thought.

"You must be right," Summer said, looking down. She kicked at a hard clump of dirt with the toe of her red cowboy boot. "About the timing. I'd forgotten. Their names, that night, the next day, everything." Summer looked up. "What is it you're doing, exactly?"

"Right now I'm trying to reconstruct the events of the kidnapping," Bernie said. "What happened after they grabbed you off the street?"

"There was a lot of driving. Then . . . then must have come the blowout, which was when some trucker spotted them changing the flat. The trucker called it in on account of Bi—on account of the kidnappers wearing the ski masks, which seemed kind of weird to him. That gave the cops the clue to the van. After the blowout, we went to a house—maybe out in some isolated place, since it was so quiet. They kept the hood on me the whole time, except for when they gave me a shake and a burger."

"Did you see their faces?" Bernie said.

"They kept the masks on," Summer said. "I fell asleep, and when I woke up, one of them had gone to pick up the ransom."

"Where?"

"Out in the desert somewhere. I'm not sure I ever knew. The one who'd gone for the ransom called when he had it. Then the other one dropped me off at an abandoned gas station, actually not far from here, although there's nothing left of it now."

"Was he the one who'd been with you in the back of the van?"

Summer nodded. "He left me there with the hood on and my wrists still cuffed. But after a while I got the hood off. That was around when the detective drove up."

"Mickles."

"I think that was his name. A very nice guy, kind of jolly."

"Jolly?"

"Laughing and smiling, that kind of thing. He took me home. The kidnappers got caught. That was that."

"How were your parents?"

"That's a strange question. They had their daughter back. How would you be?"

"Understood," Bernie said. "But I gather the five hundred grand was never found. What was their reaction to that?"

"My mom couldn't have cared less."

"And your dad?"

"My dad?" Summer said. She kicked another dirt clump, much harder. "My father was an asshole."

TWENTY-ONE

L ovely kept on chewing grass. And how strange was this? It was me who started feeling pukey! Some things are impossible to explain. I moved away from her, circled around for a bit, and laid myself down. I don't like feeling pukey. Was it Lovely's fault? I leaned in that direction.

"Meaning, among other things, your father's dead?" Bernie said.

"That's one way of putting it," Summer said.

"What happened to him?"

"Heart attack."

"When?"

"About eight years ago."

"So not associated with the kidnapping."

"No," Summer said. "He was always the heart attack type."

"In what way?" Bernie said.

"Mostly in the dishing-it-out way, until his own came around. He was the explosive type."

"Violent?"

"With anybody he thought was weaker, oh yeah. In a . . ." She stopped herself, then spoke more quietly. "In a heartbeat."

"You, for instance?"

"We're not going there."

"Your mom?"

"She lives in Florida."

"I meant—"

"I don't give a shit what you meant. She lives in Florida."

"In what circumstances?" Bernie said.

"Huh?"

"Your family took a half-million-dollar hit."

Summer gestured at the surroundings. "Does this look like poverty?"

"No," Bernie said. "But I take it you're married now."

"I brought plenty to the table," Summer said. She gave Bernie a real unfriendly look. "What are you up to?"

"Just trying to fill in the blanks," Bernie said. "What do you think happened to the money?"

"Don't know and don't care," said Summer. "Is that your angle? You're after the money?"

Oh? This was interesting. I waited for Bernie to say "exactly," or "no doubt about that," or "bet the ranch, baby." We were on our way! I could just feel it!

But Bernie said none of those things. Instead I heard, "I'd like to know what happened to it—that's not the same. And if I do come across the money, your mother will be on the receiving end."

I got up, puked, and felt much better. At that moment I heard a car coming, not yet in sight. I kept a close watch on the track that led from the corral to the driveway. Lovely went on eating grass. Was she following any of this?

"Why my mother?" Summer said.

"Assuming she's the rightful heir," Bernie said. "Normally after all these years you'd expect the money to be gone, but this time may be different."

"Why?"

"Just a hunch," Bernie said. "A two-parter, really. Hunch one—the kidnappers stashed the money somewhere safe." He'd been looking my way; now he turned to Summer. "Hunch two—they entrusted it with someone for safekeeping."

Summer gazed at Bernie. Some humans had eyes that were good at keeping you out. Hers were like that.

"And now, as I mentioned, the sentences are over," Bernie said. "Billy and Travis are out."

"Then why aren't you trailing them?" Summer said. "Why hassle me?"

Bernie gazed right back at her. "Have you seen Billy? I mean recently."

"What the hell are you talking about?"

A big fancy car came up the track. Summer moved toward it.

"If he gets in touch, call me," Bernie said.

Summer stopped and turned. "Are you out of your mind?"

The fancy car parked beside the Porsche, and two women got out and hurried over.

"Where is she?" called one.

"There—hidden behind that overgrown mutt. Lovely! Lovely! Yoo-hoo!"

I looked around for an overgrown mutt, saw none. The case had taken a bad turn. Summer joined the women, the interview abruptly over. Had it gone well? I didn't get that feeling. A big fuss started up over Lovely. She left off eating grass and sampled the sugar cubes they were practically shoving down her throat. I wanted those sugar cubes myself, even though I don't care for sugar. I wanted them badly! What if I sidled over in the nicest way and—

"Chet?"

. . .

"A lot to process, huh, big guy?" Bernie said as we drove off.

Uh-oh. We were processing? We hadn't processed since the Sneezy Siragusa case, all about a missing chef, namely Sneezy, whose food Bernie never touched, not sure why, although no one was actually missing—meaning we didn't get paid, so how could processing be the way to go? But what a bad thought! If Bernie said process, we processed.

"Where to even begin?" he said. "How about with the fact that Summer showed zero reaction when I implied that Travis Baca was not only out of the slammer but among the living? Doesn't that prove all this is in the past, as she said, no longer on her radar in any way?"

He glanced over at me, like . . . like for my opinion. I stuck my tongue out—although not as far it could go, not even close—and licked the tip of my muzzle. Hey! It was kind of dry. I licked it again.

"But in direct opposition is the near certainty that there was some sort of relationship between her and Billy. He wore a ski mask, but she recognized his voice—did you catch her start to say his name when she came to the part about the trucker? See where we're going with this?"

I gazed into the distance, saw the tops of the downtown towers, golden in the sun. My best guess? We were going home.

"A near certainty but not a dead cert certainty, huh?" Bernie said. "I hear you."

When we got home, a car was parked in the driveway, one of those big old cars with the tailfins, although this one looked all shiny and new.

"Do we know any old Caddy collectors?" Bernie said.

Not that I knew of, although there's no guarantee I understood the question. My ears went up all by themselves, letting the rest of me know it was time to be on high alert. We parked on the street and hopped out, me actually hopping, and Bernie pretty far from it. Maybe his leg was having one of its bad days, although why now, when we hadn't been on a long hike, or chased any perps through a drainage ditch, or other fun things like that? But no time to figure out tough problems, or even easy ones, my specialty, because Smoky Cabot was climbing out of the car in our driveway. He came over to us with a nice big smile, nice in Smoky's case because it shrank the tattoos on his cheeks, making them less visible. But that's just me.

He tossed Bernie a small bag of pot, the smell arriving ahead of the bag. Bernie caught it easily, the way Bernie catches things, just swallowing them up in his hand.

"Success!" Smoky said.

Bernie tossed the bag back to Smoky, who dropped it, bent to pick it up, dropped it again, finally corralling it. "I told you," Bernie said. "Yours to keep. I just wanted to know if it could be done."

"Can be done, all right," Smoky said. "A well-run operation he's got goin' there. Won't sell to just any cat walking in off the street. I had to establish my bona fides in the drug community."

Sometimes humans said things that didn't need saying. For example, why bother to point out that whoever Smoky was talking about didn't sell pot to cats? Cats don't smoke pot, or anything else. Not their type of thing at all. And I mean that in a good way, despite my history with cats, generally bad.

"Did you deal directly with Winners?" Bernie said.

Smoky nodded. "Clay Winners," he said. "First names are best, when it comes to certain sectors of the economy. Turns out we know lots of people in common. It's really just a village, in some ways."

"What is?"

"The drug business."

"People get murdered in the drug business every day."

"Did I say a friendly village?" Smoky said. "But nothing to fear from ol' Clay on that score. He's the peaceable type. Big-time, by the way. Just from a reference or two I picked up, I'd say he was one of the biggest dealers in the state, and I'm talking every substance out there."

"Yeah?"

Smoky waved his hand. "The recording studio, the festival—those are just hobbies."

"How do you know?"

"Trust me—I've got antennas like you wouldn't believe."

"You've done two stretches in the pen," Bernie said. "That I know of."

"I don't have an antenna for that," Smoky said. "But—wow!" He smacked his forehead, good and hard. That always makes me nervous.

"Wow what?" said Bernie.

"Just had an idea—a creative idea. They can come at any time in my line of work. That's what makes it so rewarding."

"You had an idea for a tattoo?"

Smoky nodded. "You're real easy to talk to, Bernie. Anyone ever tell you that?"

"What's the tattoo idea?" Bernie said.

"An antenna," said Smoky. "Maybe with rays coming out of it, ba doom, ba-doom, like it's scanning the universe."

"I like it," Bernie said.

"Want one?" said Smoky. "You can be the prototype. That's always a freebie."

"I'll sleep on it."

"That's a no in my business."

Bernie smiled, about what I didn't know. But Bernie's smile lights up the day, which is the important thing. "Do you remember a club called the Black Rose?" he said.

"On Olive Street?" Smoky said. "I was a regular, back in the day."

"When was that?"

"Way back. Tuesdays was amateur night. I played in a band at the time."

"What kind of music?"

"*Sweetheart of the Rodeo.*"

"Meaning modern country?"

"Meaning *Sweetheart of the Rodeo*. That's all we did, just cover that one record."

"What's your instrument?"

"Cowbell, tambourine, triangle, you name it."

"Still play?"

"Grew up," Smoky said. "Put away childish things."

From the light in Bernie's eyes at that moment, I expected laughter, but none came. "Would back in the day include, say, fifteen or sixteen years ago?"

Smoky shut his eyes tight, kind of scrunching up his whole face, never a good look on humans, in my opinion, and he was no exception. "Might, yeah, now that I think on it." His eyes opened. "Why?"

"Any chance you knew the owner?" Bernie said.

"Owner of the Black Rose?" Smoky said. "Course I knew him. Son of a bitch named Ronich, Sam Ronich. Every goddamn check he cut us was short. You know the type who cares about money, and only money?"

Bernie nodded.

"It's not the same as greedy," Smoky said.

"What's the difference?"

"Couldn't tell you," Smoky said. "Heard some stoner say it not long ago. I could maybe track down whoever it was."

"Don't bother," Bernie said. "Back to the Black Rose. Did you ever meet Ronich's daughter?"

"Summer?"

"Yeah."

"Cool name, huh? She's still the only Summer I've run into."

"Tell me about her."

"A looker. And kind of classy, which sure as hell didn't come from her old man. Just a kid back then, couldn't of been more'n nineteen, twenty. Always on the dance floor. Let's see. What else? Great legs."

"Did you dance with her?"

"How could I when I was up on stage?"

"What about other nights, when you weren't playing?"

Smoky shook his head. "Dancing's not my thing. How about you?"

"I used to like it, actually."

"Yeah? I'd never have guessed."

Did Bernie look a bit annoyed? "Why is that?" he said. Yes, annoyed, no doubt about it. But how come? I'd have never guessed Bernie used to like dancing, and who knows him better than me? And if he had liked dancing in the past, why not now? True, Suzie had once gotten him out on the dance floor at the Dry Gulch Steakhouse and Saloon, an event that had proved too exciting for me, so I'd had to wait outside in the car, but that had been it.

Don't forget he's a great singer, sometimes accompanying himself on the ukulele. "Mr. Pitiful," for example, is one of his very best.

"Uh, no reason," Smoky said. "Just that you're kind of a tough guy."

"Where does it say that tough guys don't dance?"

"Like, there's a book about it. Or a movie."

"Yeah, right," said Bernie.

"I could have sworn," Smoky said. "But maybe not. My apologies."

Bernie waved that away. "Not a problem. Do you recall any of Summer's dance partners?"

"You mean like by name?"

"That would be nice."

For one bad moment, I was afraid Smoky was about to do that scrunching thing with his eyes again. This job has downs as well as ups, and if you're going to be successful—as the Little Detective Agency most certainly is, except for the finances part—then you've got to be ready for the worst. But in this case the worst passed us by. Smoky kept his eyes open and said, "There was this one little dude, actually a pretty smooth dancer himself."

"Name?"

"Billy," Smoky said. "Billy Parsons."

Bernie went still for the tiniest bit of time. No one would even notice. That's Bernie, right there—all you need to know about him. And me. "Anything else stick in your mind about Billy Parsons, besides the dancing?" Bernie said.

"Not much. Decent weed."

"He shared pot with you?"

"More like he sold it. He had some source down in Sonora. This was before all the legalization. Now Mexican weed's for shit. We've got the best right here in the good ol' U.S.A. These colors don't run."

Bernie gave him a long look. "Are you stoned right now?"

"Wouldn't bet against it."

"Do you run the tattoo needle when you're stoned?"

"That costs extra," Smoky said. He blinked a couple of times. "Uh, Bernie?"

"Yeah?"

"What was that idea I had back there a little ways?"

"Antennas."

"Thanks, man. I owe you. Anything you want, just say the word."

"Billy," Bernie said. "I want to know all you can tell me about Billy Parsons."

Smoky shrugged. "There's not a whole hell of a lot. That was around the time I left town for a stretch."

"In the pen?"

"It's not nice to think the worst, Bernie. I'm talking about when I got my calling."

"That being?"

"My art. I got a scholarship to go to Amsterdam and study tattooing. Ended up spending three years there. That's where my . . . how would you put it?"

"Cosmopolitanism?"

"Exactly! That's where my cosmopolitanism comes from. When I got back, the Black Rose had closed down, and I'd moved on in life."

"You've done that," Bernie said.

"Thanks," said Smoky. "You looking for Billy Parsons?"

"Yeah. Heard anything about him over the years?"

"Nope," Smoky said. "What's he done?"

"He stole a cactus."

"At one time, I'da said so what. But now I've evolved. We've only got the one environment, if you follow. I'll keep a sharp eye." They shook hands.

We entered the house. Bernie went into the kitchen. *Guggle guggle* and then came the scent of bourbon. I stayed in the front hall, sniffing around. Nothing suspicious had gone on in our absence, but I felt uneasy. There are times when you feel stronger than life, if that makes any sense, and then there's the reverse. I gazed out the window, saw nothing but the moon in the blue sky. Bernie had explained that to Charlie; all I remembered was the pepperoni slice Charlie had slipped me under the table.

In the kitchen, Bernie was saying, "They have tattooing scholarships?"

At that moment, a plain-looking car came slowly down Mesquite Road. It slowed even more as it went by, the driver gazing at our house. Hey! I knew this driver. He'd been in a Valley PD uniform the last time I'd seen him, which was outside the yellow house near the canal in South Pedroia: the gum-chewing cop—cinnamon-flavor—who'd shown up after all the action was over. Garwood Mickles, if I'd gotten it right, nephew of Brick. And now he was here? I didn't like that, not one little bit. He didn't appear to be chewing gum now, but I could smell cinnamon anyway. I didn't like that, either.

I started barking.

Bernie came into the hall, glass in hand. "What's up, big guy? He glanced out the window where—where there was now nothing to see. I kept barking anyway.

TWENTY-TWO

Bernie stood beside me in the front hall, sipping bourbon and gazing out the window. I gazed with him. What a nice moment! In fact, it doesn't get any better, as you may or may not know.

"Clay Winners tells us drugs are anathema at Cactus Sound, but turns out to be one of the biggest dealers in the state," Bernie said. "He also says the names Billy Parsons and Travis Baca ring no bell. See what logic demands here?"

I did not. But the moment stayed nice. I shifted closer to Bernie, possibly sitting on his feet. He scratched between my ears, a spot so hard for me to reach, and did his usual perfect job.

"What if the average IQ was, say, six hundred?" Bernie said. "Would I have solved the case already? Or would the fact that everyone else involved was that much smarter as well mean we'd be exactly where we are right now? Or even worse. Maybe, Chet, the whole construct of human progress is a sham. Then what have we got?"

What did we have? Was that the question? An easy one, always my preference. What we had was me and Bernie gazing out the window of our place on Mesquite Road, some expert head scratching under way, and not a care in the world. Was it possible Bernie had somehow missed all that? I gave him a close look, something I could do from where I was without turning my head. Human eyes may not be lined up in the best possible way. No offense, and not even the point. The point was—

"Uh-oh," Bernie said.

What was this? Through the window, I saw Mr. Parsons coming out of his house. He wore striped pajamas and one plaid slipper; his other foot was bare. Maybe that was why he moved so slowly. I've never worn slippers myself, although I've . . . I've worn through a number of them with my teeth. Hey! Had I just come close to making an actual joke? That wasn't me, Bernie being in charge of the jokes at the Little Detective Agency. Meanwhile, Mr. Parsons had made his way to his car, all dusty since it hadn't been used in some time. He patted his pajamas pockets, searching for what I didn't know—certainly not keys on account of the keys being already in his hand. Bernie put down his drink, opened our door, and we stepped outside.

"Daniel?"

Mr. Parsons looked up. We crossed over onto his property. Iggy, somewhere inside their house, started up on his yip-yip-yipping. Wasn't Iggy in charge of security at the Parsonses' place? If so, they were in big trouble, which takes nothing away from Iggy, still the best pal anyone would want.

"Oh, hi, Bernie," Mr. Parsons said. "Don't mind Iggy. He means well."

"I know that, Daniel," Bernie said. "Going somewhere?"

"If I can find the damn keys. Got them on me somewhere. Just a matter of a methodical search."

"Where were you headed? We'd be happy to drive you."

"That's all right," Mr. Parsons said. "You've done too much for us already. Edna and I were discussing that just this morning."

"So you're back home together."

Mr. Parsons smiled. "That we are. Such a relief, I can't tell you."

"Is the hospice—is the nurse here now?"

Mr. Parsons's smile got bigger. "No need to mince words. It's okay to say hospice."

He kept patting his pockets: two on the chest of his pajama tops, two on the pants, all empty except for one of the chest pockets, which was sending out a biscuit smell. Iggy's biscuits were smaller than mine but every bit as tasty. I found myself closing the distance between me and Mr. Parsons.

"We know the score, Edna and I," Mr. Parsons continued. "I'm not what you'd call a believer, Bernie, but I do believe she and I will be together in one form or another. Doesn't bear closer examination than that, if you see what I mean."

"Don't think I do," said Bernie.

"Closer examination means you start asking questions like what age are we going to be on the other side. Everybody twenty-five, for example, dads and moms and kids and grandkids and great grandkids and . . ." Mr. Parsons lost his breath. His mouth made motions that reminded me of a goldfish of my acquaintance on a day when he'd somehow come sloshing out of his bowl. Bernie went quickly to Mr. Parsons, put a hand on his shoulder.

"Daniel?"

Mr. Parsons gasped, started breathing again, first wheezily, then in a more normal way. From up close his breath reminded me of the air inside a certain broom closet, the broom closet at the end of the only missing-kid case we hadn't solved. Not quite true: we'd solved it all right, but too late. The kid's name was Gail. Mr.

Parsons was much, much older, but his breath smell and that last lingering one in the closet were almost the same.

"I'm fine, Bernie, just a momentary . . . bump," he said. "Like a bump in the road." He patted a chest pocket again, patted it with the hand that held the keys, and this time stuck his hand in the pocket and withdrew the biscuit. He gazed at his palm, now holding the biscuit and the keys. He looked up with a kind of vague triumph in his eyes, hard to describe. "Knew I had 'em somewhere."

I took the biscuit from his hand, as gently as I could. Bernie did the same thing with the keys.

"How about I do the driving?" Bernie said.

"You're not in our will yet," said Mr. Parsons.

"I'm sorry?"

"We're putting you in the will as soon as the lawyer stops by. Can't believe we didn't think of it sooner."

"I don't want to be in the will," Bernie said.

Mr. Parsons put a hand on his car, maybe to steady himself. "You don't?"

"It would be an honor, but there's no material thing we need."

What were material things? C-notes, perhaps? If C-notes were material things, we needed them big-time. I made quick work of the biscuit and gave Bernie a nudge.

"In any case—oof," he was saying, "let me drive you."

Mr. Parsons glanced at his house. "Don't see why not."

Bernie went to unlock the car, but it was unlocked already. He helped Mr. Parsons into the front passenger seat. I ended up on the backseat, happy to start out that way. Seating arrangements often changed, in my experience. Bernie got behind the wheel.

"Where to?" Bernie said, turning the key.

"The gym," Mr. Parsons said.

Bernie nodded. I watched him in the rearview mirror. This particular nod was very close to the nod he has for when things make sense, the only difference being that his eyes shifted slightly, namely to the passenger seat side. "Any particular gym, Daniel?" Did that mean something didn't make sense after all? I would have wondered about that but around then was when I discovered a not-unsizable chunk of biscuit somehow forgotten under my tongue. Iggy's biscuit, which made it all the tastier. I hope that's not bad of me.

Mr. Parsons was silent for a bit. Then he said, "I'll have to think."

"I didn't know you've been going to the gym," Bernie said.

"Oh, no, not me," said Mr. Parsons.

"Someone else has been going to the gym?" Bernie said.

"Well, maybe not going, precisely," Mr. Parsons said. "But she has some association with it." His voice sharpened, rose to a level I'd never heard from Mr. Parsons before, a level that made me nervous. "Let me think, goddamn it!"

"No problem," Bernie said. He let go of the wheel, sat back, looking straight ahead.

Mr. Parsons snuck a glance Bernie's way. From that angle, I could see just one of his eyes, of course. Hope you can picture this; I'm doing my best. At first, that one eye was glaring and angry. At Bernie? I wasn't buying that at all. Then the glare and anger faded and that eye got moist. Mr. Parsons put his head in his hands. "You're such a good man, Bernie," he said, or something like that, his hands muffling the sound. "I hate lying to you."

"We're going somewhere else?" Bernie said. "Not the gym?"

"It's not that." Mr. Parsons rubbed his face, leaving a snotty smear on one cheek, and straightened up. "Afraid you'd think me a fool, so I wasn't truthful about . . . about some of what I told you about Billy."

"You mean his peripheral involvement?" Bernie said.

"Peripheral involvement? I don't understand."

"In the kidnapping," Bernie said. "Falling in with bad people, all that."

"No, not that," Mr. Parsons said. "Billy has the sweetest nature, down deep. Not even all the awful things that happened in prison can change that."

"He told you about awful things in prison?"

"Not in so many words. But something's eating inside him, and that was never true before."

Something eating inside someone? Oh, no. What could be worse? How I wished I hadn't heard that! And . . . and maybe I hadn't. I leaned in that direction, leaned as hard as I could.

"What did he say exactly?" Bernie said.

Mr. Parsons shook his head. "Not much exactly," said Mr. Parsons. "Certainly not in front of Edna."

"Was this the same time when he asked for the money?"

"In the form of a loan," Mr. Parsons said.

"To go to school, as I remember."

"Forestry management. Edna found the program and recommended it. More wishful thinking on our part."

"So what was the money for?" Bernie said.

Mr. Parsons shrugged. "We sent him care packages—as many as they allowed. But after eight or nine years, our visits . . . tailed off. Edna's a trooper. It was hard. I'm talking about the maximum-security building, always with Billy behind glass. And then when the girlfriend came along, he preferred to schedule his visiting times with her. At least we thought so at the time. But maybe it was a rationalization. One of my biggest weaknesses, Bernie. I envy your strong-mindedness, can't tell you how much. Blinds you, in this case to Billy's anger."

"Billy's angry at you?"

Mr. Parsons nodded, dabbing at his eyes. That spread the snot smear around a little more. Bernie fished under the seat, came up with a paper napkin, not too dirty, and cleaned up Mr. Parsons's face. Mr. Parsons didn't seem to notice. "Angry because we stopped visiting. We still called on the phone every Sunday. His anger caught me by surprise. And Edna . . . well, poor Edna. I just had no idea the visits meant so much to Billy. He was always monosyllabic, often cut them off early. But there I go again—rationalizing."

"So Billy revealed this anger for the first time when he came to discuss the loan?"

Mr. Parsons stayed silent for what seemed like a long time. I don't mind sitting in an unmoving car if we're at Donut Heaven, say. But we were not. Right around then I noticed what you might call a tiny flaw in the rear seat upholstery.

"I don't like where you're leading me," Mr. Parsons said at last.

"Where's that?" Bernie said.

"To a place where decisions get made on account of guilt."

"What decisions are we talking about?"

"Edna's and mine," said Mr. Parsons. He wrung his hands. That always bothers me, hands being a bit like tiny people, and you never like to see people in distress. "To fund Billy's business venture."

"What kind of business venture?"

"A start-up," said Mr. Parsons. "Now just give me a moment and I'll get this right."

His lips moved, but no sound came out. Hey! My lips were moving, too! When it comes to leather upholstery there's a kind that looks like leather but smells like plastic. That was what Mr. Parsons had in the backseat of his car. I prefer real leather, although I'm not fussy.

"The securities recovery sector," Mr. Parsons said. "That was it. Billy needed capital to hire some staff."

"I'm not familiar with the securities recovery sector," Bernie said.

"Neither was I. Now I am. But don't ask me to explain it." He laughed, laughter that suddenly cut off. "Stiller's Gym! That's the name. It was on her jacket. Do you know Stiller's Gym, Bernie?"

"I know where it is," Bernie said. "Whose jacket are we talking about?"

"Oh," said Mr. Parsons. "The girlfriend. Didn't I mention her? She's very pretty."

"What's her name?"

"Dee. She came by yesterday, wearing the jacket. The satin kind. I noticed the name on the back." He leaned forward. "So shall we get started? That is, if you're still willing."

"Was Billy with her yesterday?"

"He was at a staff meeting with the twins."

"The twins?"

"He hired twin brothers. Billy says they finish each other's sentences! And Dee was only dropping off some papers."

"What kind of papers?"

Mr. Parsons started patting his pockets again. "Thought I had them right here. Whole point of the exercise."

Bernie's voice, gentle already, got more so. "What kind of papers?"

"Mortgage papers. A very smart kind of mortgage Billy found for us. It pays you instead of you paying it!"

"A reverse mortgage?"

"Something like that," Mr. Parsons said. "Dee was going to come around for the papers in a day or two, but my thinking is let's move things along, start those checks flowing!" Then came more pocket patting. "Where in hell—?"

Bernie switched off the engine. "Let's go in the house and look for them." He opened the door. *Yip yip yip*: Iggy had it dialed up to the max. "Chet? How about you wait here?"

Wait here? What sense did that make? I got to my feet, made my reaction clear.

"Chet? Need you to step up now, big guy."

Barking can sometimes change to yawning in a flash, just one of life's little surprises. Bernie led Mr. Parsons into the house. Not long after, he came out alone, reading some papers. He let me out of Mr. Parsons's car, his eyes still on the papers, and we crossed over onto our property. Bernie stuck the papers in the glove box of the Porsche.

"Securities recovery," he said, slamming the glove box closed so hard the whole car shook.

We hit the road.

TWENTY-THREE

"Tell you one thing right now," Bernie said. "I don't want to get like that. But here's the catch—do you even realize you're like that when you're like that? See how life twists against you? It's not just a long road. It's a long road that yees and yaws and bends you like in a funhouse mirror."

Of this I understood zip, except it was something about mirrors. Every once in a while I catch sight of a very tough-looking customer in a mirror and give him what for in no uncertain terms. Then those terms get less certain and soon after that a message comes through: it's me, Chet the Jet! Do I always tell myself this will never happen again? You bet! So no harm, no foul!

Bernie was quiet for a while. When he spoke, it was in a real quiet voice. "London. What could be so bad? We'd find something, right? You and me."

Was this about finding things? At the Little Detective Agency we always found whatever was out there to be found. Don't forget we had my nose going for us.

After that, Bernie gave his head a quick shake, reminding me of me. "Here's where we are, big guy," he said. Hmm. I could see perfectly well where we were: stuck in traffic at one of the ramps under or over Spaghetti Junction, primo territory for getting stuck in traffic. I waited for Bernie to say something about Spaghetti Junction, but instead he said, "Summer Ronich—did we like her? Not me, big guy—ostensible kidnap victim, is alive and well, all seemingly way behind her. Of the two kidnappers, one, Travis Baca, dies in a freak accident on his last day at Northern State. The other, Billy Parsons, in on the loose, with twenty grand of his parents' money and schemes for some business venture. Billy's also involved in the theft of a saguaro from state land. Someone—Billy being suspect one—killed Ellie Newburg, Department of Agriculture agent working the saguaro case. The detective on the murder is Brick Mickles, who solved the kidnapping fifteen years ago." Traffic started up. "What else?"

What else? Wasn't that more than enough?

"The ransom," he continued a little later, as we left the freeway for surface roads. "Half a mill, never recovered." We parked in front of a gym—I could see shadowy weightlifters through the big window in front—and hopped out of the car.

"Stiller's Gym," Bernie said. "Has a muscle-head rep. That's all I know."

Maybe a bit too much knowledge, in fact? Muscle heads sounded not too good, made me a little uneasy. Bernie opened the door and we went inside.

I'd been in gyms before, some fancy—Leda's for example, always filled with fresh flowers—and some not. Stiller's was of the not fancy variety—dinged-up wooden floor, barbells, dumbbells, stands, and racks, everything colorless and worn-looking. Were those two dudes at the bench press muscle heads? Couldn't see it, myself. Muscle necks, yes, for sure—necks that would have amazed you, as thick as human thighs you sometimes see at all-you-can-eat buffets—but their heads seemed rather small.

"Seven, eight, one more, you pussy, one more," screamed the muscle neck who was watching.

The muscle neck on the bench and doing the actual lifting made sounds, but nothing you could call human speech. The bar wobbled halfway up, and his face turned the color of a vegetable I have no time for whatsoever, namely beets. Bernie feels the same. We went past them, through an amazing air pocket practically boiling over with their smells, and headed for a boxing ring at the rear of the gym. There were no pussycats to be seen. I thought I came close to grasping what Bernie meant by muscle heads.

We're big boxing fans, me and Bernie, have a fine collection of great fights, which we break out when Bernie's in a certain kind of mood, like after we've had Charlie for a weekend and now he's gone. The Thrilla in Manila! And what about No Mas, and Ward-Gatti 1? Don't get me started!

We had no one like any of those guys in the ring at Stiller's Gym. What we had were two skinny-legged dudes huffing and puffing and throwing haymakers that made swishing sounds in the air and landed no place.

"Elbows in," called a lean little man who sat on a stool behind the ropes, a towel around his neck, a pencil behind his ear, a clipboard on his lap. "Stick and move, stick and move. Basic physics, for chrissake."

One of the skinny-legged fighters glanced over and said, "Physics?" Or something like that—hard to tell with the big mouthpiece he had on. Pay attention, skinny-legged fighter: that was my thought as another haymaker slowly came his way and then BAM. Well, not BAM, but it did glance off the side of his padded head gear, just over the ear. He cried out and staggered into the ropes. The other skinny-legged guy danced around like he was champion of the world. Bernie's face suddenly opened up in a great big smile.

"LeSean?" he said, approaching the little lean guy on the stool.

The little lean guy looked up. Then his face cracked open just like Bernie's, smiling big. "Bernie?"

LeSean rose off the stool, or perhaps Bernie simply picked him right up. They hugged and slapped each other's backs for quite some time before I'd had enough and squeezed my way in between.

"Who's this good-looking dude?" LeSean said.

"Chet," said Bernie.

"The jealous type, huh?"

"Doing his best to keep it under control."

LeSean laughed, meaning Bernie had said something funny; about whom I had no idea. "Lookin' not bad yourself, Bernie."

"You, too."

"No ill effects?"

"Nah."

"Leg okay? Didn't seem too good last time I saw you."

"No complaints," Bernie said. "How're you doing?"

"Same—no complaints." He reached out, touched Bernie's arm very lightly. "Won't never forget what you did that day."

"Long time ago," Bernie said, waving away whatever that was all about with his hand. "You own this place?"

"These days I'm tryin' not to make mistakes like that," LeSean said. "I manage an up-and-comin' welterweight from over in Negrito, ref Golden Gloves, work with a few fighters around town."

Bernie gestured over his shoulder to the two fighters in the ring, now listening in from the other side of the ropes.

"Nah," said LeSean. "Corporate types. There's a market, believe it or not, givin' lessons to corporate types. Matter of fact, want to step in for a quick demo of what stick and move is all about?"

"With one of them?" Bernie said.

LeSean laughed. "Corporate types like to sue. I meant with me."

"Not a chance," Bernie said. Meaning Bernie didn't want to box with LeSean? That made no sense. I'd seen what Bernie could do with his hands many times, often to much bigger dudes, which LeSean was not. "But maybe you can help me with something."

"Take five," LeSean said. The two fighters left the ring and headed for the watercooler, both on their cell phones before they arrived. "What's up?"

Bernie handed LeSean our card.

"Cool flower," LeSean said. "Makin' any money?"

"Maybe this time," said Bernie. "Know a woman named Dee Branch? She has some sort of relationship with this gym."

"Rides a Harley?" said LeSean.

"Yeah."

"Can't say I know her," LeSean said. "Seen her in here a few times."

"Doing what?"

"Kickboxing class on Wednesday nights. Some talent in that class—one or two of the girls you'd actually have to watch out for."

"Including Dee?"

"Yeah," said LeSean. "But there's other reasons to watch out for her."

"Such as?"

"The company she keeps, namely these 'roided-out twins," LeSean said. "Renzo and Albin Garza. Couldn't call them gang members, although we get some of that, too. More like professional thugs for hire."

"Where do I find them?" Bernie said.

LeSean gave Bernie a look. "Thing is, with guys like that, don't let 'em get their mitts on you."

"Stick and move," Bernie said with a smile.

LeSean didn't smile back. "Don't forget." He led us over to a desk, checked a screen, wrote something on a scrap of paper, and handed it to Bernie. "You're not the only one askin'," he said.

"No?"

"Had a detective from Valley PD in here day before yesterday. Big fair-haired guy, extra-pally with black folks, if you know what I mean."

"I don't," Bernie said.

"Like he'd been raised on the north side with me and mine," LeSean said. "I prefer white folks who act white—like you, Bernie—which is how come he got nothin' outta me."

"I act white?" said Bernie when we were back in the car.

What was this? Bernie white, in some way or other? Couldn't have been his skin, which was always nice and tan, in that reddish Bernie way. The truth is there's not much color variety when it comes to humans, not compared to how we roll in the nation within. Take me, for example: mostly black but with one white ear, which I know on account of how many people mention it in my presence. Ever seen a human colored like me? The point is humans go on and on about skin colors when it isn't even one of their strengths. And they have so many strengths: cars, tennis balls, bacon, and that's just without even thinking, which is how my mind works best.

Not far past the airport is El Monte, a part of town Bernie calls Subprimoville, for reasons of his own. Subprimoville is just about the biggest development in the whole Valley, detached and semi-detached and not detached at all houses built in what Bernie calls faux adobe style—or sometimes faux-a-dough, when it's only him and me in the conversation—going on and on to the edge of the desert. The catch is that lots of the houses are empty. I've heard Bernie explain what went down many times. It starts simple and gets gnarly. Let's leave it at that.

We stopped in front of a house at the end of a cul de sac, most of the streets in Subprimoville being cul de sacs. Two cars were parked in the driveway. Bernie checked the scrap of paper LeSean had given him, and we started across the dried-out lawn. Part way there, Bernie turned around, walked back to the car—me right beside him, of course—and took the .45 from the glove box.

"A touch slow, big guy," he said. "No denying it." He tucked the stopper in his pocket and we went up to the door. The house was quiet. Bernie slow? No way I was falling for that.

For no special reason, I was hoping that Bernie would shoot out the lock. He knocked instead. I smelled a smell a lot like the stain remover Bernie sprays on his clothes when there's a red wine spill, and mostly hidden way down deep a hint of something else. I wasn't sure about that something else, although the fur on the back of my neck started to rise, like . . . like my fur knew for sure and I didn't? Bernie raised his hand to knock again, but before he could, the door opened.

A smiling man looked out. He wore an apron over his clothes and had a mop in his hand. And . . . hey! I knew this man! Well, not exactly knew him, but hadn't I seen that big head before, a real big shaved head, the face broad but the features small, excepting the ears, ears with gold hoops in each lobe? So now it was just a question of where I knew him from. I got right to work on that. The problem is sights aren't as easy to remember in the nation within as smells. Had I caught just one previous paltry whiff of this man, we wouldn't be having this discussion.

"Hello?" he said.

Bernie nodded. I noticed that the bigheaded man was almost

as tall as Bernie, and actually broader. "We're looking for Renzo and Albin Garza."

The bigheaded man shook his head. "Must have the wrong address."

Bernie took out the scrap of paper. "Three seventy-one Paradise Circle?"

"That's right. But there's no one here by—what were those names?"

"Renzo and Albin Garza. They're twins, weightlifting types, hard to miss."

"Nope," said the bigheaded guy. "Might have been tenants. Place has been empty for months. There's a showing next week so I'm getting things shipshape."

"You work for a real estate agency?"

"A few of them. I'm in the cleaning business."

"Yeah?" said Bernie. "Have you got a card? I've been looking for something in that line."

"Wish I could accommodate you," said the bigheaded man, reaching under his apron. "But I'm completely—"

Cleaning business? I had this vague idea he was in the music business, but what happened next put a dead stop to any thinking in that direction. In fact, what happened next put a stop to everything. In short, another customer joined our party. This other customer was a little figure. He came trotting into view from the shadowy back part of the house. Whoa! That trot was my trot! My trot down to a T, whatever that meant. Did that make me happy to see Shooter? Probably not, but he was on the scene and there was nothing I could do about it. He stepped around the bigheaded dude and bumped up against me. I caught a whiff of his scent, so like mine. What was that all about? No time to figure it out. Things began to speed up. I barely had time to bump him back.

The expression on Bernie's face changed, grew very hard. "Care to revise your story?" he said.

"Not following you, friend," the bigheaded man said, his expression changing, too, and not for the better.

"No?" said Bernie. "This little fella is a direct link to a murder."

The bigheaded man's eyes shifted, just a quick glance toward the back side of the open door. He didn't say anything.

"Ellie Newburg," Bernie said. "That name mean anything to you?"

"Don't know what you've been smoking," the bigheaded dude said. "But this get-together is over." He put one hand on the doorknob, at the same time reaching around with his foot to shove Shooter back inside. Were we going to let him do that? I didn't think so, plus Bernie hadn't touched a cigarette in at least a day or two, so the bigheaded guy didn't know what he was talking about. I waited for some hint from Bernie about what we were doing next, but at that moment Bernie got distracted by more movement back in the shadowy part of the house. The bigheaded man turned that way, too. And then, from out of the shadows staggered one of the twins, Albin or Renzo, impossible to say which. His face was covered in blood—it even dripped off the tips of his Fu Manchu mustache—and he had a gun in his hand. He raised it in a very shaky way. Blood went *drip drip* on the floor, making a sound like soft rain, just before the storm.

TWENTY-FOUR

Humans have an expression: *When the shit hits the fan.* I waited a long time to see that happen, and finally did on a case we worked, me and Bernie, involving a rivalry between two CEOs, one of a plumbing company, the other in the ventilation business. It was actually a bit of a disappointment, the fan clogging up immediately and stopping dead, no dramatics. All the same, Bernie still says you've got to be ready for when fans are about to get hit with something goopy, and I knew this was one of those moments. Was I ready? You bet. Ears up high, heart pounding, my whole body ready to spring. Just say where!

Albin or Renzo—no telling which, but in terrible shape no matter who—pointed his gun in a wobbly way at the bigheaded man. A red bubble popped out of his mouth and then came a few words, soft and hard to understand. "Head or heart, Vroman?" Or something close to that. Much clearer was the look in the twin's eye—only one open, the other swollen shut, in case I left that out. You see this particular look in the eyes of someone about to murder someone else.

There was nothing wobbly about the movements of Vroman, if I'd caught the name of the bigheaded man. In one real quick motion, a kind of quickness that came close to Bernie's although not equaling it, goes without mentioning, he whipped a gun of his own out from under the apron and—BANG—put a bullet right in Albin's or Renzo's open eye. Albin's or Renzo's smell, from living to dead, changed as he toppled over. He toppled over backward, important to put that in, because it meant he crashed into a door which then swung open, revealing a kitchen lit by an open fridge, and the other twin lying in a pool of blood.

I knew one thing: this was a real bad scene. And right away it started getting worse. Vroman swung around in Bernie's direction, that gun pointed at Bernie's chest. I sprang at him—better believe it—sprang with such force and power I . . . I could have sprung to the moon. What a crazy thought! Forget it. The important thing was that I thumped Vroman good and hard. The gun went off anyway, a window shattering nearby. All that was too much for Shooter. The little fella barked a yelping kind of bark, shot out the door and toward the street.

"Go get 'im, Chet!" Bernie called. He'd already leaped on top of Vroman, had one forearm nice and tight around his neck, which meant game over every time. I tore off after Shooter.

Shooter turned out to be pretty quick for someone so small, and also had a surprisingly shifty running style, with so much sideways darting that it was amazing he made any forward progress at all. But he did! In moments, he was on the road, and then off it, zooming across a dried-out lawn toward a house with piles of mail outside the door, ears straight back, tongue flopping wildly to the side. I charged after him, sent him a clear barking message meaning stop this instant, unmissable by anyone. Shooter seemed to miss it. He rounded this house—another faux-a-dough, which I glimpsed in passing—and zipped into the backyard.

There was a swimming pool in this backyard, not big compared to some of the swimming pools you see in the Valley, and filled with scummy water. In short, not particularly inviting. Shooter turned out not to be fussy about things like that. Glancing back at me, his eyes kind of crazy, he dove straight into the pool. Did he even know how to swim? Should I have established that before diving in myself, since if he was a swimmer, then trotting around to the edge at the far end and waiting for him to emerge would have been my best move? Wow! Sheer brilliance on my part! Too bad that all came to me while I was in midair. So close to being perfect. No point in beating yourself up, a scary thing I've seen only once—the night we took down an angel duster who in truth took himself down—and never wanted to see again.

I splashed down into the pool. Yes, scummy and much too warm to be refreshing, but nothing sets you up as nicely as a swim. Was that something Shooter knew? I thought so from the way he was gliding along, just his eyes and nose sticking up above the water, the best technique when it comes to swimming. I glided around in his wake in exactly the same way, slipping toward a relaxing state of mind, but . . . but not quite into it, because all at once I heard Bernie, not the actual Bernie but the Bernie inside my head. Yes, there are often two Bernies in my life! Is there anyone luckier than me? Maybe our buddy Alfonso Breeze, a hubcap thief from Vista City who found a million-dollar scratch ticket in the gutter, and when that was all spent, did the same thing again! Or did he steal that second ticket? Can't possibly figure that out now. Back to the Bernie inside my head, and what he was saying, namely: "Go get 'im, Chet!"

Meaning Shooter, of course. Was my job to paddle along in Shooter's wake? Most definitely not! My job was to round up the little bugger and bring him back to Bernie, who by now had Vroman cuffed and ready for his orange jumpsuit. Time to step up, big guy!

Which I did, first by ramping up my paddle speed until I'd closed practically right on top of Shooter, and then by nipping at his tail, conveniently streaming along behind him. He yelped in a very satisfying way, shot me another of the those wild glances, and then swam slowly to the edge of the pool, climbed out, and sat attentively, waiting on my leadership. Except . . . except Shooter did none of that. Instead, he ramped up his own paddling speed, swerved away just as I was fixing to nip him again, and nip him in no uncertain terms, churning through the water so fast he was making waves, and the next thing I knew he'd sprung out of the pool and was on the loose, somehow giving himself a good shake while on the run—one of my tricks, by the way, not his.

I surged on out of the pool and took off after him, giving myself a much better shake than his on the way. Sunshine caught the droplets and made a rainbow around me, one of those beautiful things that come along in life now and then, but no time to really enjoy it. Shooter was already in the next-door backyard, his paws—surprisingly sizable for such a little guy—throwing up clods of dirt. I turned on the jets, caught up in no time flat or even less, flew right over him, twisted around just before landing, and faced him face-to-face, which is how I face anybody who's putting me through a lot of frustration, which Shooter was, and big time. And then . . . and then he nipped me! Nipped me right on the nose, hard enough so that I actually felt it.

And while I was still feeling it, Shooter took off again, around the side of this house, across another dried-out front lawn, onto the cul de sac and toward the house at the end, where by now Bernic had Vroman all set for booking downtown and was wondering what was taking the big guy so long. I didn't want Bernie to ever wonder things like that, so I bounded after Shooter, came down on him in a way that would send a message even to the craziest-cyed little dude out there, and stood over him in this wide stance that means "end of story."

Just in time, because at that moment the door of the twins' house, or Vroman's house, or whoever's house it was opened and—and Vroman came out, not cuffed and not wearing an orange jumpsuit. But that was Bernie, sometimes too nice. There he was, now stepping out behind Vroman, only . . . only it wasn't Bernie! Instead it was an older dude in a porkpie hat: Clay Winners, from Cactus Sound. He had a wrench in his hand like he'd been doing some repairs. And after him came nobody. Meaning we were turning Vroman loose? Or getting Winners to take him downtown? I was trying to figure all that out as the two men climbed into the pickup in the driveway, which was when Winners noticed us out on the street, me standing over Shooter.

"Dog!" Winners shouted. "Get in here!"

Shooter sprang up from under me and zipped down the street toward the pickup. My mind filled with tough questions, and it's not really the sort of mind for that. Meanwhile, Shooter reached the pickup and sprang up into the bed, an amazing leap for what I suppose would be still called a puppy, a puppy who smelled so confusingly like me. The pickup backed real quick out of the driveway, whipped around, and came roaring my way. I shifted onto the nearest lawn, saw Winners hunched over the wheel, Vro-

man making gestures from the passenger seat, and Shooter in the
pickup bed, on the side nearest me, his head stuck way out in
the wind. Just as the pickup was about to zoom past me I heard
Bernie again: "Go get 'im, Chet!" I still hadn't done my job. But
it wasn't too late—that's the kind of luck I have, especially since
we got together, me and Bernie. I leaped.

One of my very best, no doubt about it, although you couldn't
say I stuck the landing. Call it more of a scramble up and over the
side, with even a possible tumble onto the bare metal truck bed, a
tumble that sent Shooter skidding—or actually flying—into the
back window of the cab. He bounced off and skidded my way. I
gave him a stern sort of bump. What a lot of trouble he was! Now
my job was to somehow get him to hop out of this pickup with
me and hurry on back to Bernie. Bernie! Where was Bernie? Had
I gotten separated from him? How had that happened? I tried
to put it all together, but meanwhile we were picking up speed.
Also, Winners and Vroman had turned their heads to check us
out through the rear window, and I didn't like the looks on their
faces. I pawed at Shooter's shoulder, sending another clear message: We're outta here—move! He growled at me. I got set to paw
him again, much harder. Now was a good time for leaping out
and hightailing it—we were slowing down for a red light—but
before I could do anything, a strange whiny motor started up
and—and what now? A kind of sheet metal roof began sliding
overhead? How strange! If it kept on sliding like this, Shooter and
I were soon going to be—

FLOOSH. The roof closed over us, its front end thunking into
some sort of slot at the back of the pickup. Now we were in com-
plete darkness, not nighttime darkness, but the darkness you get
at the bottom of a mine when the lantern goes dead, which I hap-

pen to know about from a not-too-good past experience. Things were taking a bad turn, unless I was missing something. The truth seemed to be that Shooter and I were trapped in the bed of this pickup, headed for places unknown. I didn't want to go to places unknown, not without Bernie. Where was he? Bernie! Bernie!

Whoa. Get a grip. I was a pro, after all, unlike Shooter, who'd started to howl and claw at something metallic, maybe the side of the pickup bed, maybe the roof that had come from nowhere to shut us in; no way of knowing on account of the utter blackness around us. Howling would get us nowhere—we pros are clued into things like that—but clawing? Not a bad idea. I raised a paw, raked it across the underside of the roof, felt a thin gap, maybe where two sections met, and raked and clawed at that gap, hunching on my hind legs, summoning all my strength, or at least all I could use in this tight space. I raked, I clawed, I pushed, I growled, I—

With a shriek of the brakes, brakes so near they seemed to be shrieking right inside my head, the pickup slammed to a sudden stop. We went flying, me and Shooter together in one ball, cracking into the front end of the pickup bed, head first in my case. Did I hear laughter coming from up front in the cab?

I dreamed we were surfing, me and Bernie. I stood on the front of the board, way out in the ocean, the skyline of San Diego—where we'd gone to work on a case, all details forgotten—rising in the distance. Bernie treaded water behind me, one hand on the board. The ocean seemed to swell beneath us, an amazing force unlike any I'd ever known, and so rich in smells I couldn't keep up.

"Feel it, big guy?"

I sure did!

"Get ready."

Ready? I was the readiest I'd ever been. Bernie rolled onto the board, lay on his stomach, legs extending off the back and kicking powerfully.

"Here we go!"

And then we were zooming across the face of a mighty wave taking shape under and all around us. Bernie rose, hunching over me. I hunched, too. If hunching was how you rode the board, then I could hunch with the best of them. We made wild noises together, silent noises obliterated by the roar of the sea. Life at its best: I couldn't have been happier. Then the roar amped down and down and became a kind of mewling. The smell of the ocean faded out at the same time, vanishing completely.

I opened my eyes, saw nothing. The mewling came from under my chest. I was lying on my side, the mewler—meaning Shooter—curled up against me, trying to wriggle in even closer. We were moving, maybe moving fast. My head hurt, but I wouldn't want to call it pain. I'm a tough customer, which maybe you know by now. I growled. Shooter cuddled in tight and stopped mewling. The pickup engine roared; the tires tore at the road beneath us; we rocked one way and then another. The ride got bumpier and bumpier and began turning dusty. I didn't want to be in blackness and breathing dust. I wanted to be with Bernie.

Next thing I knew I was back on my feet, clawing again at the section division in the metal roof. All my power surged inside me, surged like the power itself had gone crazy. The two sections began to bend and bow and come apart. I saw light! And clawed and bashed even harder, using all my power plus Bernie's as well, if that makes any sense. The sections split apart, almost wide enough for me to peek out. I smelled saguaros. We were on our way! Chet the Jet! And here was Shooter, right beside me and trying to do what I was doing, even though he couldn't reach. There was hope for the little fella.

But then the brakes shrieked, and once more I shot toward the front of the pickup bed, once more head first. The light failed. Laughter.

TWENTY-FIVE

W hy didn't you put him away for good?"
       "What are you talking about?"
"When you stepped out from behind the door."
"Critiquing my performance, Vroman?"
"No, boss. Just thought this might be one of those teachable moments."

Teachable moments? Sounded familiar. I opened my eyes, found myself mostly in darkness, except for a single ray of light slanting down from above, a ray of light swirling with golden dust. Maybe a beautiful sight, although I wasn't really in the mood for beauty. Not in the mood for beauty is not the normal me, but at the moment my head kind of hurt. Nothing I'd call pain, of course—more like a bit of a distraction. Meanwhile, I felt someone warm curled up against my chest. I glanced down, saw Shooter sleeping in a contented sort of way, not a care in the world. My head started feeling better. All sorts of memory pieces were on the move in my mind. I hoped they'd get cracking and put themselves together.

"Teachable moments, huh?" I recognized that voice, the voice

of Clay Winners, and decided I didn't like it. "Ever heard of Colo-
nel Tom Parker?"

"Nope."

"Elvis Presley's manager. He was a genius at squeezing all the
juice out of every opportunity. That's a gift, Vroman."

"So, uh, you were squeezing out the juice?"

"Imagine that house with three dead bodies in it. Then imagine it with two dead bodies and one other dude—a particularly
troublesome private dick with plenty of enemies—lying there out
cold. Suppose someone at Valley PD gets a heads-up text. Tasting
the juice yet?"

"You talking about Mickles? I don't trust the bastard."

"Who would? But he's got dirty hands, and he knows we
know how dirty. That makes him reliable."

"He's going to help us frame Little for the murder of the
twins?"

"He's going to do it all by himself, Vroman. Hit the switch."

A whiny motor started up, and a roof overhead began to
open. The sun glared in, way too bright, and I closed my eyes
down to little slits.

"One thing, boss," Vroman said. "I've got the gun."

"So?"

"The gun I did the twins with. Shouldn't we have left it on the
floor next to Little?"

"Never want to be too neat," Winners said. "And guns are
dangerous. Know why?"

"Um, because they kill people?"

"Because they can be traced," said Winner. "All set?"

"Drop it on 'im."

Shadowy figures appeared in the glare above me. I got a real
bad feeling, shifted my legs under me, set to spring. But no. All

of that only started to happen, on account of how slow I seemed
to be. How was that possible? I was never slow. My anger at
being slow got my blood flowing—which made my head hurt,
although nothing you'd call pain—and I rose. With a wobble or
two? Maybe, but on my feet was the point, and ready to deal.
Bring it on!

Whoosh. I felt a strange whoosh of air, and then—oh, no! A
sort of leather cage settled tight over my head. Not a muzzle? But
yes. I twisted around, tried to bark, tried to bite, tried to shake off
the horrible muzzle, all with no result. I couldn't even open my
mouth. I knew muzzles from a long time ago, back before Bernie.
There was nothing I hated more.

"Haul 'im out."

A force began to pull me, pulling on me from the muzzle
strap or something else around my neck. I dug my paws into the
floor, only then finally cluing in on where I was, namely the bed
of the pickup, which had a steel floor, hard to grip. I slid along
to the back of the pickup and then off, falling to the ground and
landing much harder than I usually do. But it was good to feel
the ground under me. My vision cleared, and there within easy
springing distance stood Vroman, a little smile on his too-big face,
like he was enjoying himself. Could some stupid muzzle keep me
from knocking him down, showing him what was what? You
know the answer to that. I sprang.

And . . . and got nowhere. What was this? A pole? A pole
plus a muzzle? Yes—I felt the loop at the end of the pole, tight
around my neck. The pole glinted in the sunshine, a long metal
pole with me on one end and Vroman on the other. I ran sideways, hoping to outsmart that pole, if you see what I mean, then
stopped suddenly and rounded on Vroman. But the pole proved
to be smarter, easily keeping itself between us. He jerked the loop

tight around my neck, the same jerking motion fishermen make with their rods to whip hooked fish clear of the water. That kept me from breathing. I tried to bite, tried to bark, both impossible because of the muzzle. I growled. It was all I could do. I growled until I was out of breath and could get no more, on account of the neck loop. Air! I needed air, so bad.

"Should I just put 'im out of his misery?" Vroman said.

"He may prove valuable," said Winners, moving into my line of sight, his porkpie hat set back on his head in a relaxed sort of way.

"For squeezing out more juice?"

"There's hope for you yet," Winners said. Sunshine glittered on his neatly trimmed white beard. "Ease up on the loop, then work 'im with the pole, take some of the starch out." Winners turned toward the pickup. "Dog! Come!"

From the corner of my eye I could see Shooter, now awake and poised at the back edge of the pickup bed. He just stood there.

"Dog!"

Shooter looked my way. He started to pant.

"What the hell is wrong with you?" Winners said. "Come!"

"Why are you so interested in that dog?" Vroman said.

"First, he's evidence, as Little so cleverly pointed out, so we keep him close. Second, I'm going to train him to be the badass guard dog of the world. Third, it's none of your goddamn business." Winners stabbed his finger at Shooter and raised his voice. "Come!"

The little fella panted harder, but he didn't move. My mind began to form a plan, but before it got to the first step, Winners walked over to Shooter, glared down at him. Shooter's tail drooped and he ducked his head a bit, as though awaiting a blow. I wanted to do bad things to Winners and then bad things to Vroman, so bad I couldn't even imagine them.

Winners stuck his hand in his pocket and out came not a gun, or brass knucks, or any of the kinds of nasty things I expected, but a biscuit. He held it out for Shooter to see. "Come."

Shooter just stood there. Were his eyes on me? I thought so. At the same time, his little nostrils—actually not so little considering his overall smallness—started to twitch, and he stopped panting.

"Come."

Shooter leaned forward, ever so slightly, his muscles trembling, like they were pushing and pulling him at the same time. He even made a faint whimpering noise. But in the end he leaped for that biscuit. How could I blame him? I'd have done the same thing.

Winners whisked the biscuit up and away just before Shooter could clamp his little jaws around it. Shooter fell to the ground—hard and rocky desert ground with thorny bushes here and there—rolled over and scrambled back up, making another play for that biscuit, just out of reach once again. Holding it high, Winners set off toward a huge round golden tent, way bigger than a house, that stood at the base of a nearby two-humped hill. Shooter kept jumping for that biscuit all the way, coming up short every time. When they came to the tent entrance—a dark opening, bigger than a garage door—Shooter paused and glanced back at me. Did Winners give Shooter a kick at that moment? I thought so. Shooter went tumbling into the tent and a flap rolled down over the opening. The tent glowed in the sunshine, almost like a little sun itself. A flag with the image of a saguaro on it fluttered from the roof of the tent. And behind the tent rose a gigantic saguaro, taller than the tallest tree I'd ever seen: a gigantic saguaro but made of shiny metal. Workers on ladders were painting it green. Everything seemed very bright.

Vroman's eyes were on me. Some humans have kind eyes. Some have eyes that can go either way. Vroman's eyes didn't belong to either group. Maybe I was noticing this a bit on the late side. He got to work on taking the starch out of me. Bernie entered my mind immediately, in case I needed any help.

The problem with the muzzle—aside from the obvious one of how much I hated the feel of it, and how enraged it made me inside—was that after we were done with taking the starch out of me, I couldn't drink, despite my thirst. And I was pretty thirsty, no doubt about that. Plus the fact of knowing you can't drink makes you thirstier, something I'd already learned from other scrapes I'd been through deep in the desert. Speaking of scrapes, when you've survived a few, your inner starch gets harder to remove, if that makes any sense. I lay in the shade of a crumbling stone wall, forming a plan. It was a good one so far: *Bernie!*

The stone wall was part of the remains of an old hut, the kind of ruin you find out in the desert. We love exploring old ruins, me and Bernie. Once we'd found a real old US Marshall's star with a bullet hole right through it! Suzie had written a whole story about it for the *Tribune*, and we'd celebrated with steak tips at the Dry Gulch Steakhouse and Saloon. What a life!

This particular hut also had the remains of a roof, plus most of another wall. A rusty metal ring hung from that other wall, and I was attached to that ring by a thick-linked chain. Not a long chain, but long enough so that I could reach a small stone trough just beyond a low pile of stones where one of the missing walls had stood. I smelled water in that trough, maybe not the freshest or coolest water, but . . . water! I rose, not quite hopping up in my normal way, but no complaints, and made my way over to the trough. I gazed down into it. Yes, water for sure, murky, scummy, buggy. I wanted it real bad.

My hut seemed to be partway up a slope, some big saguaros masking the view, although I could make out the golden tent at the base of the two-humped hill, the gigantic saguaro, now almost completely green, and a few shirtless workers who seemed to be building a wooden stage. Was one of them taking a water break? He had his head thrown back and, yes, a clear and sparkling bottle tilted to his mouth. Maybe he was the type who had nice feelings for the nation within and would soon amble on over and share his drink. That didn't seem so crazy to me at the time, a sign I wasn't quite at the top of my game. I went back to gazing at the gigantic saguaro and noticed—maybe a little slow on the uptake—that it now had a gigantic human face and wore a gigantic porkpie hat. I was liking the gigantic saguaro less and less.

The sun slid lower across the sky, turning redder, the way it always did. A small dust cloud rose from that direction, also reddish, but that wasn't the point. The point was that dust clouds like that in country like this often meant a car was on the way. Like a Porsche, for example. Had to be the Porsche! I took off for that dust cloud, bounding—

Only there was no bounding, no taking off after dust clouds, nothing doing at all. Somehow I'd forgotten all about the chain. It brought me up short and I smacked down hard on the stony ground, the muzzle now twisted around a bit, partly covering one of my eyes. But no big deal. Vision's not as important to me as it may be to you, and besides I could still see with my other eye, at least well enough to make out the car under the dust cloud—not a Porsche, as it turned out.

I got to my feet, felt pretty dusty, considered giving myself a good shake, decided to put it off for a while. Bernie's mom—a real piece of work who sometimes shows up on Thanksgiving—says never put off till tomorrow what you can do today. Even though she calls Bernie Kiddo, I wouldn't have minded seeing her round about now, not one little bit. Maybe she was driving that approaching car; another wild thought that also seemed somewhat normal to me at the time. The car disappeared behind a rise, soon after coming into view on a curving dirt track, much closer now. The car followed a track up the mesa and parked not far from the golden tent. Then the driver's door opened and out stepped not Bernie's mom—whom I was still kind of expecting—but a very big man I didn't like even though I didn't know him that well, which wasn't my usual approach at all. But Bernie really didn't like him, so say no more. Hadn't they almost thrown down the last time they'd seen each other, outside the Parsonses' house? Yes, it was Brick Mickles.

Walking like he owned the place, he disappeared inside the tent. Over to one side, the workers finished up with their water break and got back to work. The banging of their hammers sounded very clear even though they were pretty far from my hut. Not my hut: shouldn't have put it that way. I'd be out of here and gone real soon: just a matter of time until my mind got working on the plan.

Meanwhile, a vulture circled high above, wings spread but not flapping, riding the breezes up there the way birds do. That must have been nice, although I always wonder if birds know how nice. Why are their eyes so mean and angry all the time? At the very moment I was having that thought, the vulture tilted sharply, swung around in my direction, and spiraled down a bit, now not so high above me anymore. For some reason, I began to grow more conscious of my tongue, which was feeling bigger than normal and kind of dry. It really wanted to get outside my mouth and flop around freely for a while, but the muzzle made that impossible. The muzzle, the chain, the thirst: it was almost a little too much. I gathered my strength beneath me and strained forward with all my might, getting nowhere. A small setback? Yes, but you can't let small setbacks bog you down: that's one of the rules at the Little Detective Agency, part of the reason we're so successful, if you're willing to forget about the finances. Out there by this ruined hut on a stony hill, I forgot finances and everything else except for the muzzle, the chain, and water. And don't leave out Bernie. That goes without mentioning.

The sun, red and low and fat, sat on the shoulder of a distant mountain. The sky went through all sorts of color changes, seemed to me a giant living thing. I spotted a cloud, streaky and pink. Clouds brought rain. *Come this way, cloud!* But it did not. And even if it rained, how could I get any water through the muzzle? Chet the Jet: not at the top of his game.

Over at the golden tent, the big flap opened, and Winners and Mickles stepped out. They started on a narrow path up and down a rise, crossed a flat patch, and then switchbacked up the hill toward me. Their hard shoes made crunching sounds on the desert floor. Not a very loud noise, I suppose, but it just about filled up my whole sound world. The only other thing I heard was my heart, boom-booming in its usual way. Once I'd heard Bernie say: "Chet's got a heart as big as all outdoors." You had to love Bernie.

TWENTY-SIX

I stood up and faced them as they mounted the slope. Winners, not a big guy, huffed and puffed, but Mickles, so huge, did not. They stopped, just out of my reach, and gazed at me. Winners took off his porkpie hat and wiped his forehead with the back of his arm. Then he took a water bottle from his pocket and drank, drank a little sloppily, a bubbly stream running off his chin. Oh, that lovely smell! My tongue got drier, bigger, harder. I growled, pretty much my only option under the circumstances. There were other things I wanted to do, starting with chewing that porkpie hat to bits, maybe kind of crazy.

"Sure there's nothing you're not telling me?" Winners said, tossing away the empty bottle. How I wished for Bernie at that moment. He would have made Winners pick up that bottle at the very least, or maybe even eat it, which would have been my preference.

"What are you driving at?" said Mickles, his eyes still on me.

"I laid him out pretty good is all," Winners said. "Socket wrench, right behind the ear."

"He was gone when I got there, exactly fourteen minutes after your text. Why would I say he wasn't there if he was?"

Winners shot Mickles a sideways look. "No reason I can see."

"Know your problem?" Mickles said. "You overthink."

Winners said nothing, but I could feel him thinking, so maybe Mickles was right.

"Not saying your plan didn't have its good points," Mickles said. "But it didn't work."

"So now Little's on the loose."

"Yup," Mickles said.

"I don't like him."

"Join the club."

"Not that way," Winners said. "Well, yes, I don't like him that way, too, but what I meant was he's hard to read."

"He's a private dick, paid to cause trouble. What's hard about that?"

"Who's paying him?"

Mickles didn't answer.

"You don't know?" Winners said.

"What difference does it make?" said Mickles.

"Maybe he could be paid more to go away."

Mickles shook his head. "He's not the type."

"See? That's what I mean. What kind of type is he? He can read charts, for chrissake."

"What the hell are you talking about?"

"He's dangerous, that's all. And he's on the loose."

Mickles pointed at me with his chin. "But we've got Chet."

"The dog?"

"Correct," Mickles said. He gave me a closer look. "Something happen to him? Looks kind of in rough shape. Is that blood coming out of his ear?"

"Fell off the truck," said Winners.

Mickles nodded, a slow nod that actually reminded me of one

of Bernie's, even though they were as different as men could be. "Happens," he said. "What do you know about him?"

"What do I know about the dog?" said Winners.

"Yeah."

"Stay clear of him, that's for goddamn sure."

"What else?"

Winners shrugged.

"He's an unusual dog," Mickles said. "Without him, Little wouldn't have a pot to piss in. See where I'm going with this?"

"The dog means a lot to Little?"

"Exactly. His livelihood, man. And you're right about one thing. We can't have Little on the loose, not while Billy's out there, too."

"So we're going to make a deal?" said Winners.

"You are," Mickles said. "A deal of the reneging kind. When you've got it set up, let me know."

Winners nodded.

"And this time use a gun," Mickles said.

"Any suggestions on the price?"

"For Chet? Make it something he can come up with fast."

"Ten grand?"

"Sounds right."

"Which we'll keep at the end. Call it a dividend."

"I'll want half," said Mickles.

They turned and headed back down the hill. "Half's unreasonable," Winners said. "I'm doing all the work."

"There you go again with the overthinking," said Mickles.

Winners laughed and said, "How does a third grab you?"

Mickles laughed, too. None of this laughter was the kind you hear when humans are enjoying each other's company—in fact, all I felt between them was mutual hate. Mickles said something about how a third grabbed him, but they were over the rise by that time, and a breeze had sprung up at my back, blowing their talk away. All I knew was that they didn't like each other and they were both right. As for Bernie not having a pot to piss in, Mickles was clueless. We had two toilets at our place on Mesquite Road, one in the hall bathroom, the other in the bathroom off Bernie's bedroom. Also, once when Bernie'd had maybe one bourbon too many, he'd peed into the swan fountain on the patio out back. "You didn't see this, big guy," he'd said at the time. So forget I mentioned it and stick with Bernie having two pots.

The sun vanished behind the faraway mountain, the sky turned dark purple, and shadows started roaming around. I thought about water and Bernie. Was I hungry as well? Possibly, but when you're as thirsty as I was, you don't think about hunger. Plus my face was all caged up and my tongue couldn't be free. Even if it couldn't have water, at least it wanted to feel some air. I gathered my strength again—although it didn't all seem to be there, kind of mysterious—and surged forward. The chain held me in place, and I got nowhere. That didn't stop me from trying again. And again. And some more times, way beyond two. When it comes to numbers, I stop at two, but I never stop when it comes to some other things. So later—the sky fully dark now, except for the pink glow of the city out beyond the distant mountain—when I finally crept back into the ruined hut, it didn't mean I'd stopped trying to be free. I was just taking a break. We took breaks at the Little Detective Agency, just another feature of our business plan.

One thing about this particular night: there were more shadows on the move than on any other previous night I remember. *He's afraid of shadows* is something you hear humans say—not about me, of course. I'm not afraid of shadows or anything else that comes to mind, but shadows are different when you're chained to a stone wall and wearing a muzzle. I mulled that over for a while—lying way back in the farthest corner of the hut, where the two remaining walls joined up—and then returned to thoughts of water. The best water I'd ever tasted came flowing right out of a rock in a high mountain forest on the day I first saw snow. Bernie made a snowball—what an amazing idea, would never have occurred to me, but that was Bernie—and we played us some fetch, although not for long, what with the short life spans of snowballs. Never mind snowballs. That water, flowing out of the rock, so clean and cool and perfect, took over my whole mind. "Lifeblood of the planet, right there," Bernie had told me, which I didn't get, on account of it tasted very different from and much better than blood. Sometimes Bernie's so smart no one can understand him.

If only he could be here now! He'd rip off the horrible muzzle, whip out my portable water bowl, fill it to the top again and again. I'd slurp and slurp and splash water all over the place. The fun we'd have!

Bernie didn't come. The night grew cooler. The moon rose. Just half a moon, and it was having one of those real pale nights. I preferred the moon in a warm and yellow mood. Somehow tonight's pale moon brought to mind those bleached-out bones you come across in the desert. A bad thought, and maybe because I was so thirsty I started having others, like if Winners or Mickles— or even Vroman, the worst thought of all—would only come and take off the muzzle and let me drink, I wouldn't do anything bad to them, just lie down meekly at their feet and be their friend. Oh, no! Help me, someone! But there was no one so it was up to me. I made the bad thoughts go away and replaced them with thoughts of what Chet the Jet would do to those men when he got the chance. With bells on, whatever that meant exactly. That made me feel much better, if you forgot about the thirst.

But I couldn't.

After a while, something rustled in the thorn bushes nearby. Not just something, of course, but a snake. Hard to miss the smell of snake, a bit lizardy, a bit froggy, with a strange add-on that always reminded me of a time Bernie and I searched a chem lab at the college. Bernie had picked up a test tube and said, "Just about the deadliest poison known to man." And then: "Oops!" But he hadn't dropped the test tube, meaning it was one of Bernie's jokes. There's no one like Bernie when it comes to jokes. I squeezed myself as deeply as possible into the corner of the hut. If the snake came in I could . . . I could . . . I was still figuring that out when the snake rustled off in another direction. I closed my eyes, waited for sleep to come. That's never a problem for me.

Sleep wouldn't come, or at least not come close enough. It lingered just out of reach, what could have been a dark and comforting blanket. I was too weak to make it drift that last little distance and settle over me. So I just lay in my corner, eyes open, breathing in a shallow sort of way through the muzzle, alive. In the morning I would do something about all this. For example—

Before any examples popped into my mind, I heard more sounds from outside the hut. Snake? No. Neither was it a javelina, turtle, mouse, rat, cat of any kind, big or small, and also not human. None of those things. There's only one creature that moves in those quick fits and starts, a certain type of creature following a scent, tail up high. Sure enough, Shooter came zigzagging into my hut, tail high, no question, the pale moonlight in his eyes, making them appear a bit on the crazy side. He saw me in my corner, and trotted right over, tail wagging a mile a minute, which actually turns out not to be that fast, Bernie and I having hit two miles a minute more than once in the Porsche—although not the one we have now. I'm referring to the one that got blown up. That baby could fly!

Shooter stood before me, wagging away and making a breeze that felt good. He pawed at my shoulder, just meaning let's play, but my shoulder happened to be a bit on the sore side at that moment, and I growled at the little fella. He backed away, tail drooping. Then he got another idea—in a way that reminded me of me getting another idea, kind of odd—and went sniffing around the hut. Whatever scent had caught his attention led him toward the front of the hut and outside, where he quickly disappeared in the night.

Shooter! Come back! Maybe not me at my best, trying to lean on such a little dude. I told myself not to do that again. There's nothing worse than not living up to your own standards, as I'm sure you know. And what was my standard? To be up and doing, to take charge, to be the guy. Therefore I rose and—

Except I couldn't seem to get to my feet. I was still trying—and doing pretty well, lifting my belly off the ground, legs not shaking too bad—when Shooter came zigzagging back into the hut, exactly as he'd done the first time. And exactly as he'd done the first time he trotted over and pawed my shoulder. This time I kept the growl inside. He pawed me again, tried a quick, low bark, meaning *Let's go, dude!* Oh, how I wanted to! With a real big effort, I rose to a full stand, first time in my whole life it had taken any effort at all to do that, which just goes to show you. Shooter's tail started wagging again, a moonlit blur. He barked the "let's go" bark again, followed it up with a few quick fake lunges toward the opening in the hut, just to give me the idea. No need for that: getting away from here was the number two idea in my mind, number one being water.

I gazed down at him. He gazed up at me. For some reason, I settled back down on my belly, making us more or less eye-to-eye. Around about then was when Shooter seemed to notice the muzzle.

He came a little closer, nostrils twitching. Then, closer still, he sniffed at the muzzle. He made a sort of whine, high-pitched and soft at the same time, and sniffed some more. After that, he backed away and went through the whole fake lunge, let's go thing again. He followed that up by prancing out of the hut in a slow and exaggerated kind of run, almost like he was trying to teach me, Chet the Jet, how to run. Shooter was a very annoying dude, but when he went prancing out into the night, I found myself hoping pretty hard that he'd be coming back.

Which he did, still prancing. This time he paused in mid-prance, one paw raised, and noticed the muzzle again. That led to a repeat performance—nostril twitch, whine, sniff. Only now he leaned in much closer and gave the muzzle a lick. The muzzle was partly metal but mostly leather, and had a leathery smell with some bloody under-scents, old and new. Shooter did a little more licking and then gave the muzzle a nip, the exploratory kind. He drew back quickly, as though expecting the muzzle to do something. It didn't, of course. Muzzles couldn't come and get you: that wasn't how they did their nastiness. Shooter had a lot to learn.

He stood there in the middle of the hut for a bit, doing pretty much zip. Was prancing next? That's what my money would have been on, if I'd had any, meaning if me and Bernie had any, which we did not at the moment. But I'd have lost that bet, because no prancing happened. Instead, Shooter emerged from what humans maybe call a trance and gave himself a good long stretch, head way down, butt way up, a stretch that reminded me so much of my own. A lot to learn, maybe, but some things the little fella had down perfectly.

All nicely stretched out, Shooter came over and gazed at me for some time. I gazed back. He moved in closer and licked the muzzle again, over on the side that had shifted across my eye. He licked it once or twice and then took another nip. Normally nobody gets to nip anywhere near me, but I wasn't at the top of my game, and for some reason Shooter seemed to be a special case. Don't ask me why. He nipped again a few times at the muzzle, over on the side and higher up where the muzzle felt kind of strappy against my head. Nipping soon turned to gnawing. Gnawing leather is a fine way to pass the time, completely understandable. I didn't mind at all, felt glad for his company. There was something about Shooter, although I couldn't take it further than that. His teeth—small but amazingly sharp—raked through my head and neck fur occasionally as he gnawed away. My world shrank to gnawing sounds, the smell of freshly gnawed leather, and the touch of those sharp little teeth. And then it began to shrink some more, as though . . . as though . . . I didn't want to go there, even though "there" was a place with cool water flowing out of the rocks, all the cool water anyone could ever want, lifeblood of the planet.

Bernie!

TWENTY-SEVEN

I drifted through a world that was all about gnawing, its sounds and smells. Although I'm a world champion gnawer, I myself wasn't doing the gnawing. Except in a way I sort of was. That was one strange thing. Here's another: My eyes might have been closed, but I saw the pale moon anyway, certainly felt its stony light. Even stranger, I was suddenly on the moon myself, gazing down. I saw Chet and Shooter in the ruins of an old stone hut, out in the desert. They looked like they were made of stone themselves.

And then came a new sound, a sound a lot like ripping or tearing. It reminded me of something bad that had once happened to a shoe of Leda's; this shoe had a name, by the way, kind of odd. Manolo? Was that it? Not important. The important thing is that just after I heard the ripping sound, the muzzle seemed to go slack on my face. After that the gnawing continued, but in a far-off way. Also there was no more of the pointy-toothed raking through my fur. I missed that.

I lay quiet, listening to the gnawing, missing the raking. The moon slid down a bit in the sky, brightening up the inside of the hut. I realized that Shooter had moved off. There he was, curled up near the opening of the hut, busy gnawing on the muzzle, held securely between his front paws in proper gnawing style, a style exactly like my own. There was hope for Shooter, no doubt about it.

So that was the situation in the ruined hut. Night, moon, me—not at my best and getting worse, and Shooter—still a puppy, but off to a promising start. Who knows how much longer we could have gone on like that? We never found out, because from out of the blue came an idea: What if I tried opening my mouth?

Nothing to lose. I tried opening my mouth. And what do you know? It opened right up! A little stiff and sore, maybe, but open. Was opening wider possible? Oh, yeah, baby! I opened my mouth to the max. Ahead lay all kinds of exciting possibilities; I just knew it.

How about my tongue? Could I stick it out into the fresh air where it wanted so badly to be? I gave it a whirl. And out came my poor tongue, all hard and bone-dry, but out. Out in the world! I looked over at Shooter, gnawing busily on the muzzle. He caught my look and folded himself around the muzzle in a possessive sort of way, like . . . like he'd pulled a fast one!

No way I could let that happen. The next thing I knew, I was on my feet, perhaps a bit unsteady, but up. I took a step or two in Shooter's direction. That was when the smell of the water in the trough outside the hut struck me full force, like one of those waves off San Diego. I went right by Shooter—he wriggled to the side, protecting the muzzle, or what was left of it, not a bad sight at all, how mangled it was—and made my way to the trough. What a long time that took! But when I got to the trough I lowered my face into it and drank and drank, slurping up lovely and delicious scummy and buggy water like there was no tomorrow, a human phrase I understood like never before. And guess what? There was a tomorrow! I filled myself up with the lifeblood of the planet.

How much better I felt, and practically right away! I began to notice my surroundings, including the huge golden tent, soft glows from inner lights showing through the walls in one or two places, but mostly dark, and off in the distance strange small fires that seemed to be burning here and there. I picked up the scent of burgers, faint, yes, but no one could miss that smell; no one in the nation within, I mean. No offense. I moved off to get a better—

No. I did not move off. Somehow I'd forgotten all about the chain. What does it say about a chained-up dude who forgets he's chained up? I had no idea, wished that such a bothersome question had never occurred to me.

I twisted around, got myself a good look at the chain, a thick-linked chain no one could gnaw through. But, as humans say, there's more than one way to skin a cat. I've never seen it done even one way, personally, and you're welcome to try. Just be warned that cats have a quickness you're not going to believe, and the skin that gets skinned will most likely be yours.

No time for cats at the moment. I took a step or two forward, felt the chain stretching out behind me and rising off the ground. Then I began to pull, pull hard, harder, my hardest. In my mind, I heard Bernie. *Show 'em what you got, big guy.* Oh, I will, Bernie, I will. Can you see me? I'm pulling harder than my hardest now, ramping up to pull even harder than that, and ever harder than that, and—

CRASH! From back in the hut came a crashing sound with a lot of boom mixed in, a sound that reminded me of a mine cave-in that Bernie and I had seen in an up-close and personal way. I went flying past the trough, landing hard, which made my achy body achier. Who cared about that? Not me, amigo. I picked myself up, turned, and saw Shooter racing out of the hut, or rather what was left of it. And was he yelping or what? Scared out of his little mind: a gratifying sight. As was the present state of the hut, the back wall in heaps of loose stones, the roof fallen in, and only the side wall still standing, although even as I watched, that side wall started falling apart as well.

Shooter ran yelping around me, kind of beside his little self. I took a few steps down the hill, not headed anywhere special, but just because I could do it. Free! I was free, and if, as I slowly realized from the dull clanking sound, the chain still seemed to be attached to my collar, so what? I walked around in a little circle, doubling back on the chain, which had a bolt attached to the last link, a bolt that must have been sunk into the wall of the hut and had now come loose. A whole lot of work had gone into keeping me from being free. That made my freedom all the sweeter! Did I feel tip-top? Maybe not, but good enough, amigo.

I gazed beyond the silhouette of the distant mountain—blacker than the night—toward the faint pink glow of the Valley sky. Then I turned to Shooter, now doing some vigorous scratching behind his ear, and gave him one of my low rumbly barks. This one meant: time to head for home, little fella. I started down the hill, dragging the chain behind me. Normally that wouldn't have slowed me down the slightest bit, but I wasn't quite normal. Somewhat achy, yes, and more than that: hungry. When had I last eaten? I was trying to remember when it struck me that Shooter didn't seem to be by my side. I looked back up the hill and there he was, not far from the water trough, scratching behind his other ear. I gave him another low rumbly bark. He left off scratching for a moment, stared at me in a blank sort of way, and went back to scratching. Was leaving Shooter up here on the hill to fend for himself in the cards? It was not. I climbed back up and made a few gentle attempts at getting his attention, all of them failures. I took a less gentle approach. After that we started making our way down the hill, me leading and Shooter following, although he did most of his following from in front. My less gentle approach had taken something out of me, kind of strange.

We walked down the hill, turned away from the two-humped hill, the golden tent, now totally dark, and the gigantic cactus man, and started across open desert. The chain clunked along behind me, sometimes catching on a stone or a bush in a very annoying way, forcing me to tug at it on a night when I didn't seem to have many tugs in me. Meanwhile, Shooter was doing a lot of prancing and zigzagging in the moonlight, mixed in with sniffing under rocks where he had no business sniffing, not with snake scent so strong in the air. I plodded on—hate to put it that way, but it's true—giving him the odd growl or low rumbly bark, totally ignored each and every time.

The strange fires I'd spotted from up at the hut drew closer, scattered across the desert floor. How many? More than two, less than one of those huge numbers humans mention, like gazillion. The breeze was in our faces, a cool breeze carrying scents of wood smoke, pot smoke, and burgers. I tried to pick up the pace and after what seemed like not too long, caught up to Shooter. He was wriggling around on his back, moonlight gleaming in his eyes. I closed in and gave him a look. He sprang up, shook off some dust, most of it in my face, and we moved on.

Up ahead a dry wash appeared, cutting across our path. We went down into it, crossed over, and came up the far side, where a huge gate rose in the night, two tall wooden posts with a metal banner, hung with guitars, joining them at the top. Shooter and I walked through this gate and moved toward a circle of tall saguaros, some standing, others lying on the ground beside recently dug holes—recently dug holes smelling faintly moist, even out here—their roots wrapped in burlap. A sort of walkway marked by two rows of white stones led through the saguaro circle to the gate, as though this was the fancy entrance to something or other. Before I could take it any further, I noticed a big camper parked in the shadows.

I went over and sniffed around the camper. Somehow Shooter was already there, busy laying his mark on one of the wheels. A good idea, no arguing against that, but it meant now I had to lay my mark on top of his, and I wasn't sure I had anything to mark with, having been so thirsty for so long. I raised my leg and, yes, laid my mark on top of Shooter's. Nothing you'd call a strong and commanding spurt, more like a dribble, but something, at least. I was digging down for more when a man spoke inside the camper.

"You hear rain?"

"Huh? Don't rain here. What's the matter with you?"

"Thought I heard rain."

"Go to sleep, for chrissake. We gotta have them goddamn plants in the ground by eight sharp."

"Why?"

"Why what?"

"Why the whole thing?"

"What whole thing?"

"In a circle. All that."

"Symbolism. Cactus Man's all about symbolism."

"Huh?"

"Just go to sleep."

Silence.

And then: "If it's rainin', those holes'll get all messed up."

After that came snoring. I moved away from the camper. And what was this? Shooter sidling back over to the wheel and raising his leg? Like he was going to lay his mark on top of mine? Who did he think he was? I hurried back as best I could what with the chain and not quite being at full strength, and gave him a bump to remember. He tumbled away, scrambled up, and trotted off—actually in the direction I wanted him to go—his tail wagging happily in the moonlight, like everything was breaking his way. I followed him. Whoa! That wasn't it at all. Change it to I moved in his footsteps, but in the lead.

Up ahead I caught sight of one of those fires I'd seen from above. It was burning near a tall flat-faced rock. Human shadows moved on that rock, and as we closed in I saw a familiar night-time desert scene: humans sitting around a campfire. The smells of pot and burgers grew stronger, also booze and cocaine. Shooter ran on ahead, maybe not the best idea, and I was trying to ramp up my own speed when the chain caught on something behind me. I circled back, got myself untangled, looked for Shooter and found him poised in the darkness just beyond the campfire light, one paw raised in a hesitating sort of way. I caught up with him and hesitated myself.

What we had here were a bunch of youngish humans, men and women, wearing not much in the way of clothing—nothing at all if you ignored what they had on their heads. Not so easy to do, since they were all wearing antlers, some of them really huge. We stayed put, me and Shooter, watching these antler-wearing naked humans smoke and drink and talk, mostly about black holes and what would happen if you fell in. I myself had been in more than one black hole and knew that what happens is you claw your way up, but they were having trouble figuring that out. All in all, a scary sight. The only good thing about it was the platter of freshly cooked burgers set on a cooler at the edge of the light. A man and a woman lay on their backs on either side of the cooler, gazing up at the sky.

"All the black spaces between the stars are the holes?" the woman said.

"Pretty much," said the man.

Neither of them showed the slightest interest in the burgers, although they could have reached over and grabbed a couple without even bothering to sit.

"So we'd be falling up to the sky?" the woman said.

"According to Einstein," said the man.

"Wow," said the woman.

Which was around when I noticed that Shooter had changed his position a bit, now stood on his hind legs, his front paws resting on the edge of the cooler. Whoa! But whoa didn't seem to be in the little fella's game plan. With a quick sort of head jab, he snatched a burger off the top of the stack and darted into the shadows. What was I waiting for? This wasn't like me at all. I moved in on the cooler—

"I hear, like, chains dragging across the desert floor."

"That's what we've come to cut loose from, babe."

"Cool."

—and snapped up pretty much the whole stack. They were cooked right through, which always shows burgers at their best, in my opinion.

My strength started coming back, like a real big dude waking up inside me. On the other hand—a human expression you hear every day—Shooter seemed to be weakening. I was leading from in front now and had to turn back more than once to prod him along. "If we had three hands, we'd think differently," Bernie says, a scary idea in many ways. I thought about Bernie as we headed in the direction of that pink glow, thoughts like *Bernie!* and *Bernie!* The pink glow came no closer, but I'd been around long enough to know that was just a trick of the wide open spaces.

We went down into a narrow canyon, now beyond all the campfires except for one, a very small fire at the base of a small tree, mostly just a glow with a flame or two flickering up. I wasn't hungry anymore—a little pukey, if anything—and had no desire to see more antlered humans, but because of the narrowness of the canyon, we had to pass close to the fire, in fact to the very edge of its light. A man and a woman sat by this campfire. No antlers, fully clothed: I thought things were looking up until I noticed that the man was loading a revolver: the rounds glinted as they clicked into the chamber.

"Shh," said the woman, her voice low. "Do you hear something out there?" She turned toward the man. Her face had been shadowed by the brim of a cowboy hat she wore but now I saw it clear: a hard face surrounded by lots of soft blond hair, a face I knew. It was Dee Branch. Right away I thought of our slashed tires. True, Dee hadn't done the actual slashing, but she'd been the wheelman on the escape, and that made her a something or other in the eyes of the law. I don't forget things like that.

The man rose, real quick, flicking the chamber closed. He was a little longhaired dude with lots of ink on his arms. I knew him, too, of course: Billy Parsons. In the firelight I could see that his face looked a lot like his mom's, if old Mrs. Parsons was his mom, just a guess on my part; plus he didn't look exactly like her—more like his mom on an unhappy day. Also, old Mrs. Parsons didn't have a snakehead tattoo on her cheek; I was glad of that. Billy and

Dee peered into the night, although with no hope of spotting us, human vision being pretty much useless in the dark.

This was a confusing moment. Wasn't the whole case about finding Billy? And now I'd found him! Chet the Jet! Found him, yes, but what next? Was it possible to somehow corral him and drag him back to Bernie? Or would it be better to go get Bernie and bring him here? I was leaning in that direction, especially in light of that revolver in Billy's hand, when Shooter chose that moment to give himself a good shake. His ears flapped with a sound like gunshots in the quiet of the night.

TWENTY-EIGHT

Billy—one of those speedy little guys—dropped down on one knee, squinting into the darkness, the gun up and pointed in Shooter's general direction. Dee was just as speedy, maybe more so. She whipped out a gun of her own from somewhere, rolled away from the fire, and froze in excellent firing position, a move I've seen Bernie do to good effect more than once. This was looking like what Bernie calls a live-to-fight-another-day scenario, meaning our move was to back silently away into the night and then hightail it. The problem we had was Shooter's unfamiliarity with Bernie's advice. He trotted forward toward the fire.

"Hey," said Dee, rising and putting her gun away. "It's a puppy."

Billy rose, too, the revolver still in his hand, but now pointed down, which was how I like to see weapons, except for ours.

"Look how cute!" Dee said. "C'mere, cutie pie."

Was there any chance "cutie pie" meant me? A good one, I thought, and stepped into the light. Dee and Billy both stepped the other way.

"Whoa," Billy said. "This one's a huge version of the puppy."

Dee's eyes narrowed. "Recognize him?"

"Recog—?" Billy began. And then: "The dog who took down the twins?"

"And belongs to that detective buddy of your parents."

Their guns came up again, pointed not at me and Shooter, but into the darkness, sweeping back and forth like they were afraid of someone—who, I didn't know. Plus there was no one out there; the breeze was blowing from that direction, totally scentless when it came to humans. Billy knelt, fished around in a backpack, found a flashlight. He switched it on and the two of them walked into the darkness, aiming the beam here and there. I sat and waited. Shooter went over to where Dee and Billy had been sitting and sniffed the ground.

"He's gotta be out here," Billy said. "Dogs don't just drop out of the sky."

My ears went right up. Raining cats and dogs is something you hear humans say, and it's a sight I've always looked forward to very much. Was Billy saying that it couldn't happen, at least not for dogs? But it could happen for cats? I didn't like how this was going.

Billy and Dee wandered around for a while. "Think your parents sent him after us?" Dee said. "To get the money?"

"You know they're not like that," Billy said.

"Not everyone's as nice as you."

"I'm not nice."

"Yes, you are," said Dee. Then came a faint smacking sound, the kind you hear from a kiss on the cheek.

"But they are," Billy said. "Which is how come I'm paying them back, that's for sure."

"What about the reverse mortgage scam?"

"Goddamn you, Dee—it's not a scam. It's just good, you know, tax planning."

Then came some silence. They moved farther away, the beam sweeping back and forth over rocks, bushes, emptiness.

"Billy?"

"Don't start."

"You don't even know what I'm going to say," Dee said.

"You're gonna say fuck all this, let's just take off for Alaska or someplace. Can't do that. No way I'm walkin' away from what's rightfully mine."

"I was going to say Costa Rica," said Dee. "You know I hate the cold."

Billy laughed. He had a nice laugh, kind of like Bernie's actually, but not as deep.

"We love each other," Dee said.

"I know."

"So what else matters?"

"Wish it was that simple," Billy said. He shone the light on his watch.

"Where are the twins?" Dee said.

"Should be on their way."

"They were supposed to be here at six."

"Stop worrying. Think they'd walk away from a payday like this?" The flashlight beam made a few more sweeps and Billy said, "Nobody out here."

"Then where did the dogs come from?" said Dee.

The beam swept around and shone on me. I rose, just in case—of what I wasn't sure. But I've been around, know a thing or two, such as in dustups it's better to begin on your feet.

"Sure it's the right dog?" Billy said, coming closer.

"The detective called him something. What was it? Chet, maybe?" Dee looked right at me and said, "Hey, Chet. What's doin'?"

That sounded nice and friendly. Nice and friendly makes my tail start up—that's just the way it is.

"Right dog," Dee said.

I couldn't have agreed more. Dee and I were thinking as one: I was the right dog, no doubt about it.

"But," Dee went on, "he's in rough shape. Is that a chain?"

"Musta broken free," said Billy. "I wonder—"

He moved toward me. Even though they knew I was the right dog, meaning everything between us was nice and pally, I found myself backing away.

"What are you doing?" Dee said.

"Maybe we should keep him for now."

"Why?"

"Might be useful," Billy said. "Just a hunch."

"I don't see how—"

With no warning, Billy shot forward and made a grab for the chain. A quick little dude, as I've mentioned, but of course I was quicker and—except for some reason, this one time, I turned out not to be quicker. Billy got hold of the chain, gripped it tight. I tried to pull away. He got dragged along but didn't let go. I pulled harder, ready to haul little Billy clear across the desert if I had to. During all this I happened to notice Shooter, now sitting by the fire and watching the goings-on with his head cocked to one side.

"Don't hurt him," Dee said.

"For chrissake, I'm not hurting him. I'd never hurt a dog. And why am I always the one who—"

I never found out where Billy was going with that one, on account of this small figure who came streaking in and bit him on the ankle. Perhaps not what you'd call a real bite, although definitely more than a nip. In any case, enough for Billy to cry out, "Ow! What the hell?" and let go of the chain. Shooter and I wheeled around in one motion—like we'd been practicing this for treats, had it down cold—and took off into the night.

It turned out to be maybe the longest night I remember, except I don't really remember it. Did we come across a mostly buried pickup that reminded me of Ellie? Maybe. Did the chain get heavier and heavier? That sticks in my mind. Did Shooter stop for naps more than once? I'm pretty sure about that, too. Also some blood might have leaked out of one of my ears, blood that I believe Shooter licked off in a companionable sort of way. After that we followed the moon into ranch country—ranch country being kind of obvious from all the horse and cattle smells—but ranches also meant humans, and I hadn't been having much luck with humans so I kept my distance, plodding along. Shooter, long past the prancing stage, plodded along behind me. From time to time I caught myself letting my head hang down a bit, raised it right back up, and pronto. We weren't having any of that. Much later, in the darkest part of the night—the moon having disappeared, who knew where—I glanced back and noticed that Shooter's head was hanging, too. I turned and nudged it back up in its proper place. We weren't having any of that from him, either.

My mind began shutting down, not an unpleasant feeling. I grew less and less aware of my body, on the move and never stopping, except for Shooter's naps. Plod plod, big plods and little plods, like PLOD PLOD plod plod and then there'd just be PLOD PLOD, which was when I'd turn and find him zonked out on the ground. I stayed on my feet during those naps, standing over him, not totally sure that once down I could get back up again. How strange was that? So this was the situation: mind shut down and body out of touch. All that was left was a heartbeat, boom booming away.

The sky grew misty, and the stars disappeared. We moved through a sort of cloud, nothing to see but stony ground, all cracked and thorny. Then the mist began to clear and in the distance I saw the downtown towers. And not too long after that, I spotted the airport tower. The canyon that backs onto the end of the last runway just happens to be the same canyon that backs onto our place on Mesquite Road, which you might not know, just one of the helpful discoveries I've made in my career.

The sun was shining as we made our way up the canyon. From above, planes came gliding down, one after another, wings gleaming, a very nice sight. How slow and heavy they seemed! I felt pretty slow and heavy myself, and the chain was now gaining weight with every step I took. We climbed a long gradual slope, PLOD PLOD plod plod, the chain getting caught—again!—in a spiny clump of greenish brush. I circled back, tugged a few times, prodded Shooter back on his feet, and pushed on.

From the crest of the slope we had a long view of the canyon, crossed by a dry wash I knew well, and speckled with housing clusters along the ridge tops. We belonged to one of those clusters—I even thought I could make out the big red flat rock that marked the path up to our back gate. But maybe not. Maybe I was wishing too hard. If wishes were horses is a human expression you hear from time to time. Horses are prima donnas, in my experience, so if wishes were prima donnas . . . That was as far as I could take it. My mind drifted to Lovely, the tiny horse who belonged to Summer whatever her last name was, the kidnapping victim, if I'd gotten it right, although she didn't seem as much like a victim as other victims I'd known, if that makes any sense. I was just on the point of thinking that it did not, when a figure appeared down in a draw not too far ahead, if a draw was one of those strange places where the ground is sloping up in all directions.

Forget draws. The important thing was this figure, who turned out to be a man, a tall man who seemed to be wearing some sort of white headband, and had binoculars around his neck. We keep a pair of binoculars in the Porsche, useful for divorce work, which we hate at the Little Detective Agency, on account of—

The man began to run in our direction. Did I know that run? Oh, yes! A surprisingly fast run for a big man, and if one leg didn't appear to be working as smoothly as the other, that was only on account of his wound, the poor guy. By that time, I was running, too, the chain a great big nothing, a mere balloon, floating behind me! We came together at the head of the draw, me and Bernie.

He picked me up. Tears flowed from his lovely eyes, not a Bernie thing at all. I licked them up. It turned out Bernie's tears were the best I'd ever tasted. No surprise there. He patted and patted me. I noticed that his headband was actually a bandage, kind of bloody. Bernie was also noticing things, starting with the chain. His face went harder than I'd ever seen it, even on the night when we'd opened up that broom closet, too late. He unclipped the chain from my collar and hurled it as far as the eye could see, or at least pretty far.

Next Bernie noticed Shooter, at that moment pawing at his knee. Bernie picked Shooter up and held him, too. Not a move I'd tolerate normally, but this one time I let it go.

Amy's our vet. She's a big, strong woman with big strong hands that know what's what. She patched me up in no time, good news since even though I like her, I don't like hanging with her, not in her office. So when it was time to go, I went. As I hopped in the car—not quite hopping, more like climbing, I heard Amy say, "Who did this to him?"

I watched from the shotgun seat. They stood in the doorway of Amy's office, Bernie looking down at Amy, but not by much.

"I don't know," Bernie said. "But I'm going to find out."

Amy gazed at him. Short hair, no makeup, jeans, and a T-shirt: she was the no-nonsense type. "Glad to hear that," she said. "But I've got a question. You might say it's none of my business. I think it is."

"Go on," Bernie said.

"Have you ever thought about the rightness or wrongness of putting Chet in dangerous situations?"

Bernie stood there, still wearing the bloody bandage, looking a bit pale. "In the beginning," he said, so quietly I almost didn't hear, meaning real quiet.

"And?"

Bernie took a deep breath. His voice grew stronger. "And I decided he loves what we do. If he could choose, he would have chosen this."

"A little on the convenient side, perhaps?" said Amy.

"That doesn't make it false," Bernie said.

Amy gazed at Bernie. He gazed back. What was this about? Why the delay? I was ready to peel on out of here. I barked, just getting my two cents in, which doesn't sound like a whole hell of a lot, so who could mind?

They both turned in my direction. Amy shook her head, at the same time with a little smile on her face.

"Still our vet?" Bernie said.

"Of course," said Amy.

Why wouldn't she still be our vet? This dillydallying was all about nothing. I barked at a volume less easy to ignore.

• • •

So good to be back home. Shooter took two steps into the front hall and settled into napping position. Bernie and I went into the kitchen. He took out a pill. "Amy says you have to take this."

I backed away. Bernie opened a cupboard, found a bottle of pills, swallowed a couple. "See?" he said.

I did not.

"All right, all right."

He went to the stove, whipped up a very small burger, stuck Amy's pill inside. That was better. For some reason my pill-taking method had escaped his mind for a moment. No one's perfect. I set off through the house, sniffing my way from room to room, just normal security procedure. After that I lapped up some nice clean water from my bowl and sat in a patch of sunshine, feeling pretty good, my head nice and empty. When I snapped out of that, I went looking for Bernie.

I found him asleep in his bedroom, bloody bandage still on his head. Bernie sleeping in the middle of the day? Unheard of. I climbed up and lay beside him.

Sometime later the bedside phone rang. Bernie's eyes snapped open. "Good grief," he said. He glanced at me, reached for the phone, ended up just missing, and knocking it onto the floor. Leda's voice came out of the speaker.

"Bernie? Where the hell are you?"

He fumbled for the receiver, said, "Leda?" into the wrong end, fumbled some more and got it right. "What's up?"

"What's up? Are you kidding me? I've been trying and trying to reach you."

"About what?"

"You're not serious?" I heard kids in the background. "Your only child's—as far as we know—birthday?"

"Oh my God."

"To which I made extra sure to invite you—to try to invite you—in plenty of time to avoid a repeat of last year's unpleasantness, to put it euphemistically."

Bernie was on his feet. "I'm on my way."

"Empty-handed, I assume."

"What does he want?"

"Red Desert Chronicles, Volume Four."

"What's that?"

"The hottest video game on the market. Is something wrong with you, Bernie? You sound out of it."

Bernie raced into the bathroom, soon raced back out, bloody bandage now gone, replaced by a bunch of Band-Aids stuck on at different angles. We hurried to the front door—nothing like being on the move! I was close to tip-top already—and Bernie had his hand on the knob when he paused and looked at Shooter, stirring slightly on the floor, as though we'd messed with his nap. Shooter could be very annoying, as I may have mentioned. *Bernie, let's roll.*

But we did not roll. Instead, Bernie went on gazing at Shooter. At last he said, "Wakey wakey, little guy. How about a ride in the car?"

Huh?

TWENTY-NINE

W e drove into High Chaparral Estates and parked in front of Leda's house, a real big one, but there were lots of even bigger ones on the same street. In case you're interested, I was riding shotgun, with Shooter on the little shelf in back, although at the beginning he'd actually made a play to reverse our seating arrangement.

A bunch of kids were leaving the house, clutching party bags and climbing into shiny new cars idling on the street. Charlie, Leda, and Malcolm stood on the front step, waving good-bye. We went up the path and all their mouths changed, Leda's lips turning down, Malcolm's sort of disappearing, and Charlie's opening in a nice happy smile.

"Sorry we're late," Bernie said. "Happy birthday." He gave Charlie a hug. Charlie hugged him back. "I've brought you a present," Bernie went on. "His name's Shooter."

Then all eyes were on the little fella, who'd chosen that moment to lift his leg in front of what looked to me like a rosebush.

"You what?" Leda said. "Without consulting me? Absolutely no way. Where in hell do you get off—"

Shooter finished up at the rosebush and . . . and trotted over to Malcolm, a bit of a surprise. Malcolm has a very long face, but also very long feet with very long toes, and he was wearing flip-flops. Shooter went right to those long feet and without the slightest hesitation began licking those very long toes in a thorough fashion.

"Heh heh," said Malcolm. "Heh heh. Have to admit he's kind of cute, huh, Leda?"

"What?" said Leda. "What?"

"Shooter, you said?" said Malcolm.

"That's right," Bernie told him.

Malcolm's eyes narrowed. "Has he had his shots?"

"Tag's right on his collar," Bernie said.

Charlie was jumping up and down. "I can have him? I can have him?"

"What?" said Leda. "What? And how come he looks so much like Chet?"

"That is interesting," Bernie said.

"Can I have him? Can I have him?"

Shooter kept working on Malcolm's toes.

"Heh heh, heh heh."

"He won't be any trouble," Bernie said.

"And who cares about a little trouble?" said Malcolm.

"What? What?"

We split soon after that, just me and Bernie, Shooter remaining in High Chaparral Estates. He was in Charlie's arms, last I saw, licking Charlie's face. Licking Charlie's face after licking Malcolm's toes? I went back and forth on that, but in the end it didn't bother me. I found myself wondering about the taste of Malcolm's toes and made another of those mental notes.

We met up with Captain Stine at Donut Heaven, parking cop-style, driver's-side door to driver's-side door. He passed Bernie a cruller.

"They changed the recipe."

"Why?" said Bernie, taking a bite, also tearing off a piece and handing it to me.

"New baker. Also illegal, but he believes in the war against obesity."

Bernie did some chewing, a thoughtful look on his face. I did some chewing, too, with no clue about the look on my face, my only thought being, *Ah, cruller.*

"Not as good," Bernie said.

Then send some more my way. I had no complaints about this new cruller, or whatever the hell they were talking about. Hey! I was feeling kind of feisty all of a sudden: just one of those private moments of enjoyment that come around from time to time.

"Change is the only constant," Stine said.

"So I've heard," Bernie said. He glanced at me waiting somewhat patiently for more cruller. "But I don't believe it." He flipped me most of what was left. Sometimes in life you can feel when things start to break your way.

"What happened to you, by the way?" Stine said. "You look like shit."

"Wasn't put on earth for my looks," Bernie said, or something like that: hard to tell with his mouth full. Plus Bernie was the best-looking human you'll ever see, so what I thought I'd heard didn't even make sense.

Stine sipped his coffee. "Anything on Ellie Newburg?"

"Why would I have anything? You're the cop."

"Don't start. We've got zip so far."

"Take Mickles off it and see what happens," Bernie said.

"What are you trying to tell me in your charmless way?"

"And reopen the Summer Ronich kidnapping."

The furrows on Stine's forehead deepened. "I got your email.

The file's lost somewhere in the changeover—one of thousands, so don't even go there. Meaning you'll need to give me a hint, Bernie. Throw me a bone."

I went on high alert, eyes glued to Bernie's throwing arm. He raised it, but only to swallow some coffee. Coffee scent filled the air. I'd have smelled a bone if one was anywhere nearby or even somewhat distant, and I did not. Humans can be puzzling.

"Mickles ran that case," Bernie said. "The file would have been lost, changeover or not."

"Is this some kind of obsession?" Stine said. He glanced at Bernie, saw the expression on his face, then looked away. "Care to fill me in on the backstory, you and him?"

Bernie shook his head.

"Matter of fact," Stine said, still not looking at Bernie, "I've done some digging on my own."

Captain Stine a digger? No dirt under his fingernails, and even if he'd used a shovel, there'd be traces of fresh earth scents on his clothes—especially if he wore cuffs on his pants—and there were not. Once I'd discovered a Cheeto in the cuff of a dude's pant leg. What a day! Actually, the same day I was Exhibit A, down at the courthouse, and the dude with the Cheeto in his pant cuff was the judge. There'd been a short recess after that, although I myself hadn't returned.

"Managed to locate a source," Stine went on.

"Oh?" said Bernie.

"Hector 'Kid' Infante."

"He's a lifer."

"Does that rule out anything he says?"

"Not necessarily," Bernie said.

"The Kid's got fourth-stage prostate cancer," Stine said. "Not that that's dispositive about anything. He told me the story of his arrest. More like a summary execution, actually, until you happened along. Who threw the first punch, you or Mickles?"

"Check with Internal Affairs."

"I did. The Kid told IA that you threw the first punch and that Mickles hadn't been abusing him, all those cuts and bruises coming from a brawl he was in earlier that evening. Then came your demotion, et cetera, et cetera. Now he's saying Mickles cuffed him and beat the crap out of him, you pulled Mickles off, Mickles slugged you and you . . . you did what you do. What's the truth?"

"What do you think?"

"And why would the Kid lie to IA?"

"What do you think?" Bernie said again.

"Don't know," Stine said. "But here's a theory—Mickles made a deal to go easy on the Kid in exchange for his IA testimony and then double-crossed him."

"It's a theory," Bernie said.

"Funny thing about Mickles," Stine said. "He's got his little fiefdom all right, but after the thing with the two of you, his trajectory stalled, even though you were the one who crashed out. There'd been talk about him as chief of D's, maybe chief of the whole department. All that ended. You know why?"

Bernie shook his head.

"It wasn't that people had suspicions about what had really gone down between the two of you, a white-hat–black-hat deal. It's that everyone had been a little afraid of him, and then you beat him to a pulp. He lost his mojo. A chief needs mojo."

This was hard to follow. Neither of them was wearing a hat. I'd never seen Stine with a hat on; Bernie does have a sombrero that comes out at parties—not often but at the same time too often. The only hat that came to mind was the porkpie worn by Clay Winners.

That got me thinking about his pal Vroman, at which moment my teeth sent me a message, just a sort of hi, we're here.

"There was no beating to any kind of pulp," Bernie said.

"Suit yourself." Stine crumpled his coffee cup, wiped his hands. Tiny cruller crumbs caught the sunlight. "Anything else I can enlighten you on?" he said.

"Like?"

"Like, for example, there was a double homicide out in El Monte two days ago, along that stretch where all the subprime loans went down. The victims were twins—the only twin double homicide in the whole history of Valley crime. I looked it up. Only identical twin double homicide, I should've said—there've been three fraternal twin doubles. First report from the scene came from a corporal name of Garwood Mickles. Nephew of Brick, which was news to me."

Bernie said nothing, but his thoughts came my way, fast, deep, dark.

"Both shot in the head at close range with a .45. You've always been partial to a .38, as I recall."

"Still am," Bernie said.

"Good to know."

"But we actually don't have one at the moment."

"No?"

"On the bottom of the Gulf of Mexico—a long story."

"I believe it. So what's in the arsenal these days?"

"A .45."

"Ah," said Stine.

Bernie checked his watch.

"Nice seeing you," said Stine. "One other thing—Carl Conte from Agriculture called me. More saguaro thefts out past Rincon City, twenty or thirty. All within three or four square miles of the first one."

Bernie turned the key. "How's the baby?"

"Cries at the sight of me."

"He'll go far."

Bernie was quiet as we rode away. His eyes had an inward look and his hands seemed to be doing all the driving. Didn't worry me one bit: those were the best hands in the world.

After a while, he glanced my way. "You okay, big guy?"

What was this? Why wouldn't I be? I started panting a bit.

Bernie nodded. "Something bothering you, huh? Thought so."

Nothing was bothering me. Where was he getting this? I panted a little harder.

"Amy's a smart woman," Bernie went on. "Also afraid of nobody. So how about the rightness or wrongness of putting you in dangerous situations?"

Oh, I got it. He had to be talking about letting his hands do the driving while his mind was someplace else. And I had no problem with it, as you know. The panting stopped at once.

"What are you telling me? Okay? Not okay?"

Poor Bernie. He looked so worried. I put a paw on his knee, and we lurched forward in a way that never gets old.

"Chet! How many times do I—" And then he started laughing. Life couldn't be any better than this. So why not just keep driving and never ever stop? I tried to think of a good reason.

And was still trying, maybe not very hard, when Bernie said, "Need to understand the sequence back in Subprimoville. Vroman—whoever the hell he turns out to be—had already shot the twins when we arrived. Actually can't say he was the gunman for sure, because there was another person in the house, namely whoever stepped out from behind the door and coldcocked me. Any chance you know who that was?"

Me? I wasn't following this at all.

"But one thing's practically for sure—Vroman and whoever was behind that door killed Ellie Newburg. Shooter's the proof."

Whoa! Shooter had done something good? What about the big guy? Luckily enough, my tail was in easy gnawing reach.

"Stop that."

I paused, which can look a lot like stopping, if done right.

"Billy Parsons and his buddy Travis Baca kidnapped Billy's girlfriend, who at the very least went along with it. They were clumsy almost beyond belief, and Mickles busted them. The ransom was never found. Billy does his time, gives his parents a stolen cactus, hits them up for money. Then he hires his girlfriend's twin 'roid-head buddies. What for? Something about the securities recovery sector, according to Daniel. What were they up to? Whatever it was, Vroman and whoever else was in on the murder of Ellie Newburg didn't like it, not one little bit." Bernie glanced at me. "Fair summary so far?"

More than fair. The best summary possible, whatever summaries might be.

"Also fair to say there's something in the case file that Mickles couldn't live with?"

I had no idea. But how nice to be riding in the Porsche! Was the engine running a little rough? I heard a faint *chewhee chewhee*, that took me back to some major repairs a while back, although the *chewhee chewhee* had grown to a *kerchunk kerchunk* that even Bernie could hear long before the engine had actually fallen out, so we were A-okay for now.

Sometime later, we were out in the desert. I'd seen this stretch before, got the feeling we were not far from where we'd found Ellie. Bernie turned off the blacktop, followed a dirt track that led around some big rocks, and ended at the base of a big hill. Lots of saguaros grew on the hill, making it look green even though it wasn't. A small tent stood by the only tree in sight. We parked at some distance from it and made our way up the hill, coming to a hole in the ground after not too long.

We gazed down into it. No one there. After that, we climbed a little higher, came to another hole and then another. Bernie was taking pictures when the tent flap opened down below and a woman came out. She stared up at us.

We walked back down and approached the tent. "Hi," Bernie said.

"Hi," said the woman, a very young woman, possibly of high school age. I'd had some experience with high school kids, all good. "That your dog?" she said.

Bernie nodded. "His name's Chet."

"He's beautiful."

Nothing wrong with high school kids, possibly the very best human type! Something must happen later in life that . . . I couldn't take it any further.

Meanwhile, the tent flap opened and a couple more kids came out, pushing a wave of pot smell through the air.

"Dogs can go to the festival?" one said. "Wish I'd known."

"Festival?" Bernie said.

"Cactus Man," said the kid. "We're hopin' to sneak in before it opens."

"Shut up, you moron," said the last kid who'd come out. "What if he's security?"

"I'm not security," Bernie said. He glanced up the hill. "I'm interested in cactuses. Someone's been stealing them."

"You work for conservation?"

"Kind of," Bernie said. Then he nodded a decisive kind of nod. "Yeah, we do."

"Cool," said one of the kids.

"We're big on conservation," said another.

"So why not tell him?" said the girl who'd first come out of the tent.

"Tell me what?" said Bernie.

The kids exchanged a look.

"It'll stay within this circle," Bernie said.

"Circle?" said a kid.

"The three of you and the two of us," said Bernie.

"Chet's part of the circle?"

"Certainly."

The kids nodded to one another.

"Well," said the girl, "when we got here, they were driving away with a saguaro."

"In the back."

"Like, of the pickup."

"Yeah?" said Bernie. "Who's they?"

"The festival people."

"It said 'Cactus Man.'"

"Like, on the door of the pickup."

"So what does this even mean?" the girl said.

"It means the Cactus Man men are stealing cactuses," said a kid.

"Looks that way," Bernie said.

"I meant the deeper meaning," said the girl.

THIRTY

B ack in the car, Bernie drank water. He looked a bit pale, which made me worried, and then he swallowed some pills, and I worried more.

"Someone got me a good one, big guy. Bet you even know who."

I tried to think.

"Same person who chained you up? And where did all that happen?"

A memory swam into view: ruined hut, golden tent, gigantic cactus man towering up to the sky.

Bernie closed his eyes, rubbed his forehead. I squeezed up against him. He smiled, gave me a pat, turned the key. We drove back to town.

And soon were back in South Pedroia. We parked in front of Cactus Sound and went to the door. Bernie was about to knock when our wino buddy—sitting on a barrel a few doors up the street, paper bag in hand—rose and came our way.

"Spare any change? Preferably the paper kind."

Bernie reached into his pocket. "If we came here every day, you'd be rich."

"Nah," said the wino, taking the money Bernie gave him, "I'd just be drinkin' off the top shelf." He raised the paper bag, took a nice big swallow from the bottle he had inside, and paused. "Meaning I seen you before?"

Bernie nodded.

The wino peered at him and then at me. "Got a vague memory," he said. He made a cackling sound that scared me, although it might have been laughter. "As opposed to what, huh?"

"I didn't say anything."

"No, you're all right. And this dog here seems familiar."

"Chet's his name. He was with me the other night."

"Other night, huh? Like the dark side of the moon. But spittin' goddamn image, all I can say."

Bernie went still. "You're saying Chet looks like some other dog?"

"Yeah. Doncha think?"

"Who's this other dog?"

The wino bent down, lowered his hand, palm down. "'Bout so high, hangs out here."

"Here on the street?"

"Nah. The studio, Cactus Sound. The asshole loves the little guy, only goddamn thing he's loved in his whole life, other'n money."

"The asshole have a name?"

"Just about anyone I ever met," the wino said. "But I'm talkin' about Clay Winners."

"Owner of the studio."

"'Mong other things." The wino took another long swallow.

"Like dealing drugs?"

"Wouldn't know nothin' on that score." He squinted at Bernie over the top of the bottle. "You a cop?"

"No."

"Don't like cops."

"Do they like you?"

The wino cackled again. "Sure as hell do not, with a capital goddamn N." He took another drink, looked disappointed, turned the bottle upside down, and shook it. Nothing came out. He placed the bottle carefully against the curb. "Guess I'll catch up on some shopping," he said. "Nice talkin'."

"Before you go," Bernie said, "how well do you know Clay Winners?"

"Asshole and me go way back," the wino said. "Worked for him practically a century, felt like."

"Doing what?"

"Janitor, messenger, coffee boy—you name it. Till he canned my sorry ass."

"Way back, huh?"

"Way, way back."

"Far enough back to remember Billy Parsons?"

"Snatched that little cutie—what was her name?"

"Summer Ronich."

"Somethin' like that."

"What was that all about?" Bernie said.

"Hell if I know," said the wino. "Some crackpot idea. Crackpots the both of them—Billy and . . ."

"Travis Baca."

"Somethin' like that. Scared so shitless it was funny."

"You're talking about Travis?"

The wino burped. "Beg pardon," he said, covering his mouth. "Talkin' 'bout the both of them, him and Billy. They showed up here after it all blowed to smithereens."

"Here at the studio?"

"Met Winners in the inner sanctum."

"What's that?"

"Like in the church. Never been to church?" He glanced down at the empty bottle in the gutter.

"Don't go away," Bernie said, moving toward the car.

"Huh? Where to?"

Bernie popped the trunk, came back with a bottle of bourbon that looked pretty full, handed it to the wino.

"Well, well," said the wino, examining the label. "Reminds me of my golden youth." He took a careful little sip. "Ah."

"All yours."

"Much obliged."

"Getting back to the inner sanctum," Bernie said.

"What we called Winners's office." The wino licked his lips, long and slow. "Like he was the pope, kind of thing."

"And Billy and Travis went in there when they were on the run?"

"Not for long. They were gone real fast. Not that real fast did them any good. They were cooked." He took another drink, more than a sip this time. "Cops musta been right on their heels. Detective showed up maybe the next morning."

"Detective?" Bernie said.

"Real big guy—your height but . . ." The wino spread his hands out wide. "He went into the inner sanctum, too."

"With Winners?"

"Uh-huh."

"What did they talk about?"

"Couldn't tell you. I was just passin' by. Cleanin' toilets, so musta been a Wednesday. Hated cleanin' toilets. Musicians, you know?"

"Did you ever see the detective again?"

"Nope. But I saw Billy."

"You saw Billy?"

"Hardly recognized him. Prison'll do that to a man."

"So this was recently?"

"Sure."

"He came here?"

"That's right. Walked right past me, no time of day, like I was a stranger, and went in. I heard this shouting match from inside. Little while later, some flunky came out and tied one of them cactuses—"

"A saguaro?"

"Yeah. Tied a saguaro to the roof of Billy's car. Then Billy came outside and drove off, his face all red, like . . . like a real embarrassed kid. Winners and that motherfuckin' hoodlum stepped out to watch him go, had themselves a good laugh."

"Hoodlum?"

"For real," said the wino. "Name of Vroman. You don't wanna go near him. He's what you might call a stone killer. No heart inside, if you see what I mean."

"Any killings you know about for sure?"

"Don't know about for sure, but I'd kind of like to know the story of that . . ." He glanced at me. "Getting a bit confused here with the dogs." He raised the bottle toward his lips, but Bernie snatched it away.

The wino backed off a step or two. "Thought we were friends."

"Friendship's a two-way street."

"So the unfriendly types always say."

Bernie gazed at him, then made a little nod. "Fair enough." He handed back the bottle. "But right now I need you at your sharpest, that's all."

"What for?" The wino held tight to the bottle but didn't make any attempt to drink.

"Your clearest memories," Bernie said.

"My memories is kind of muddy," said the wino. "Goin' back to childhood."

"Maybe you're out of practice. Weren't you going to say something about the puppy who looks like Chet here?"

"Hey! How'd you know that?"

"Just a guess."

"But I hardly knew it myself. You're like a genius or somethin'."

Tell me something I don't know, Mr. Wino!

"The puppy," Bernie said.

"Right, the puppy—a puzzlement, put it that way. Turned up right here riding with the nice lady."

"What nice lady?"

"Kind of like you—gave me a gratuity. Not everybody does. Hardly anybody, truth be tol'. Can't blame them. 'Course, if I spiffed myself up . . . but then I wouldn't have to . . ." His voice trailed off. He gave the bottle a quick peek.

"The nice lady had the puppy with her?"

The wino nodded. "Rode up front in her truck. She got out, slipped me a couple bucks, went inside."

"The studio?"

"Yeah. Dog stayed in the truck. She left the window cracked open. He stuck his little snout out. I remember that clear as a bell. Then the lady come out with Winners. He got in the truck with her and they took off. I headed on down to Red's—"

"What's Red's?"

"Bottle shop. Run by thieves, but it's the closest." His mouth opened, closed, opened again, revealing not much going on by way of teeth. I started feeling bad for him.

"And?" Bernie said.

"And what?"

"Did something happen after that?"

The wino nodded. "Purchased me a pint of Night Train." He held up the bourbon. "This is a different story, friend. Reminds me of the possibilities in life." All at once he looked worried. "I get to keep it, right?"

Bernie nodded. "Anything else come to mind about that sequence?"

"Sequence?"

"Lady, puppy, Winners."

"Sequence, huh? I like that word. See quench, like you're the man." The wino's eyes, dull until that moment, went brighter. "And what if another see quench starts up on that, the end turning into a new beginning?"

"Not following you," Bernie said.

What was this? The wino getting angry? "Why the hell not? Simple thing." He muttered to himself, then said, "Jeep comes around from the back."

"From behind the studio?"

"Alley with parking."

"You saw it on the way back from Red's?"

"How many times I got to tell you?"

"It followed the lady and Winners?"

"And the puppy. Thought you was smart."

"Who was in the Jeep?"

"Vroman," said the wino. "Din't I say so? He was drivin' and he was still drivin' when they come back."

"Who's 'they'?"

The wino cocked his head to one side. "Maybe you's not so smart after all. Vroman, Winners, and the puppy."

"The lady?"

"Not her. End of see quench." The wino gave Bernie a quick sideways look. "You sweet on her or somethin'?" he said.

"She's dead," Bernie said.

"Condolences," said the wino.

"All because she found out they were stealing cactuses."

The wino nodded. "The legit part is a disguise. They take what they want." He glanced at the door to Cactus Sound. "Fixin' to start up another see quench?"

"Yeah."

"Shit out of luck—they're all split for the festival." He offered Bernie the bottle. "Thirsty, friend? Happy to share."

"I'm driving," Bernie said.

The wino's eyes went dull.

"One thing about kids," Bernie said. "They know how to sneak into places."

News to me! I had a pretty high opinion of kids to begin with; now it rose even higher. We pulled up to the base of the hill where we'd seen the kids. No sign of them now, and their little tent was gone.

"So what we'll do," Bernie went on, "is follow the kids, let them show us the way."

Following the kids? Was that it? Easy peasy. I picked up their individual scents before we got out of the car, although even if I hadn't, it wouldn't have mattered: we'd caught a break when it came to tracking, namely garlic and vinegar potato chips. Not my favorite potato chip—a bit too much, in my opinion—and not the point. The point was that one of those kids was packing garlic and vinegar potato chips. I could have followed them with . . . with my nose closed. What a crazy thought! No repeats of that, if you don't mind.

Bernie got the backpack out of the trunk, filled it with water bottles, snacks, flashlight, binoculars, a box of ammo. Then he rummaged around under the seats, found the holster, strapped it on, and stuck the .45 in place. Open carry? We hardly ever did that. This was shaping up as a special night. Bernie stepped away from the Porsche, paused, went back for the bottle of pills in the glove box. He swallowed some, more than two, and we hit the trail.

It wasn't quite night yet, what with a fiery light blazing on one side of the sky. But stars were already popping into view overhead. Every time you looked, there were more. Once I heard Bernie explaining all about the stars to Charlie. Could have listened forever! Did I understand even one little thing? No. What I loved was Bernie's voice, although I can't say I was unhappy when Charlie said, "Dad? Now can we have dessert?"

Some of that fiery light reflected off the butt of the .45 and also Bernie's eyes. I felt pretty good. This was much better than a desert walk with Shooter. Not once did Bernie curl up for a little nap, and it wasn't just that. There was nothing like a walk with Bernie, plain and simple. I moved closer to him. He gave me a pat. "Moon'll be up soon, big guy." And the very next time I checked, there it was, slightly shaved down from the night before. Bernie knew it all.

We followed a stream of garlic and vinegar potato chip scent down a long draw and up the far end. Some low mesquites stood at the top, and we paused there, taking in the view. I've seen plenty of nighttime desert views, but not one like this. For starters, in the distance we had that gigantic cactus man, all lit up in bright colors and sometimes strobing from his eyes, strobing bothering my own eyes more than just about anything. A little closer rose the big golden tent, now glowing like the sun, and between the cactus man and the tent stood the stage. Too far away to see the band, but I could hear their music, faint in the night, mixed with shouts from the crowd, some of which sounded surprisingly clear. Down on the flats, the circle of saguaros—stolen saguaros, if I was in the picture—was also all lit up, and searchlights shone on the entrance gate, where I could make out a line of people. A barrier made of yellow tape—like crime scene tape except wider—ran from both sides of the gate into the distance, and flashlight beams bobbed here and there along the insides of the barrier.

"That'll be security," Bernie said. He pointed. "And there are our kids."

I caught their shadowy forms on the flats, moving toward some house-sized rocks that interrupted the flow of the tape. No lights shone near those rocks. Kids: you had to love them.

"Let's go," Bernie said. But we didn't start right off. Instead, he turned my way, knelt, looked right in my eyes, and gave me a real big hug. Not our usual MO on this kind of night, but very nice all the same.

THIRTY-ONE

The kids were long gone by the time we reached the big rocks, and the sounds and smells of the festival were a lot stronger. Pot, cocaine, booze of many kinds, human sweat, Porta-Potties: a rich mix, but not strong enough to mask the scent of those garlic and vinegar potato chips. I could even separate out the potato part, by the way, which may surprise you.

We moved past the rocks. A flashlight beam was poking around to one side, too far off to reach us. We went the other way, circling toward the two-humped hill, looking like white stone in the moonlight. As we got closer, we could see people climbing the hill, all of them stony white themselves. Also they weren't wearing much in the way of clothing, although some were masked and others had antlers on their heads. Not the antlers again? But yes.

We started up the two-humped hill, soon passed a naked pair of antler dudes peering at their cell phone screens. "Anything?" one said.

"Just one bar, but . . . nope, it's gone."

"So no pizza? How the hell are we . . . ?"

Bernie and I kept going, but as we did I spotted a big dude in the shadows of a sheer rock wall cut out of the hillside: a clothed, unantlered dude, although he wore a white mask that covered his whole face. I sniffed the air and caught no whiff of him at all, the cool night breeze blowing in the wrong direction. A few steps later, I turned to check on him. He was gone.

We reached the dip in the two-humped hill, mounted the other side, and looked down. Wow! We were practically right on top of the golden tent. Flaps were open on all sides and people went in and out. Little fires burned here and there on the desert floor, and a big crowd was in wild dancing motion in front of the stage, the musicians dancing wildly, too, except for the drummer, who looked like she was chewing gum. Fireworks burst nonstop all over the night sky. The breeze rose up in our faces, carrying the smell of lots of humans in high excitement. Did the smell spread from one to another, carrying the excitement with it? No clue. All I knew was that I myself was not a fan of big excited human crowds, no offense. And meanwhile, I'd left out the most amazing part of the whole scene, namely the gigantic cactus man, now glittering in Christmas tree light colors, its eyes strobing back and forth across the desert like . . . like it was searching for something. All of that added up to a sort of roar that filled the night, hard to explain.

Bernie shrugged off the backpack, took out the water bottle, and my portable bowl. He was thirsty already? Not like Bernie at all. He poured some water in my bowl, which I tasted, just being polite, and then tilted back his head and drank. His face turned stony white, and for a moment he looked . . . sort of older, hard to explain. He paused, throat exposed to the moon, and glanced down at me.

"What you growling at, big guy?"

No idea. But whatever I was growling at deserved it. I was sure of that.

Bernie slung on the backpack, and we started down the hill, steep at first, which meant a lot of zigzagging for Bernie and a lot of waiting for me, and then leveling out a bit. We were partway down the easier section, not too far from the bottom of the hill, when a second, smaller roar started up inside the big one. From behind a clump of barrel cactuses—their sharp spines, about which I could tell you plenty, sparkling brightly, what with all the light going on—came a motorcycle accelerating fast, front wheel raised in the air. A woman drove and a man sat behind her, both with long fair hair, streaming out behind them. She drove like she knew what she was doing. He looked like he knew what he was doing, too, if you can say that about a guy just riding on the backseat. What else? He had a silver gun in one hand. This was turning out to be a primo night for open carry. We knew these motorcycle riders, of course: Billy and Dee.

"Chet! After 'em!"

We ran, me and Bernie. Had I ever seen him run faster? I almost had to run myself, just to keep up with him. Did he stumble a bit when we hit the bottom, falling and losing the backpack? Maybe, but he was back on his feet before you'd even notice. Meanwhile, the motorcycle zoomed through one of the tent flap openings and into the golden tent.

"No, Billy!" Bernie shouted, a shout lost in the surrounding roar. I hardly heard it myself. We raced across flat ground, leaping right over—at least in my case—some antler people sitting around a fire, and charging into the tent.

In our business, a lot can be going on all of a sudden, and the trick is to . . . something or other. Bernie says it all the time; maybe he'll say it again someday. But for now, here's a clue: when you're not sure what's next, watch Bernie. So: I watched Bernie.

He was taking in everything at the speed of light, the fastest speed going, just another thing I know on account of him. When Bernie's taking things in at the speed of light, you can see the light speeding in his eyes. Who's more alive than Bernie? Nobody is the answer, amigo. And here's what we had to take in: a bar and buffet at the most distant part of the tent, with a few people drinking and eating those drinking snacks on tiny napkins, snacks which often, as in this case, include shrimp wrapped in bacon; a bunch of musicians lazing around on some couches, their instruments around them; and a sort of office with a few desks, off to one side; all of this lit by big lanterns that hung from above.

Bernie took all that in in no time flat, figuring out what mattered as only he can do, namely the scene over in that office: Dee on the bike and revving it, and Billy off the bike, gun pointed right at the head of a man who backed away clutching a—what would you call it? A cash box? Yes, a cash box. The man backing away, porkpie hat somewhat askew on his head, and his whole face sort of askew as well, was Clay Winners.

Bernie ran toward all that, me at his side.

"You owe me five hundred grand," Billy was saying, his voice shaking. When human voices shake, we've got big trouble, in my experience.

"Didn't we put that to bed?" Winners said.

"You really thought I'd be satisfied with a goddamn cactus?" Billy said.

"I thought you'd be satisfied with staying alive."

"You were wrong."

Winners held the cash box tight to his chest, like a baby. "Point one," he said, "there is no five hundred grand."

"What the hell are you talking about?" Billy said.

"Mickles grabbed half right off the top," Winners said.

"Why'd you let him do that?"

"Figure it out."

Dee cut the engine, got off the bike. "To save his ass, Billy." She reached down, slipped a knife out of her boot. "We'll take the rest—two fifty."

Winners backed another step, bumping up against a table. "Time marches on—how come you're still not getting the message?"

"Message?" Billy said. "Fifteen years in the pen and you get a cactus? That's the message?"

"I'm talking about getting what happened to the twins," Winners said. "Can't make it any clearer. How stupid are you?"

Billy made a sound almost exactly like the snarl we have in the nation within. Things happened fast after that, so fast I didn't pay attention to running footsteps just on the other side of the tent wall, probably a mistake. First, the knuckles of Billy's trigger finger went white. Then Bernie shouted "No!" and grabbed Billy's shoulder. The gun went off anyway, but nobody got hit. Instead, an overhead lantern shattered and burst into flames. The flames jumped straight up to the tent roof, licked at it, and got huge. Screaming started up all over the place, a sort of piercing layer above the roar. I was looking up like everyone else, which was how come I didn't see Vroman until it was a little on the late side. He came bursting into the tent, a shotgun in his hands. Dee saw him first and slashed at him with the knife. But from too far away. He clobbered her with the shotgun barrel, and she went down. Bernie leaped in front of him. The light around us changed to bright red. Bright red burned in Bernie's eyes. Vroman raised the shotgun, a look in his eyes that meant pleasure was on the way.

He didn't know Bernie. Bernie stepped inside—so fast! so smooth!—and batted the barrel aside with one hand. With his other, he threw that sweet uppercut. It caught Vroman square on the chin. Vroman's eyes rolled right up and he toppled over, landing on his back. Next thing I knew I was standing over him, his throat between my teeth. A growl like I'd never heard rose up, drowned out all the roaring.

"No, Chet, no," Bernie said, not loudly, but I heard. I felt his hand on my collar, very gentle, and let Bernie pull me off. That was when a huge section of flaming roof came floating down, wrapping itself around Winners like an enormous coat of fire. For a moment he just stood there with his mouth open, cash box to his chest. The he cried a horrible cry and struggled wildly inside the burning fabric, which clung to him harder with every move he made. The cash box came flying out of what now looked like a bonfire. Bernie caught it in midair. Winners's cries faded down to nothing; fire sounds amped up the other way.

Billy pointed his gun at Bernie. "Give."

Dee rose, her nose bloody and twisted, but steady on her feet. "Enough, Billy."

Billy looked at Dee in surprise and slowly lowered the gun.

"I should take you in, Billy," Bernie said. "For the crime of throwing your parents under the bus." A bit confusing: the only bus I recalled in this case was the school bus with the mean driver, and the Parsonses hadn't been on the scene. "But I just don't feel like it," Bernie went on. He tossed Dee the cash box. "Anywhere you can lay low?" he said to her.

Dee glanced at the cash box like she couldn't believe she had it. "I've got a cousin in Matamoros," she said.

"Adios," said Bernie.

They hopped on the bike, Dee cranking the engine, Billy on the back with the cash box.

"Wait," he yelled to her. He opened up the cash box, grabbed a wad of banded-together money, and flipped it to Bernie. "Make sure they get this." Then Dee gunned it and they took off, out of the fire and into the night.

Yes, by that time we were in the middle of a great big fire, the whole tent in flames from one side to the other. I could feel my fur getting singed, not a good feeling at all. We ran, me and Bernie, just as more flaming roof came down, falling like a blanket over Vroman and what was left of Winners.

Outside everyone was running and screaming. We ran, too, but didn't scream. We don't actually scream in the nation within, and Bernie's not a screamer. The whole tent went up with a huge *BOOM* and we got thrown to the ground. We picked ourselves up, scrambled, rolled, scrambled some more. Fireworks went off in another boom, and the sky exploded in all kinds of color. We came to rest against the base of cactus man, on a tilt now but still strobing away.

Bernie and I sat there, side by side, catching our breath, eyes glued to the fire, no longer spreading across the ground, but growing higher and higher. That was when the big, broad man in the white mask stepped out from behind the leg of cactus man. We turned to him real quick, but he was ready, had a gun trained on us before we could get to our feet.

The man spoke. The breeze was right now, carrying his scent, so I knew who he was before I heard the sound of his voice. "Familiar with the word 'nemesis,' Bernie?"

Bernie nodded.

"You're mine." He took off his mask. It was Mickles, of course, the strobe lighting up and blanking out his face. "So you can imagine how good I'm feeling right now." He glanced over at the fire. "You've actually simplified my life tonight."

"Because there's no one left who knows you extorted two hundred and fifty grand from a kidnapper?"

"Winners couldn't really be called a kidnapper," Mickles said. "More like a trustee."

"How did you find out he was holding the ransom?" Bernie said. "By promising Billy and Travis you'd cut them a deal, even let them go?"

"They're scum," Mickles said. "You know that. Scum's owed nothing. That's not the problem. The problem is you're wrong about nobody knowing. You know, Bernie." He pointed the gun at Bernie's head. Not his poor head! A crazy thought at the time, perhaps, but I knew Bernie's head had been bothering him. And now this! I got mad. And when I'm mad, I'm at my very fastest. I sprang.

Mickles started to swing the gun my way, but he wasn't quick enough. I hit him on the shoulder, spinning him around, and the gun went flying. Then Bernie was on him. They wrestled around. And what was this? Mickles on top? He punched Bernie right in the mouth and blood poured out. I charged in. After that came some more wrestling around and a moment later we were all on our feet.

Bernie grabbed Mickles by the collar, got in a couple good ones. Mickles got in a couple of good ones of his own. That made Bernie mad, just as mad as me. We're a lot alike in some ways, don't forget. He bent, coiled up all his strength, and threw the uppercut.

Maybe not landing it square on the chin, but close enough. Mickles staggered back against the leg of cactus man, hitting it hard. The strobing stopped and I heard a strange metallic sound from overhead. Mickles hadn't gone down, something of a surprise, although his face was a satisfying, bloody sight. Except what was this? He was reaching into his jacket, pulling out a little gun? I—but I had no time to do anything, because something cracked high above, and an instant later a huge hat—a porkpie hat, but made of sheet metal—came plunging down, brim first. The edge of that brim sliced deep into Mickles's head. He went down the way humans do when it's forever.

Hey! We were getting lots of help from above tonight! That was unusual and very nice. I turned to Bernie. Bernie turned to me. He grinned and said, "Saved by cactus man, big guy. Didn't that girl ask about the deeper meaning of—"

And then stopped right there. His eyes closed. He—my Bernie—slumped to the ground and lay still.

There was lots of crying in the next little while. I saw Captain Stine crying and Nixon Panero. Also old Mr. and Mrs. Parsons, and Amy the vet. Lots of cops, perps—and cooks, too, plus bartenders. Plus Leda. And Charlie, which was the worst. Can't leave out Suzie, who cried plenty but turned out to be the strongest.

I myself was going out of my mind, but finally Suzie got them to let me visit the hospital. They had Bernie in a room by himself. He lay on a bed, eyes closed, pale. There were no tubes or anything like that connected to him. Maybe that was what Suzie was talking about when she said, "What's going on? Where's the ventilator?"

A nurse shook her head.

We went to the side of the bed. Bernie's hand lay on the sheet. He has the most beautiful hands in the world, as I've probably mentioned way too much. I gave that beautiful hand a lick. It felt cold.

Then slowly, so slowly it almost didn't happen, the hand moved a bit. It rose the tiniest height off the sheet, turned the tiniest bit, and came to rest against the side of my neck. Bernie's hand gripped me, so weakly you couldn't really call it gripping. But I knew he was holding on tight. I know Bernie.

ACKNOWLEDGMENTS

There'd be no Chet and Bernie series without the hard work of my crack researchers, Audrey and Pearl. They show up every day and work for treats. A writer can't ask for more than that.